HEARTBREAK CAFE

Heartbreak Cafe

PENELOPE J. STOKES

FJC
STOKES
2009

BERKLEY BOOKS, NEW YORK

THE BERKLEY PUBLISHING GROUP
Published by the Penguin Group
Penguin Group (USA) Inc.
375 Hudson Street, New York, New York 10014, USA
Penguin Group (Canada), 90 Eglinton Avenue East, Suite 700, Toronto, Ontario M4P 2Y3, Canada
(a division of Pearson Penguin Canada Inc.)
Penguin Books Ltd., 80 Strand, London WC2R 0RL, England
Penguin Group Ireland, 25 St. Stephen's Green, Dublin 2, Ireland (a division of Penguin Books Ltd.)
Penguin Group (Australia), 250 Camberwell Road, Camberwell, Victoria 3124, Australia
(a division of Pearson Australia Group Pty. Ltd.)
Penguin Books India Pvt. Ltd., 11 Community Centre, Panchsheel Park, New Delhi—110 017, India
Penguin Group (NZ), 67 Apollo Drive, Rosedale, North Shore 0632, New Zealand
(a division of Pearson New Zealand Ltd.)
Penguin Books (South Africa) (Pty.) Ltd., 24 Sturdee Avenue, Rosebank, Johannesburg 2196,
South Africa

Penguin Books Ltd., Registered Offices: 80 Strand, London WC2R 0RL, England

This book is an original publication of The Berkley Publishing Group.

PRINTING HISTORY
Berkley trade paperback edition / August 2009

Library of Congress Cataloging-in-Publication Data

Stokes, Penelope J.
    Heartbreak cafe / by Penelope J. Stokes.
        p. cm.
    ISBN 978-0-425-22844-9
    1. Widows—Fiction. 2. Restaurants—Fiction. 3. Female friendship—Fiction.
4. Mississippi—Fiction. 5. Domestic fiction. I. Title.

    PS3569.T6219H43 2009
    813'.54—dc22   2009004052

PRINTED IN THE UNITED STATES OF AMERICA

10 9 8 7 6 5 4 3 2 1

Acknowledgments

To the following people, I owe a debt of gratitude for their faith in me and their belief in this novel:

To Claudia Cross, my agent, and Wendy McCurdy, my editor.

To Dorri, Deb, Jim, Jerene, Joyce, Sandi, Carlene, Joe, and Letha—and the memory of dear, loving Bob—for their unfailing support, encouragement, and love.

To Pam, whose presence makes all the difference.

To Stewart Cubley, founder of The Painting Experience, who graciously gave me permission to incorporate my own process painting workshops into this novel. I highly recommend the experience to anyone who wishes to go deeper in the spiritual and emotional journey. For more information, visit the website at www.processarts.com.

And finally, a special note of thanks to Annie Danberg, who shared her time and heart with me, and whose penetrating questions helped me face what was hidden in darkness. Better than therapy, Annie, and a heck of a lot more fun.

Prologue

"There's two things in life a man can't get enough of," my mama told me. "Good cookin' and good lovin'."

By *good lovin'* she meant sex, of course. But since she had never in all her born days used the *S* word, she wasn't about to start saying it right out in public in front of God and everybody, on the steps of the Chulahatchie Baptist Church the day I married Chase Haley.

Ironically, it was the combination of good cookin' and good lovin' that kept my daddy from walking me down the aisle that bright June morning. Four years before, the night of my junior prom while I was out experimenting with another kind of Southern Comfort in the back of Juice McPherson's pickup truck, Daddy had a heart attack on the living room floor, right in the middle of Mama's blue braided rug.

Daddy was a big man, tall and broad and padded with years of Mama's Southern cooking—fried chicken and sweet potatoes, biscuits and cornbread and crowder peas cooked with ham hock, fried okra and fried green tomatoes and fried summer squash. Mama was a bitty little thing, thin and scrawny as a baby bird, hardly any meat at all on her bony frame.

As I imagine it—because Mama'd never say so, not in a million years—it took quite a bit of effort to wedge herself out from under his bulk. Then she had to jerk him into some clothes—which was some kind of challenge on a man as big as Daddy—and open the blinds, and take down the old bed sheet tacked over the glass in the living room door.

With one thing and the other, by the time she got him and herself decent enough to call emergency, he was gone.

The paramedics from the volunteer fire department had known Mama and Daddy all their lives. They learned everything they knew about Jesus in Mama's second-grade Sunday school class, and everything they knew about throwing a curve ball from Daddy's Little League team. So they didn't mention the buttons on his shirt done up all cattywampus, or the fact that he wasn't wearing any boxer shorts.

They knew how to keep their mouths shut, all right. It was a sign of respect. But I imagine. I imagine.

And so I married Chase Haley without my daddy there to give me away. Now, thirty years later, Mama's gone too, and most of the people I grew up with in Chulahatchie have buried their own parents and married off their kids.

Lots of things change. But what Mama told me still holds

true: No matter how old a man gets, he still wants good cookin' and good lovin'.

The good cookin' is what I do best.

I got a suspicion Chase is getting the good lovin' someplace else.

In a town where everybody knows your name, everybody knows your business, too. You think you got secrets, you're living in Fantasyland.

Everybody in Chulahatchie, Mississippi, talked—men and women alike. Gossip flowed around us like the Tennessee-Tombigbee at flood stage. And there was no such thing as whispering. Any hint of scandal, and you might as well blow the noon whistle over at the Tenn-Tom plant or ring the big bell in the steeple of the Methodist church. The only time people hushed was when the subject of the gossip was within earshot.

That's how I knew, or came to suspect, that my husband, Chase, was on the prowl.

It was on a Friday morning at the Curl Up and Dye. I had an appointment with DeeDee Sturgis to get a haircut, and the minute I walked in the door I knew something was up. The bell over the door jingled, everybody turned to look, and the whole place went silent.

"What?" I said, staring around the room. Stella Knox ducked back under the hair dryer and buried her face in a copy of some ridiculous tabloid. All I could see was her eyebrows—which needed a good plucking—and a headline about Britney Spears being pregnant with an alien's baby.

Rita Yearwood, who was halfway through a trim, swiveled back toward the mirror and examined her fingernails. DeeDee had stopped mid-snip and stood with the comb raised in one hand and the scissors in the other as if somebody had pulled a gun on her.

"What?" I repeated.

"Nothin', honey," DeeDee said, but her eyes cut to the left, a sure sign she was lying. "Rita was just telling us this hilarious story about her youngest grandbaby, and . . ." She fizzled to a halt and shrugged. "Guess you had to be there."

In the mirror beyond DeeDee's shoulder, I saw the reflection of a woman I barely recognized—short and dumpy in ill-fitting black pants and a pale blue knit top, her graying hair a mess of grown-out layers, her cheeks flushed with two feverish spots of red. Lord help me, I looked every day of fifty and a whole lot more. Maybe I should get a facial, too. And a manicure.

I sat down on the wicker loveseat and waited. Conversation resumed, the normal beauty-shop buzz, but for some reason it didn't *sound* normal. The laughter seemed forced, the smiles false and deliberate. Every now and then I caught a glance that carried weight and significance, but it obviously wasn't meant for me.

"DeeDee," I finally said, "I'm going to take a rain check on this haircut. I can wait another week, and I just remembered there's something I've got to do."

I left with my gut churning and my hands trembling. For ten minutes I sat behind the wheel of the car, staring at a dead moth smeared across the windshield. They had been talking about me, that much was clear.

But why was I so certain it was also about Chase?

I cranked the car and was just starting to back out of the parking place when Hoot Everett came barreling through the square in his old Chevy pickup. He hadn't looked where he was going, of course, but even if he had, Hoot was eighty-three and blind as a bat with cataracts, and everybody knew just to keep out of his way.

I waited until my heart rate slowed, then made my way around the courthouse and out onto Old Tupelo Road toward Tenn-Tom Plastics, Inc.

The plastics company had been up and running for about three years now, turning out parts for car interiors—dashboards, center consoles, door handles. It was boring work, but it paid pretty well, and most everybody, Chase included, considered it a godsend. Nobody could earn a living farming anymore, and when the feed plant had shut down, six hundred people from three counties had lost their jobs on a single day. Tenn-Tom Plastics saved Chulahatchie from oblivion.

Still, I could never approach the plant without cringing. The CEOs might be richer than God, but they hadn't spent a dime of it on aesthetics. No trees, no grass, no landscaping of any kind. Huge and sprawling and ugly, the monstrous building looked as if it might have been constructed of giant Lego blocks, slapped down on fifty acres of asphalt and surrounded, like a prison, with a twelve-foot chain-link fence.

I paused at the gate, and Fart Unger came out from the guardhouse to lean against the car. Fart's real name was Theodore, but he'd gotten stuck with the nickname in elementary school, so long ago that nobody gave a second thought to its origin or meaning anymore.

He was a tall, skinny man, bald as a chicken's egg, with a ruddy complexion. I remembered him as a third-grader, short and porky with beady eyes and bright red hair. The perfect target for school bullies, a little boy custom-made for nasty nicknames. By the time he was in high school, however, Fart had shot up to six four and become the best basketball player in northeast Mississippi.

He was a hero—the local boy made good. North Carolina State gave him a full athletic scholarship, but when he blew out his knee his sophomore year, he came home to Chulahatchie to do what everybody else did: settle down, get a job, raise a family, try to make ends meet. And do your best to abandon your dreams before they destroyed you.

"Hey, Fart," I said. "How's Brenda and the kids? You got a new grandbaby, isn't that right?"

He grinned down at me, fished his wallet out of his back pocket, and handed over a picture of a round, pinkish blob. "Bertie came home last weekend and brought her to see us. Cutest little thing you ever laid eyes on. Her name's Diana. We call her Piglet."

I shook my head and returned the photo. "You of all people oughta have more sense than to saddle a child with that kind of nickname."

Fart laughed. "Didn't hurt me none." He patted the window ledge. "You here to see Chase?" A shadow passed behind his eyes, something furtive, almost frightened.

"Yeah. He forgot his lunch."

Fart's gaze darted around the empty car, and I knew I hadn't fooled him. I scrambled for an excuse. "He's got a bunch of comp time from last month; I thought maybe I'd surprise him and take him out to Barney's. Friday's catfish day."

I've never been a quick thinker or a particularly good liar. Chase raved about my cooking; he'd take my leftovers over Barney's catfish any day of the week. Besides, Barney had quit serving lunch two years ago.

Fart gave me a sympathetic look, one of those glances men can never seem to cover up.

"Tell Brenda I'll call her. We'll have dinner soon," I said as he waved me through the gate.

It was only eleven-thirty. I drove through the parking lot, up and down the rows, but Chase's truck wasn't there. At ten 'til twelve, I pulled up in a visitor's space and went into the office.

Tansie Orr, the office manager at Tenn-Tom, sat with her head down at the computer, typing furiously. "Be with you in a sec," she said without looking up.

I waited, watching the top of Tansie's head. Her roots were showing, two inches of glossy brown shot through with gray, and then, abruptly, bushing out into a brassy blonde, overtreated and fried to a frizz. She'd look better natural, I thought; the salt-and-pepper suited her coloring. Besides, no fifty-year-old woman should even think about platinum blonde unless she's consciously going for the cheap hooker look.

At last Tansie raised her head, and I saw that expression again—that fleeting glimpse of pity quickly covered by a smile. The kind of look you give a cancer patient when the doctor starts talking about quality time.

"Hey, Dell," she said, too brightly. "What are you doing here?"

"I thought maybe I could get my husband to buy me lunch," I said, reprising the lie I had concocted for Fart Unger.

Tansie bit her lip. "Gimme a minute." She clanged through a steel door marked EMPLOYEES ONLY and left me standing there with a knot in my stomach the size of Stone Mountain.

I kept my eyes on the clock over the door. Two minutes ticked by. Three. Four. The noon whistle blew. I'd heard it often enough in town, the faintly mournful sound of a train in the distance, headed off to exotic places. Up close, it blasted with a force that left my eardrums ringing. It had to be loud, I supposed, to be heard above the noise in the plant.

At five after twelve the door opened again. Beyond it I could hear indistinct voices and shuffling movement, a stampede of steel-toed work boots headed for the lunchroom. Tansie shut the door behind her and stood shifting from one foot to the other.

"Um," she said, "seems like Chase isn't here. His supervisor said he left around eleven, took the afternoon off." Her eyes darted to the coffeemaker in the corner, to the fluorescent light above her head, looking anywhere except into my eyes. "Guess he had some overtime coming," she finished lamely, as if this explained everything. "He, ah, didn't tell you?"

I forced a laugh. "Come to think of it, he might have said something about going fishing. I just forgot."

I ran for the door before I had to face that pity again.

For the next two hours I drove aimlessly around town—through the square, twice, to the Piggly Wiggly, down every street in every neighborhood, even out past the river camp where Chase went fishing, just in case. But his truck was nowhere to be found.

There was nothing else to do but go home.

I cooked all afternoon: cornbread, turnip greens, creamed corn, squash casserole, chicken with homemade dumplings—everything Chase liked best. Even a chocolate chip cake with double fudge frosting.

Five o'clock came and went. At six I went out onto the front porch and watched the sun set. At seven I stood on the back deck and looked at the lights shimmering on the river.

At eight o'clock I put the food away.

At nine I sliced the cake and ate three pieces without tasting it.

At ten I went to bed.

At eleven-fifteen the telephone rang.

It was the sheriff. Chase was dead.

· 2 ·

In a small town like Chulahatchie, everybody knows everybody, but precious few really know. Some folks you just smile at and say hey when you meet them on the street, but they've never crossed the threshold of your front door, and you've never set foot in their house, either. Some you sit with at church potlucks and high school football games, exchange recipes, and get together for coffee. Some come to your house for a fish fry on Saturday night or to watch the Falcons get beat on Sunday afternoon. A few, very few, include you at family suppers and birthday parties and Thanksgiving dinners.

But in a whole lifetime there's usually only one or two people you can call near midnight when your world falls apart.

Mine was Antoinette Champion.

Toni and I had been best friends since kindergarten, got our braces the same week, double-dated to the senior prom, got drunk together for the first time and swore we'd never touch the stuff again. We were maids of honor at each other's weddings and had no secrets.

At eleven-twenty on the night Chase died, she answered on the second ring. "God, Dell, you mean that ass of a sheriff told you this on the phone? He didn't come to the house?"

"No," I said. "Just the phone call."

"The man's an idiot. What did he say?"

"I don't remember," I said, trying to clear the cobwebs from my head. "Something about a nine-one-one call, and the EMTs finding Chase at the river camp, and transporting to the hospital. Other things, too, details. But he might as well have been talking to a fencepost. I don't know, Toni. I just don't know."

"You're in shock," she said. "What are you going to do now?"

I was shaking with the kind of cold that comes from the bones, from the inside out. I took a breath and tried to stop the shudders, tried to sound strong. "I'm going to do what has to be done," I said. "I'm going to go down to the hospital and talk to the doctor and claim the body, and then tomorrow morning I'm going to make arrangements for the funeral."

"You shouldn't be alone. I'll meet you there."

For a fleeting instant I flirted with the idea of refusing. "Okay," I said. "Thanks."

*   *   *

When I got to the emergency room entrance of the hospital, Toni was already waiting outside, smoking a cigarette. I don't know how she got there so fast. All I did was throw on some clothes and head out the door, but there she was, two steps ahead of me, as usual.

She crushed the cigarette under her tennis shoe and pulled me into her arms. "I'm so, so sorry," she murmured into my hair. She was crying—I could feel the warm wet tears on my neck and hear the crack in her voice. But when she let me go, she swiped her eyes and blew out a breath. "You okay?"

"Yeah. Let's get this over with."

The doctor on call in emergency looked like Doogie Howser, small and blond and slight. The name stitched over his pocket was DR. LATOURNEAU.

"You're not from around here, are you?" Toni said. I poked her in the ribs to shut her up, but she didn't take the hint. "Are you a real doctor?"

He raised his eyebrows at her. "Yes . . . ah, ma'am. I'm fully qualified, I can assure you."

"Fresh out of med school, I reckon," Toni persisted. "Ole Miss?"

"UT, Memphis," he said.

"You don't sound like you're from Memphis. You sound like a Yankee."

"Toni," I said, "let's just get on with it." I ignored her protests and faced the doctor. "I'm Dell Haley. You have my husband, I believe."

The puzzled look on his face told me he hadn't the faintest idea what I was talking about. "Your husband?"

"Chase Haley. Fifty-five, big guy—the sheriff said he'd been brought here."

Blank stare. No response.

"In the ambulance?"

At last the fog lifted. "Oh, yeah. The heart attack. DOA."

"Charming bedside manner," Toni muttered, loud enough for him to hear. "You and the sheriff must have gone to the same school. Sensitivity U."

At least he had the grace to look abashed. "Sorry," he mumbled. "If you'll come with me, Mrs. Haley." He took my arm in what he undoubtedly thought was a solicitous manner and steered me toward the stainless steel double doors, turning his back quite deliberately to shut Toni out.

She was having none of it. She followed along behind, swearing under her breath, the soles of her tennis shoes pounding like a heartbeat on the hard tile floor.

The examining room was a small cubicle surrounded by filmy draperies in the ugliest mustard-colored fabric I had ever seen. The room seemed infused with a pungent, astringent smell, like rubbing alcohol and singed flesh. On a bare, cold stainless steel gurney, Chase lay naked, barely covered by a thin cotton sheet. I couldn't look at him.

Dr. Latourneau pulled a thin metal clipboard from under Chase's left thigh. It stuck a little; the flesh wiggled, and my head swam. Toni reached out an arm to steady me. The doctor didn't notice.

"Call came in to nine-one-one a little after nine o'clock," he said, reading from the notes on the chart.

"Who called?" Toni interrupted.

Doogie recoiled like he'd been slapped upside the head, and studied the chart. "Doesn't say."

"Well, there's gotta be something there." Toni jerked the chart out of his hands and scanned it.

"Sorry," the doctor said, but he didn't sound one bit sorry. "You can't have access to the patient's private medical information." He pried the clipboard out of her fingers and clutched it to his chest. "Maybe the sheriff's office will have more information about the source of the call."

"Yeah, like he knows his ass from his elbow," Toni said. "Okay, so what else?"

He went back to the chart, holding it up between himself and Toni so she couldn't see it. "EMTs responded to find a white male, mid-fifties, in cardiac arrest. They administered CPR at the scene and transported, but by the time he got here . . ."

I didn't hear the rest. At nine o'clock I had been pigging out on chocolate chip cake with double fudge frosting, cursing my husband for ruining my nice dinner and sure, very sure, that he was off somewhere having a roll in the hay with some bimbo in a ten-dollar motel.

"Will there be an autopsy?" Toni demanded.

I've watched way too many episodes of *CSI*. An image of Chase sliced open and peeled back on a coroner's table slapped me back to reality. "Who said anything about an autopsy?"

Toni turned to me. She had seen plenty of medical crime dramas in her time, too. "They oughta do an autopsy to determine cause of death. Maybe it wasn't a heart attack. Maybe—"

The Boy Wonder interrupted. "Cause of death was clear. The attending ER physician signed off on it. If you want an autopsy, you can request one, but—"

"No," I said. "No autopsy."

"All right." He made a notation on the clipboard and handed me a brown paper bag with the Piggly Wiggly logo stamped on the front. "These are his personal effects. If you'll just sign here, we'll release the body to the funeral home. He'll be there by nine tomorrow morning."

I stared unseeing at the paper he held out, the pen poised uncertainly in midair. "Right here." He guided my hand toward a line at the bottom. I signed. "I'll leave you alone with him now, so you can . . . ah, say your good-byes."

An expression something like relief shot across his face as he took the clipboard and left the room. His soft-soled shoes made little squeaking noises across the tile floor, a mouse scurrying away into its hidey-hole.

At last I mustered the courage to look at my dead husband. His eyes were closed, and his hair—gray around the temples and darker on the sides and top—looked matted, as if it had dried all sweaty. His bald spot was showing.

I combed through the hair with my fingers, covering it up as if it were some obscene private part that shouldn't be showing in polite company.

His flesh was ash-gray and waxy, with a tinge of blue around the lips and under the eye sockets. When I touched his arm, it gave slightly under the pressure of my fingers, like the skin of a water balloon.

The sheet, apparently, had been pulled up over his face, and whoever turned it down had done it carefully, evenly, smoothing it out as if preparing a bed in a fine hotel. I almost expected to see a foil-wrapped chocolate on his forehead, the kind we got every night when we took an anniversary cruise to the Caribbean so many years ago.

The memory sliced through me like a dull paring knife on a green apple—pressing its edge against the resistant skin, bruising, ripping. Not a clean, quick cut, but a painful, jagged tearing.

Toni's arm went around my shoulders, drawing me back to the present. I could feel the warmth of her body at my side, caught a scent of tobacco and spearmint gum and Chanel N° 5. Her breath came in ragged gasps; she was crying.

For the first time all night I looked at her. Really looked.

Toni had always been attractive—to tell the truth, a whole lot prettier than me. She was tall and leggy and blonde, the kind of Southern girl/cheerleader/beauty queen good looks that might have marked her as an airhead if she hadn't been so dang smart. And down to earth. And loyal.

Some people are described as drop-dead gorgeous. Toni Champion was drop-dead *good*. If I lived a hundred lifetimes, I could never have a better friend.

Over the years I reckon I quit noticing how beautiful she was on the outside and just appreciated her heart. Now, in this moment of crisis, I noticed. She still had the legs that went on forever, the slim figure, the high cheekbones, the wide blue eyes. Her blonde wasn't natural anymore, but it suited her, not like Tansie's platinum color. Tonight she had it twisted up in a knot with a pencil stuck through it. Somehow on Toni it looked good.

Everything looked good on Toni. Everything except grief.

Her face was haggard, exhausted, with dark circles under her eyes and a little bit of leftover foundation creased in the fold under her neck. Anyone who observed us here, staring down at Chase's lifeless body, couldn't have told who was the widow and who was the friend.

My gaze followed hers back to the man on the gurney. The sheet was folded halfway down his chest. The dark tanned V beneath his chin ended just above his breastbone. His shoulders and upper arms were white, and a little mole I had never noticed before stood out like a tick against his pale skin. The patch of hair on his chest was gray and curly, and beneath the surface I could see bruises the color of storm clouds, purplish gray.

"God," I whispered, "this is what we need children for. Nobody should have to go through this alone."

I heard a sob catch in Toni's throat. It was a stupid and thoughtless thing to say, and I cursed myself silently for it. Because although Chase and I were never able to have children, my best friend *did* have a child—a son. A son now dead and buried in the graveyard on the north side of town, spitting distance from where Chase's final resting place would be.

His name was Stanley, after his great-grandfather, but everybody had called him Champ. He was a terrific kid—athletic and funny and smart, the star pitcher on his Little League team.

Toni told her husband, Rob, she didn't want Champ to have that shotgun for Christmas, but Rob didn't listen. A boy had to have his own gun, didn't he? He was eleven years old. Time to learn how to hunt, time to bag his first deer. It was a rite of passage for both father and son.

After the accident, the stress was too much for Toni and Rob's relationship to bear. He accused her of blaming him, and the truth was, she did. It was all his fault, teaching his son to swagger around the county like a redneck with a shotgun slung over his shoulder.

It only took one mistake. Set it against a fencepost while he climbed through the barbed wire, and the next thing you knew—

I tried to push the memory away, but it wouldn't go far. Toni knew a whole lot more than I did about grief, about the pain of losing someone too soon. She lost twice, lost everything, all in one year. Rob couldn't take it anymore, and finally, one day, he just got in his truck and drove off. They weren't divorced, but the paperwork hardly mattered. Last I heard, Rob was living with some woman up around Dahlonega, Georgia, and Toni didn't care.

I reached for her hand.

"Can you come home with me tonight?"

She nodded and swallowed hard. "Sure."

I'm sure some shrink would say I was feeding my pain, but by the time we got to the house I was ravenous. I warmed up the chicken and dumplings, heated the squash casserole, got out the chocolate chip layer cake. It was two A.M. by the time we finished, and while Toni put the dishes in the dishwasher, I opened the Piggly Wiggly bag and pulled out my husband's personal effects.

Someone, a nurse probably, had neatly folded and stacked his belongings. His wristwatch was on top—not the everyday one, but the nice gold-colored Bulova I gave him for Christmas last year.

Something gnawed at my brain, something not right. He should have been wearing his work clothes, but here were his cordovan loafers and navy dress socks. His blue oxford button-down with the windowpane checks, the shirt I had bought him because it reminded me of one he took on our honeymoon trip thirty years ago. His good khakis with the belt loop coming loose in the back, the one I hadn't gotten around to sewing back on yet.

This wasn't his stuff, my mind tried to tell me, but it was. I knew it was; I recognized it. His worn brown wallet was there—eighteen dollars in cash, a Visa card, and his driver's license with a picture of him scowling into the camera.

In a habit born of years of doing his laundry, I felt in the pockets of his pants. A handful of change, the keys to his truck, his Swiss army knife with the chipped handle. And something round and gold and heavy.

His wedding ring.

I didn't want to see this. Didn't want to know. Didn't want to have confirmed what my mind and heart already told me. But I steeled myself and kept going, a lumpy, determined, middle-aged backhoe digging and digging to find the truth.

And I found it. There, at the bottom of the pile, neatly folded beneath a clean undershirt.

A pair of brand-new briefs.

Not white cotton, like my husband always wore. Not

sagging and misshapen with the elastic stretched out. Not the underwear of a fifty-five-year-old man in a thirty-year marriage.

New briefs. Black silk bikini briefs.

All doubt vanished. The floodgates opened, and despair, which had been dammed up and waiting at the edge of my subconscious, rushed in to drown me.

"Whoever thought up these rituals for the dead ought to be drawn and quartered and roasted in the third circle of hell," Mama told me after Daddy died.

She was right. The whole thing seemed barbaric, surreal. Once word got out that Chase was dead, the whole town ground to a halt as if somebody had jerked the emergency brake on a fully loaded freight train.

People flocked to the house, bringing tuna casseroles and macaroni and cheese and homemade apple pies, fried chicken and brownies and peanut butter cookies and huge tin pans full of pork barbecue.

The women clustered in the kitchen like hens around scratch, clucking and ruffling their feathers and vying to be queen of the chicken yard. The men crowded into the living room, sweating in their unfamiliar suits, balancing plates on their bony knees, eating and telling stories about Chase and sometimes laughing, until they caught sight of me lurking in the doorway.

My hunger binge had long passed; I had thrown up everything I ate the night Chase died and hadn't touched a bite since.

"Come on, honey, you got to eat something," Rita Yearwood urged, pressing a plate of fried chicken and cornbread into my hands. I hated Rita's cornbread. I got no idea how she could mess up something that simple, but it tasted like the yellow pollen that comes out of the magnolia trees in the summer time. Kinda resembled that pollen, too, all flat and caked together.

DeeDee Sturgis stood nearby with a somber expression on her face. She didn't say anything, but she was itching to get her hands on my hair—I could see it in her eyes. *Poor Dell, didn't get a chance to get her hair done, and then her husband goes and dies, and she's stuck at the funeral looking like that . . .*

Without warning my head began to swim and the walls started to close in, just like the hot flashes and panic attacks I used to get when I first started going through the change. I pushed past Rita and ran for the bathroom. I was still heaving into the sink when Toni came in and shut the door behind me.

"You okay?"

"Yeah, great. Don't I look it?" I ran some cold water into my hand and rinsed my mouth out. "Why can't they just leave me alone?"

"Because that's not what people do when someone dies. They bring food. They come to call. They pay their respects."

"Respects?" The word stuck in my throat. "Everybody out there knows what Chase was up to. They *know*. And they're all pretending that nothing's wrong, that everything's normal, that I'm the grieving widow who's lost her faithful and loving husband—"

"Look," Toni said, "why don't you lie down and rest for a while? I'll tell everybody to go on home, that you'll see them at the funeral later this afternoon."

"What about the food?"

Of course, I'd think about the food. And all those women messing around in my kitchen.

"I'll take care of it." She laid a hand on my shoulder and chuckled. "You won't have to cook for months."

"Assuming I'd want to eat DeeDee's tuna casserole," I said. "It tastes like hair."

"It's made with clippings from the shop," Toni said. "Didn't you know? That's why she never gives out her recipes."

We both started to laugh—the kind of wild, hysterical giggling that takes you over and can't be stopped. "Her secret ingredient!" I whispered, but it came out as more of a squeal.

We laughed and laughed, leaning against the sink in the bathroom with our arms around each other. For a minute or two I felt like a teenager again, and then, without warning, the tears came. I couldn't stop them, any more than I could stop the giggles—great wracking sobs, wrenched from my gut and dragged out into the open against my will.

"Come on," Toni murmured. She led me into the bedroom and helped me onto the bed, then took my shoes off and covered me up with the quilt Mama had made me for my wedding day.

Through the open doorway I could hear shuffling and muttering. "She'll be all right," Toni said to somebody. "She just needs to rest."

Then she shut the door behind her and left me alone with my pain.

Open caskets are, in my opinion, vulgar and tacky and totally unnecessary, but in a town like Chulahatchie, everybody expects to have the opportunity to view the deceased and show their ignorance by saying things like, "Don't he look natural?"

When I die, I hope somebody has the good sense to cremate my remains and use the ashes to feed the azalea bushes. The last thing I want is to be laid out in full view of God and everybody wearing too much rouge and Kiss Me Pink lipstick.

Besides, Chase didn't look one bit natural. He looked dead.

My husband was, in life, a man of many passions. Good cookin' and good lovin', certainly, but other things, too, like storytelling and laughing and high school football and funnel cakes at the county fair. He'd been an all-state wide receiver once upon a time, and a second-stringer at Mississippi State, and when we married he still had rock-hard muscles and that charming, crooked little smile with a dimple in his right jaw.

Over the years the muscles went flabby, but he kept the smile. That man could charm the pants off—

Well, off of someone. That much was clear.

And now he was dead, squeezed into a mahogany casket with his head on an ivory satin pillow, looking about as natural as a waxwork of Elvis in Madame Tussauds.

"He's dressed real nice," DeeDee Sturgis whispered in my ear. "But his hair could use a trim." She didn't say a blessed word about *my* hair. Still, that I-told-you-so look was in her eye.

At that moment it took a lot to keep from laughing right in her face. DeeDee didn't know what I knew. Nobody else knew, except for Toni. It was our secret, a brief moment of sweet revenge: Chase was getting buried in the clothes he died in. Or, more precisely, died out of.

The pale blue windowpane-checked oxford. The khakis, all freshly washed and ironed, with the belt loop sewn neatly back on. The navy socks and cordovan dress shoes.

Right down to the black silk bikini briefs.

If my husband was going to die being unfaithful to me, the least he could do was be ashamed of his underwear in the afterlife.

· 4 ·

I didn't cry at the visitation. I didn't cry at the funeral, either. I didn't cry at graveside, when I saw Toni staring off over the hill toward her son's tombstone. I didn't even cry the night after, alone in the eerie sleepless silence of a world without my husband's grunting snores.

I cried, of all places, in the glass-walled cubicle of the Chulahatchie Savings and Loan, at ten minutes 'til noon on a Monday morning when nine-tenths of the population was lined up depositing their paychecks from the previous Friday.

I never liked Marvin Beckstrom. In school he had been a geeky, defensive little boy who grew up to be a geeky, defensive little man. Maybe it was all the teasing he got as a child, I don't know, but education didn't improve him one bit, and becoming manager of the bank supplied him with just enough power to swell his head. He was short and scrawny and intellectual looking, with acne scars and over-sized horn-rimmed glasses. A brittle, large-eyed insect in a custom-tailored suit. Behind his back everybody called him the Bug, and that was the nicest of his nicknames.

He had a habit of jingling his keys in his pocket, as if to remind everybody exactly who was in charge here, and the smirk on his face told you that he never forgot one iota of what people said about him in junior high. If you'd ever in your life offended Marvin Beckstrom, there'd be a sleet storm in hell before he'd even think about approving your loan.

My appointment was at eleven-fifteen. He kept me waiting until quarter to twelve, just because he could. I sat in the straight-backed chair outside his glass-walled box, twisting my hands in my lap and feeling like I'd been called to the principal's office for acting up in class. Meanwhile people came and went, watching me with somber expressions and occasionally saying "hey" but not meeting my eyes.

Once the rituals were over and done with, nobody knew what to do with the newest widow in town.

Finally the door opened.

"Come on in, Miz Haley," he said, ushering me into the inner sanctum.

Miz Haley? He'd known me since second grade and never in his life called me *Miz* anything.

"So am I supposed to call you *Mr. Beckstrom* now?" I blurted out. "Since when did we get so formal?"

He quirked an eyebrow and smirked at me. "Just trying to be professional, Dell. This is, after all, a difficult time for all of us." He leaned forward across his polished mahogany desk. "How are we doing?"

The condescension in his voice ran under my skin like a whole colony of invisible fire ants. "Well, let's see," I said, making no attempt to conceal the sarcasm. "I'm fifty-one years old, I just buried my husband, and I got a call from your secretary this morning telling me I urgently needed to come down here and discuss my finances. How do you think *we're* doing?"

It was a mistake, backing him in a corner like that, but I couldn't help myself. His eyes narrowed and a muscle in his jaw tensed, and in that moment he reminded me of a Chihuahua baring its teeth to a rottweiler. He leaned back in his chair and slid a green file folder to the center of his desk blotter.

"Fine," he said. "Setting the niceties aside, here's your situation. As you may know, Chulahatchie Savings and Loan holds the mortgage on your house—"

"Mortgage," I repeated. I sounded like a mentally deficient parrot.

"Yes, mortgage. The loan secured by your property."

"I know what a mortgage is," I said. "We've lived in that house for thirty years. Surely it's paid off by now."

The smirk returned, and with it the condescending tone. "Dell, I'm aware that many women of a certain age—" He paused and looked up.

I bit my tongue until I tasted blood but managed to say nothing. Apparently satisfied, he nodded and resumed his little speech.

"Many women of a certain age, like yourself, have

always depended upon their husbands to provide for them, and to take care of financial affairs. Unfortunately, this does not always serve them well when their spouses die, ah, unexpectedly."

He was right, although I wasn't about to admit it. I had always let Chase handle the finances. I kept the household checkbook, paid the monthly bills, bought groceries, but as long as there was money in the account, I didn't question it.

I glared at him. "Spare me the lecture and cut to the chase, Marv."

A flicker of amusement ran across his face at the unintentional pun. "Cut to the chase," he repeated, just in case I hadn't caught it. "All right, here's the bottom line." He paused dramatically. "The house is mortgaged to the hilt. Chase refinanced it to buy the river camp and the boat. And his new truck, of course." He withdrew a sheet of paper from the file and handed it across the desk. "There's the summary. All told, you have thirty-five hundred and change in checking and debts totaling about a hundred and thirty-two thousand."

I couldn't breathe, couldn't think. I was sinking, sure as if Marvin Beckstrom had tied a rock around my leg and tossed me in the Tombigbee.

I lunged for a lifeline, a floating branch, anything. "What about a pension? Life insurance?" My voice cracked and shook, and I stared at my hands. When I looked up, the smarmy little cockroach replaced his smug expression with an attitude of concern, but not fast enough. I caught it.

"Everybody lost their pensions when the feed plant closed

down and Ray Kaiser skipped town with the cash," Bug said. "Chase was only vested at Tenn-Tom two years ago, so don't expect his pension to amount to much. And apparently he opted for the minimum life insurance—twenty thousand."

Twenty thousand. Plus thirty-five hundred. I've never been any good at math, but it didn't take some kind of Mensa genius to figure out what this meant.

"You might be able to sell the river property," Marv said as if reading my mind, "although I wouldn't count on it in this market. The truck's worth five or six thousand, I'd guess."

"And he paid what? Twenty-four, twenty-five?"

"Depreciation." Marvin shrugged. "If you're careful, you could probably live for a year on the cash from the life insurance," he said. "But if you want my advice—"

I didn't. Didn't want his advice, and sure as fire didn't want to spend another minute of this life looking at his goggle-eyed, self-righteous face. I didn't want to cry, either, but the tears were already choking me, and I was going to be sick, right here, right now, right in the middle of his plush green carpet.

I ran for it. Pushed my way out the door, broke through the line snaking its way around Pansy Threadgood's counter, bolted into the ladies' room, and locked myself in the handicapped stall.

For a full five minutes I stood there hanging over the toilet, salivating like one of Pavlov's dogs while my stomach decided it didn't have anything to throw up. When I was fairly sure I wasn't going to retch, I closed the lid, sat down on top of the toilet, and wept.

Damn him.

Damn him for leaving me like this. Damn him for buying that godforsaken river camp, for mortgaging the house, for not considering for a single minute what might happen to me when he was gone. Damn him for his selfishness, for his infidelity, for all the times he came home late and wormed his way out of an argument by being cute and charming and flattering.

"Damn you, Chase Haley!" I yelled. "Damn you for living, for dying." I slammed a clenched fist against the bathroom wall.

It hurt—hurt bad—but I didn't stop. I couldn't. "I hope you rot in hell. I hope you burn to a crisp. I hope—"

"Dell?" Someone was tapping gently on the stall door. "Dell, honey, are you all right?"

I peered through the crack and caught a glimpse of frizzy blonde hair. It was Tansie Orr, probably here on her lunch hour from Tenn-Tom. "You need some help, hon? Let me in."

Against my better judgment I opened the stall door. She stood there for a minute, looking down at me, then took charge, unrolling about six yards of toilet paper and pressing it into my hand. "Blow your nose, honey, you're all snotty," she said.

I got up, went to the mirror, and squinted at my reflection. She was right; I was all snotty. My nose and eyes were red, and there were black tracks running down my cheeks. Right then and there I vowed that, even if my eyes disappeared completely between my crow's-feet and the folds of my eyelids, I'd never wear mascara again.

Tansie was standing behind me, watching me in the mirror. "Guess you got some bad news from Squeaky, huh?"

In spite of myself, I smiled. It was another of Marvin's childhood nicknames, along with Mouseturd, Roach, and Chickenhead. I nodded.

"He's a pure-D sumbitch, that's for sure," Tansie said amiably. "What'd he do to you?"

"He told me the truth."

"God, I hate it when that happens." Tansie shook her head sympathetically and pulled me into a hug. She was five or six inches taller than me, which placed my face right at bosom level. The fumes of Estée Lauder made my eyes burn, and I nearly suffocated in her cleavage before she let me go.

She leaned against the sink and flossed between her two front teeth with a long red fingernail. How she typed with those claws was a mystery even Agatha Christie couldn't solve. "Listen, honey," she said. "You're in some kind of a spot. God knows there's a whole bunch of us who'd be in real deep doo-doo if our husbands went and died on us. But if you want my advice—"

She waited for her cue to continue. I shrugged and repressed a sigh. "Go on."

"Well, look. I been thinking. Tank took me to Asheville last year at Christmastime, remember? We stayed at this gorgeous Victorian B&B—that's a bed-and-breakfast, you know. Real nice place, run by a widow lady."

She met my eyes expectantly. I had no clue what she was getting at.

"So?"

"So you could do that, Dell. You *could*. You got a Victorian house and an extra bedroom. You could open up your own B&B right here in Chulahatchie."

The woman was insane. Certifiable. For one thing, my house wasn't Victorian. It was just old. It only had one bathroom, unless you counted the half-bath that was so cramped Chase couldn't get into it without getting stuck. The small extra bedroom had always been used for storage, since we had neither attic nor basement. It was currently stacked with cardboard boxes full of Christmas decorations, and dead geraniums that got caught in the first freeze, and a bunch of Chase's old fishing gear that he brought home from the river camp to fix and never got around to it.

Besides that, Chulahatchie wasn't exactly a hotbed of tourism. Nobody came here unless they had to, or got lost and took the wrong exit off the highway, or were desperate for gas, since the Pump 'n Run was the last chance between here and the Alabama line.

A B&B in Chulahatchie? It was ludicrous.

But I didn't say any of this to Tansie. She meant well, bless her heart, and she looked so happy to finally be able to come up with such a great idea. Like she'd been waiting her whole life to say something smart and important, something nobody else had ever thought of.

As it turned out, Tansie wasn't the only one willing to give me the benefit of their infinite wisdom. I might've appreciated it, too, if any of it had applied to me—if I'd had a college degree or secretarial training or a brain for numbers. If I could lift sixty pounds or haul boxes or load trucks. If I hadn't been a fifty-one-year-old woman with no training, no experience, no money, and no prospects.

"Free advice," Mama used to say, "is worth every cent you pay for it."

All I could do was cook. And I couldn't for the life of me figure out how that was gonna help.

· 5 ·

Two weeks after the funeral, I was in the kitchen taking the last batch of fried apple pies out of the skillet when the doorbell rang.

I couldn't quite get the hang of this cooking for one. Every horizontal surface in the kitchen was covered with fried pies—pies on cooling racks, pies on paper towels, pies in a long flat Tupperware for freezing. Chase loved them, couldn't get enough of them. And even though he wasn't here to enjoy them anymore, I cooked them anyway. It just wasn't in my nature to stand by and see all those apples go to waste.

I fished the last of the pies out of the grease, turned off the gas, and went to the door to find Boone Atkins standing on my front porch.

I had spoken to Boone at the visitation and funeral, of course—he was there, just like everybody else in town, but we hadn't really talked. When other people were present, Boone tended to keep his distance, like he had a plastic bubble around him nobody else could see. It shielded him from the ugliness folks manifested toward him, but it kept him from getting close to anybody, too.

Except for me. I was Boone's best and only friend, because everybody else in town thought Boone was gay.

In this day and time, that might not seem like such a big deal, at least not in New York or San Francisco, or even in Memphis or Birmingham. But in Chulahatchie folks tended to be suspicious of anything out of the ordinary, and here ordinary meant straight, white, and Baptist. Or maybe Episcopalian, if you had money and good taste.

Boone was the librarian at the Chulahatchie Public Library. He'd lived more than forty years in the house he was born in, except for the time he went to Oxford to get his library science degree. When his father died, Boone stayed on and took care of his mother, and when she passed, he inherited the house.

He was a quiet, gentle soul who had three loves in life: music, books, and art. That made it worse, of course, since it meant he fulfilled just about every stereotype on God's green earth.

What finally sent everybody over the edge, though, was after his mama died, when he redecorated, and painted that nice little white house a color called Marvelous Mauve with the trim all done up in Plum Passion. It was more subdued than it sounds, and really gorgeous, if you ask me, but it didn't set too well with folks who already had their suspicions about him.

Chase couldn't abide Boone—called him the "little fairy faggot" behind his back. I know because he said it in front of me, once.

Only once. I swore if I ever heard it again I'd kill him first, and then divorce him. He kept quiet after that, but he didn't have to say it out loud to communicate his displeasure about my friendship with Boone.

And Boone wasn't stupid. He never came to the house. We'd have lunch every week or two, always when Chase was at work, and usually in Starkville or Tupelo or sometimes even over in Tuscaloosa, where we weren't likely to be recognized. It was kinda like carrying on a love affair without the love.

Except that there was love, of a different sort. Boone understood parts of me that nobody else had ever seen, not even Toni. We talked about novels and ideas and creativity. He recommended books to me, and asked my opinion about things, and made me feel smart even though I wasn't nearly as educated as he was.

Boone was my lifeline to a world beyond Chulahatchie. But a secret lifeline. Always a secret.

Now Chase was gone, and I reckoned I could have anybody I damn well pleased inside my house. It was an odd feeling, and a liberating one.

"Hey, Boone," I said. "Come on in."

He hesitated for a second or two, stared down at the doormat, then glanced around the deserted street as if to make sure no one was watching. At last he stepped over the threshold and gathered me into his arms.

He hugged me for a long, long time, holding on very tight. "Dell," he said.

That was all, just "Dell." But it was enough.

When he let me go, I stepped back to look at him. I could never get over how handsome he was, even though I'd known him forever. He was a few years younger than me—forty-something, forty-five, maybe—but he looked thirty. Broad shoulders, dark hair and eyes, a little cleft in his chin. Handsome enough to be a heartbreaker, if the situation had been different. He didn't look like a librarian, that much was certain.

I frowned at him. "How come it took you so long to get here?"

He didn't answer just yet, but followed me back to the kitchen. "Something smells wonderful."

"Fried apple pies. I just finished. Sit down and I'll make us a pot of coffee."

He settled at the kitchen table and watched me while I put the coffee on and piled a plate with the fresh apple pies. Boone had the ability to be quiet without being uncomfortable, something most people can't do to save their souls.

I finally quit ginning around the kitchen and sat down. Boone gave me about thirty seconds, then leaned forward with his elbows on the table and his chin in his hands. "What are you going to do, Dell?"

It was so sudden and so blunt that I laughed out loud and sprayed coffee halfway across the table. "Not much for small talk and superficialities, are you?" I said.

"Not with you." He took one of the pies and bit into it. "This is wonderful, Dell. Just sweet enough, lots of cinnamon. The crust is so flaky—except for the part you spit on." He grinned. "Answer my question."

"The answer is, I don't know."

"Well then, I'll answer *your* question. I waited this long to come and see you because when someone dies, everybody gathers around the grieving family members for a couple of weeks, and then it's business as usual. People go back to their lives. They forget, because they're not living with it, that the pain and lostness and unpredictability of grief go on and on and ambush you when you least expect it. When you're grieving, you need people there after the funeral is over, after the food is gone, after the closets have been cleaned out and the thank-you notes written. I know you've got Toni, but I want you to know that you've got me, too."

His face wavered in my vision, like he was underwater, or like I was looking at his reflection in the bottom of a well. I blinked back the tears. "Thank you."

"It's okay to cry, Dell."

"So they tell me. But I'm having trouble with that, Boone. I can't seem to cry for the right reasons—because I'm sad, or because I've lost my husband of thirty years, or even because I'm lonely. I only seem to cry when I'm mad. I mean *really* mad, furious enough to throw things or punch a hole in the wall."

He gazed at me with an expression I hadn't seen very often—tenderness, and understanding. "You've got plenty to be mad about."

I took a bite of one of the pies but couldn't taste it. It stuck in my throat like a lump of Mississippi red clay. "You know everything that goes on in this town, Boone," I said when I finally got it down. "Tell me the truth."

"The truth about what?"

"About Chase. I know he was having an affair, and nobody can tell me different. But I don't know who, or where, or when. Everybody's talking about it, except to me.

"They found him at the river camp that Friday night, but I went out there in the afternoon, and his truck wasn't there. Somebody called nine-one-one, but I don't know who."

"Why do you need to know?" he asked.

"I need to know because I need to know!" I said. "Call it natural curiosity. Call it retribution. Call it anything you like. I want the truth." I put my head in my hands and swallowed hard. "I can't walk down the street in this town without wondering: Was it her? Or her? Or maybe her? Who can I trust? People avoid me or talk in whispers behind my back or give me this look of pity that makes me want to throw up. I just wish I knew. Then maybe I could get on with my life and things could get back to normal."

Boone smiled and put his hand on my arm. The touch of his flesh felt warm and solid, real. The realest thing I'd felt in a very long time.

"It's not going to be normal," he said quietly. "It's never going to be normal again—or at least it will be a different kind of normal. Everything's changed. You may never have all your questions answered, Dell. If you knew *who*, you still wouldn't know *why*. If you knew *why*, you still wouldn't know *how*—how your husband could do such a thing, how you could be so blind as not to realize."

He paused and looked long and hard at my face, as if trying to see something hidden behind my eyes. "I don't know who it was," he said. "But Chase *was* at the river camp. His truck was parked around back, under the deck. It's still sitting there, right where he left it."

I thought about this for a minute. "Yeah. I guess I wouldn't have seen it from the road. He always just pulled up in front of the door. But if he had some woman out there—"

"Maybe he thought you might come looking for him."

A rush of gratitude welled up in me for this man, this dear, sensitive, honest man. He didn't try to argue me out of the conviction that Chase had been unfaithful. In his own way, he confirmed my suspicions, validated my emotions. At that moment I loved him more than I ever thought possible.

"Thank you," I said.

"For what?"

"For not trying to talk me out of this, or explain it away, or spare my feelings by convincing me it's all in my head."

"No good ever comes from living with self-deception."

The knot of anxiety in my gut loosened up a little, and I ate another fried pie and refilled our coffee cups. I told him about the mortgage, and the life insurance, and the reality that I had about eleven months and nineteen days before I'd be out on the street sleeping in a cardboard box.

He listened without interruption, only muttering something under his breath when Marvin Beckstrom's name came up, something that sounded like *poisonous little toad.* When I was done and came up for air, he was smiling.

"What?"

"Nothing. I was just thinking that probably everybody in this town has an opinion on what you ought to do next."

"You got that right. Tansie Orr suggested I open a bed-and-breakfast."

He gave me a disbelieving look and then grinned

broadly. "That woman is a candidate for the Whitfield State Hospital."

"Tupelo Psychiatric would be closer," I said. "But you should have seen her face, Boone. She thought she was being brilliant, like she had discovered some new principle of quantum physics or proved Einstein's theory of relativity."

"Bless her heart."

This made us both laugh. In the South you can say anything about anybody, and you're not being bitchy as long as you qualify it with, *Bless her heart.*

"So," I said finally, "you got any bright ideas about how to keep your old friend out of the poorhouse?"

"As a matter of fact, I do have one suggestion."

"Well, don't hold back, honey. Let me hear it."

He took a sip of coffee and sat back in his chair. "Play to your strengths."

"What the hell does that mean?" I said. "Haven't you been listening? I have no salable skills. I don't have a college degree, I'm too old for manual labor, and—"

"Play to your strengths," he repeated. He picked up another fried pie, saluted me with it, and took a bite. "Mmm. Delicious. Dell Haley, you are without a doubt the best cook east of the Mississippi and south of the Mason-Dixon Line."

And, as Boone knew I would, I finally got it.

· 6 ·

On the west end of town just off the square was a little store-front I had passed by a million times without even noticing. It had been boarded up for so many years that the newspapers covering the front windows still had the Katzenjammer Kids in the comic strips. It sidled up to the Sav-Mor Dollar Store parking lot on the left, and on the right shared an ancient brick wall with Runyan's Hardware.

When Boone produced a key and ushered me inside like he was presenting me with the Taj Mahal, I was sure he had lost his mind and would end up sharing a room at Whitfield with Tansie Orr.

The power was off, but enough daylight was coming through the papered-up windows to see that the place was a mess. It had the dank feeling of a building closed up too long, and yellowish grime coated every surface—a combination of grease and nicotine, my nose told me. Beneath that smell was the faint odor of mice. Something scuttled behind a baseboard. I was sure I had died and gone straight to hell.

Boone, however, was in heaven. "Just look at this place!" he said.

"I'm looking."

Apparently my tone indicated I wasn't impressed. He came over and put an arm around my shoulders. "Don't look with your eyes," he said. "Look with your heart. Look with your imagination. Look with your *soul*."

I swear, sometimes I think the man deserves his reputation. Still, I tried to humor him.

All along the back, directly across from the front door, ran a long counter with swiveling stools. The side walls were lined with high-backed booths, most of the red vinyl seats split open with the stuffing coming out. In the center of the room were six or eight square Formica tables that dated back to the fifties.

I guess I wasn't doing too good at what Boone called "looking with my heart." My eyes kept getting in the way.

"Look up," he said. "What do you see?"

"I see a ceiling about to fall on my head."

"It's tin, Dell. It's original." He went over and rubbed his hands along the countertop. "This is marble, the soda fountain counter from when this place was the old drugstore. And come here—"

He dragged me through a swinging door into a kitchen with a huge cast-iron eight-burner stove, two ovens, and a massive grill. "See, there's a big walk-in freezer, and a huge fridge—okay, that will have to be replaced, but there's plenty of pantry space. It's perfect."

"It's old," I said. "It's filthy."

"It's vintage," he said, undeterred.

"All right," I conceded. "Maybe it does have potential. But you know I can't afford to buy—"

"That's the beauty of it," he interrupted. "You don't have to buy it. You can lease it—cheap. I talked to Marvin Beckstrom, and—"

"Hold on. Are you telling me this place is owned by Chulahatchie Savings and Loan?"

"Well, yes, but—"

"Absolutely not. There is no way in hell I'm doing business with Chickenhead Mouseturd. He thinks I'm an idiot. You should have seen the smirk on his face when he told me—"

Boone came over and put his arms around me. That little bit of tenderness did me in, and I started to cry.

"Then prove him wrong," he whispered. "Prove to Marvin Beckstrom, and to this whole stupid back-assward town, that you're worth more than they give you credit for."

That night at Toni's house I picked at my chicken pot pie and told her everything—about my finances, about Boone's bright idea, about the old diner and what awful shape it was in and how scared I was about the future.

"It's brilliant," she said when I had run out of words. "It's so brilliant I wish I had thought of it."

"I could lose everything, right down to the gold crown on my left molar."

"Yeah, but think of the possibilities," Toni said. A wistful, nostalgic expression came over her face. "Remember when we were kids, and that place was a diner?"

"I remember when it got shut down for health violations," I said. "Besides, who'd come, when we've got Barney's, and McDonald's up on the bypass, and Fiesta Mexicana?"

"Everybody would come. Barney's only serves dinner. Fiesta Mexicana is a roach pit," Toni said. "Besides, that's not the issue. The issue is, this is perfect for you. What do you love most? Cooking. What do you do best? Cooking. Can you think of a better way to earn a living?"

"Well, no, but—"

"I swear, Dell Haley, you can be so dense sometimes!" She sighed dramatically. "You've been married to Chase since you were twenty years old."

"Twenty-one."

"Don't pick nits with me, girl. You'd been twenty-one for all of three days. And besides that, we both know that numbers don't tell the whole story. At twenty—or twenty-one, if you insist—you may be able to vote and reproduce and buy liquor, and you may be sporting a woman's body, but nothing else is grown up yet. Not your mind, not your heart, not even your God-given common sense. Shoot, a woman doesn't even know herself until she hits thirty or thirty-five. Maybe even forty."

"I'm sure you got a point in there somewhere."

"The point is, you lived Chase's life, not your own. He

made all the decisions, or else you made decisions based on what he wanted and needed. Now he's gone, and it's your turn. For God's sake, Dell, take a risk. For once in your life, take a chance and see what you can do."

"Boone said the same thing to me, almost in those exact words."

"Boone is a smart man. Very, very smart." She gave a crooked little grin. "About everything except the color of his house."

Once word got out that I'd leased the old diner and was planning to open a restaurant, people flocked in to see what was going on. It reminded me of the year the Tombigbee flooded, and half the town was standing out on South River Street watching to see how deep the water was going to get. Some of them hadn't spoken a word to each other in ten years, but there they were, scratching their heads and laying bets on the high-water mark and joking around like long-lost cousins at the Baptist church homecoming. Nothing brings folks together like a good disaster.

Evidently you didn't even need a full-blown catastrophe to lure folks out—just the hint of impending doom. Half the people in Chulahatchie came to see the show. I reckon a number of them actually did place whispered bets on how fast I'd crash and burn. Others just stood around shaking their heads and predicting ruination and generally being useless and in the way.

Tansie Orr had to put her two cents' worth in, of course. "I'm tellin' you, Dell, you shoulda thought about a bed-and-breakfast instead."

"Naw," DeeDee Sturgis said. "You shoulda come and worked for me. You could make good money doing those new acrylic nails."

I wished I'd had a comeback for this. What I wanted to say was that no sane woman in Chulahatchie County would pay for acrylic nails. Except for Tansie, and she was standing right there, so I had to keep my mouth shut.

Marvin Beckstrom sidled up and ignored the venomous look Tansie was giving him. "This is a bad idea, Dell. You could lose your shirt."

As if I didn't already know that. But dang if I'd give him the satisfaction of hearing it come out of my mouth. "Thanks for the encouragement, Marvin," I said.

The sarcasm passed right over his head. "Just being realistic, Dell. I told you—"

"I know what you told me," I said. "But you leased me the place anyway, didn't you?"

He raked his eyes over the derelict building and shrugged. "Business is business."

"Yeah," I said. "So why don't you go mind your own business and let me get back to mine."

He ambled off toward the square with his hands stuck in his pockets, jingling his keys and whistling. Anybody else looking on woulda seen a cheerful little man without a care in the world. I saw a black hole of despair, sucking all the life and energy right out of me.

Dang, that man could turn a wedding into a funeral just by showing up.

· 7 ·

Mama always said you could tell your friends from your enemies by the ones who didn't say "I told you so."

Boone took a week of his vacation time to help me get the place in shape. Toni showed up every day after school. Fart came with his tool belt and extension ladder. Even Tansie and DeeDee came to help.

I was in the kitchen staring at the mess and getting absolutely nothing done when I heard the argument start up. "Boone, no!" Toni yelled. "Absolutely not."

Glad for a reason to abandon the disaster area, I went out into the dining room. "What's going on?"

"Boone wants these, can you imagine?" Toni held out a fistful of color chips. "Purple Sunset and Sweet Surrender, for God's sake."

"Have you ever been in an upscale restaurant in your

50

life?" Boone said. "These are fabulous colors. Peaceful, yet compelling. Very avant-garde."

"Avant-garde, my ass," Toni said. "Lord help us, Boone, are you auditioning to be a stereotype? I'd think you might've learned a thing or two when you painted your house purple."

"Let me see," I said. Toni handed over the cards. "What's this one?"

Boone squinted and turned up his nose. "Chocolate Whip? No, Dell. You want something more vibrant, more alive. This is so . . . so *taupe*."

Toni glared at him. "Taupe is good. It's neutral, but not white. And it will go nicely with the wood floors and the burgundy booths."

"Why do the booths have to be burgundy?" Boone said. "We could recover them in a deep plum faux leather—"

I shut my eyes and took a breath. "Boone," I said when I was finally calm enough, "I appreciate your sense of style, but we don't have money for plum faux leather. We'll fix the seats that need it, and leave the booths the color they are. And besides, I like this Chocolate Whip. It reminds me of the Yoo-Hoos I used to drink when I was a child."

"You did *not* drink Yoo-Hoos," Boone said. "Those things are nasty."

I grinned at Toni and shot her a wink. "They're delicious. And even better with a MoonPie. You should try it sometime."

Boone gave a little shudder. "There is no culture in this town. None whatsoever."

"That's what you're here for," Toni said. "To make us all a little more—what did you call it? Avant-garde."

But Boone wasn't listening. He snatched the color sample out of my hand and went to buy four gallons of boring old taupe paint.

Fart watched the argument between Boone and Toni with a little grin on his face, but he didn't comment. Instead, he climbed his ladder to the ceiling and began reattaching the tin tiles overhead. I went back to the kitchen, but still couldn't make heads or tails of what I oughta do in there. It seemed absolutely overwhelming. All of it: the sheer volume of physical work that needed to be done to get the place in shape, the never-ending details that had to be attended to—and most especially, the money that was draining out of my bank account like blood from a severed artery.

Lord help me, I must be out of my ever-loving mind.

I was still standing there, frozen and frantic, when Tansie Orr pushed open the swinging door to the kitchen and smacked me on the backside. Behind her, DeeDee Sturgis came hauling buckets and mops and about ten gallons of ammonia.

"Get out of the way, Dell," Tansie said. " 'Less you wanta get scrubbed and rinsed down the drain."

I got out of the way. The two of them went to work scouring the kitchen while I cleaned out the pantry closet and put in fresh shelf paper. A couple of times I heard Tansie swearing under her breath as she sacrificed two fingernails to the cause, but to her credit she never uttered a single word of complaint.

It took a full week and a whole lotta elbow grease to get

the place in shape, but by the time we got the floors waxed up and the booth seats re-covered, I was beginning to understand what Boone meant by "seeing it with my heart." I vowed to myself never to doubt him again.

Still, I was constantly anxious about the money. When all was said and done, it took most of my twenty thousand dollars to replace the refrigerator and pay for permits and inspections and get the kitchen stocked. Every time I wrote a check, I felt the lump in the pit of my stomach get heavier, and I couldn't help wondering if I was digging my own grave.

It was the little things that shocked me most—the price of ketchup and paper napkins and salt-and-pepper shakers. We had to hire the guy from Bug Blasters to bomb the place and get rid of all the critters. I felt like I was, quite literally, stuffing money down a rat hole. But it had to be done. I was already committed.

It was like when I went mud sliding when I was a little girl. We'd set out in the summer rain, find the tallest, slickest bank on the river's edge, and shoot down the red clay into the water below. I was always scared—afraid of the height, afraid of the speed, afraid of the brown river zooming up toward me. But up there on the top, there wasn't any question of chickening out because all my friends were egging me on. And once I started the long slide down, there was no way to stop. I just had to take the risk, face the fear, and see it through to the end.

Problem was, mud sliding couldn't land you in the poorhouse.

I'd grown up in the looming shadow of the poorhouse the

way some children live with the fear of the boogeyman under the bed. Not that we were poor, or even in danger of being poor. But every time I left a light on, or didn't shut the door all the way, or stood with the icebox door open looking for something to eat, Mama would say, "Child, you're gonna drive us right into the poorhouse."

At an early age—four or five, maybe—I got the impression that the poorhouse was a kind of dungeon where families were locked up, kids and all. Clamped in irons with water dripping on our heads and rats scuttling around waiting to eat us when we fell asleep.

Later, in history class, I learned about debtors' prison, and the realization that there really was a literal poorhouse, where people had to go to pay for their financial sins, scared the bejeebers out of me. Never mind that America did away with debtors' prisons in the nineteenth century; the idea still haunted me, and I couldn't for the life of me figure out how you were supposed to pay your debt if you were locked up in a cell.

I don't reckon Mama intended her poorhouse threat to instill such fear in me; it was just an expression. But she'd been a child during the Great Depression, and had probably seen breadlines or heard my grandmother talking about Hoovervilles and unemployment. When you come that close to the poorhouse, it no doubt leaves an impression on you.

By the time I grew up, I'd lost my terror of the poorhouse. I used the expression now and then, but there wasn't enough juice in the fear to keep me from risking every dime I owned on this insane scheme of Boone's. Now it came back full force in my nightmares, in images of dank holes and barred windows and scuttling sounds that made my blood run cold.

I'd done it—gambled everything on the slim chance that I'd be able to make this cafe into a going business. I could almost hear Mama's voice echoing in my ear: "Child, you're gonna drive yourself right into the poorhouse."

Finally, everything was finished. We passed inspection and were ready to open, and by some miracle I had managed to pay cash for everything and still had enough left to hold me for a month or two. Or so I hoped.

I still wasn't sure I was in my right mind. I could feel the nervous breakdown skulking around the corner, waiting to jump me. I couldn't get a clear breath, and my jaws ached with clenching my teeth. Truth was, I expected to go under and drown at any second, expected Marvin Beckstrom to walk through the door and tell me I was flat broke. I reckoned this might just be the biggest mistake I'd ever made in fifty-one years, and I've made some doozies.

On the day before my grand opening, everybody who had helped showed up to see the transformation. Boone and Fart appeared with two tall ladders and put up a huge, hand-painted sign:

HEARTBREAK CAFE
Good Cookin', Southern Style

Boone came down off his ladder, struck an Elvis pose with one hand in the air, gyrated his hips, and began to sing:

"Well-a since my baby left me, I found a new place to eat,
In Chu-la-hat-chie, Mis-sis-sip-pi, down on West Main
   Street,
Ah-well I, I feel so hun-gry baby, I feel so hun-gry baby,
I feel so hun-gry, I could die."

Everybody laughed and applauded. And maybe the name was appropriate, all things considered. I was scared out of my wits every time I thought about what I was doing, every time I looked at my dwindling bank account balance. But I figured, all right, it's done now. No turning back.

"Well, open the door," Toni said. "Let us in."

I'll never forget that moment if I outlive Methuselah. The afternoon sun coming in through those clean windows, glinting off the marble counter and shining across the hardwood floors. The exposed brick on the side by the hardware store, and the wall of booths with a view of the Sav-Mor parking lot.

I reckon by Birmingham or Atlanta standards, it pretty much looked like lipstick on a pig, but even if that was true, I was still in hog heaven. I thought it was absolutely wonderful.

And it belonged to me.

Well, me and Chulahatchie Savings and Loan.

I pushed Mama's warning out of my mind, made three pots of coffee, and passed around apple pie and peach pie and lemon meringue pie. "All right, everybody," I said. "Bright and early tomorrow morning I'll be serving breakfast starting at six-thirty, and I expect y'all to be here."

"Where's your menu, Dell?" somebody called out.

"Don't have a menu," I said. "Whatever I cook, that's the menu, take it or leave it."

"If it's anything like this pie," Fart Unger said, "that'll work for me."

· 8 ·

January's the time most people resolve to turn over a new leaf—lose fifty pounds, quit smoking. Drink less, save more, get their taxes done early for once. Usually by April 14 at 11:00 P.M., those same folks are sitting at their kitchen table lighting one cigarette off another, snarfing down chocolate or swilling beer, and pulling their hair out over their 1040s.

I didn't wait 'til January. Chase died the third week of April, just about six weeks shy of our thirty-first anniversary. The Heartbreak Cafe was set to open the first week of June. By the time renovations were done, I had settled on two goals: first, to survive, and second, to still be financially afloat by the end of the year.

Mama probably woulda said those were pretty modest aspirations, but given the circumstances, I figured my best chance of success was in aiming low.

I've always been an early riser. I'd get up with the sun, fix Chase his breakfast, send him off to work, and, if the weather was nice, sit out on the back deck and puzzle over the crosswords while I had a second cup of coffee. Didn't need to rush; I could pretty much do things in my own time, in my own way. Long as I kept a decent house and put regular meals on the table, nobody questioned how I spent my day.

The Heartbreak Cafe changed all that, and mighty quick.

That first morning I got to the cafe well before dawn. I wanted to give myself plenty of time, since I had to heat up the grill and make scratch biscuits for breakfast, and stir up some pancake mix, and put the grits on. I figured on plenty of lulls during the morning, enough to make cornbread, set the vegetables cooking, put together a meatloaf, and fry up some chicken.

God's honest truth, I had my doubts anybody would show up. Still, I had to be ready just in case.

But I wasn't in my own kitchen, and everything seemed to take longer than I thought it should. Before I knew it, the sun was coming up and it was nearly six-thirty and I hadn't remembered to start the coffee or write the menu on the blackboard over the pass-through window.

That's how I came to be on a stepladder with my butt to the entrance when my first paying customers walked in.

The bell over the door jingled, and I nearly fell off the ladder. Fart Unger was standing there, and Boone Atkins, and about a dozen big burly guys in jeans and boots, men I didn't know from Adam's house cat.

I pulled myself together and made the coffee, took orders, served·up bacon and eggs and sausage and grits and biscuits. Fart Unger sat with his elbows propped on the table, grinning at me like the cat with the canary.

I went over to refill his coffee cup. "You got anything to do with this, Fart?" I asked.

He beamed. "Those guys"—he pointed to one of the booths—"work with me at Tenn-Tom Plastics."

"Yeah, I thought I recognized some of them. But what about the rest of these people? How'd they find me?"

"I got a cousin up at Amory who drives trucks. He put the word out on the CB that the best cooking in three counties is right here in Chulahatchie." He pointed out the window at the Sav-Mor parking lot, where several semis sat idling. "You gonna give me a cut of the profits?"

"You gonna get in there and cook?"

By quarter to eight the truckers had finished their breakfast and gotten back on the road, leaving pretty good tips and promising to recommend the place to other drivers. Fart and his buddies went off to work. Only Boone was left, alone in a booth near the back, drinking coffee and reading.

"You want a refill?"

He looked up. "Yes, please. And a little company, if you've got time."

I got a cup for myself, filled them both, and sat down opposite him. I felt like I'd already worked a twelve-hour shift. I'd gone all jittery inside, the way I do when I get an overdose of cold medicine or too much caffeine. But I hadn't had so much as my first cup of coffee yet.

"You all right?" he said.

"I think so. I'm not real sure. I feel kind of—"

"Overwhelmed?"

"That's one word for it. 'Drowning' might be more accurate." I sipped at my coffee and felt myself calming down a little. "When I came in this morning I was terrified nobody would show up. And now—"

"Now you're not sure you want them to?"

"It's just so . . . well, so *much*. Cooking, serving, pouring coffee. Making sure everybody's happy, everybody's got what they need. Remembering stuff like this guy wants extra butter, that one asked for Tabasco. And they all want to *talk* to me."

Boone glanced at his watch, closed his book, and slid out of the booth. "Get used to it," he said, giving me a quick kiss on the cheek. "Something tells me you're going to be the most popular woman in town."

I don't know about being the most popular woman in town, but I was a shoo-in for the title of Most Frazzled.

Day in and day out, it was always the same. I dragged myself out of bed at four-thirty and drove around the square while the birds were still asleep. When the lunch rush was over and I shoulda been at home putting my feet up and watching Oprah, I still had to count the till and mop the floors and prepare the menu for the following day. Make stew out of the leftover roast beef, or chili out of the meatloaf. Wash vegetables and bake pies and prepare casseroles and have stuff in the fridge ready to go the next morning.

I sure didn't have time to do any of that prep work while

I was flipping pancakes and scrambling eggs. I barely had time to go pee.

I never got home until five or six, and half the time I still had to bake a cake or two. Most nights I'd lapse into a coma in Chase's recliner before *Wheel of Fortune* was even over. I'd come to in the middle of some infomercial about a vacuum cleaner robot that scooted around the house all on its own, or glue strong enough to pull an eighteen-wheeler. Then I'd turn off the TV, drag myself into the bedroom, and wake up three hours later to a screaming alarm and a pounding headache.

"You don't look good, Dell," Toni said to me one Saturday morning after I'd been doing this for a couple of months. "You need some rest."

"You think?" The sarcasm came out sharper than I'd intended, but I didn't take it back. I had glanced in the mirror now and then, and I could see what Toni saw. My life was a car windshield smacked by a rock. Every day the cracks fanned out farther and farther, spreading until the whole thing was a web I could barely see through. I was just waiting for it to shatter and cave in.

"I can't slow down," I said. "I'm barely making ends meet as it is."

Toni frowned. "But you've got so many customers. Looks to me like the place is full."

"Yeah, but it's like bailing a boat with a bucket full of holes. Everything that comes in seems to drain right out again."

"Are we talking finances or energy?" Toni said.

I felt a lump forming in my throat and tried to swallow it back. "Both," I said. "I'm exhausted all the time, and money's still bleeding out. I'm making ends meet, but just barely."

Toni narrowed her eyes. "What you need is some help, Dell."

I may be old, but I ain't stupid. "Don't you think I've figured that out already? Where am I gonna get the money to hire anybody?"

She didn't have an answer for that, and left with her tail tucked between her legs. I shoulda felt bad about going off on my best friend in the world, but to tell the truth, at the moment I was too dang tired to care.

· 9 ·

The Monday after the Fourth of July weekend, I went to the cafe before dawn, as usual. Even at five o'clock in the morning it was like walking into one of them Swedish saunas—hot, and so muggy it got into your lungs and made you feel like there was a concrete block sitting on your chest.

Boone always said that humidity kills brain cells, and that's why people in the South move slow and think slow and talk slow and tend to be, in his words, reactionary. I don't know about all that, but I know that Mississippi in July makes me want to go home, crank up the air-conditioning, and take a nap.

Unfortunately, a nap wasn't on my agenda for the day. I was gonna be slaving over a hot stove in a tiny little restaurant where all the air-conditioning blew out into the dining room so the customers would be comfortable, never mind the cooks back in the kitchen. I hoped those folks liked their turnip greens salty, 'cause there was gonna be more than ham hock in that pot.

Air-conditioning was the first order of business. I set the thermostat, put the grits on to simmer, mixed up the biscuit dough. I was just getting the lunch casseroles out of the icebox—homemade macaroni and cheese to go with the ham—when I heard something that, even in the middle of the summer heat, made goose bumps stand up on my arms.

Footsteps. A bang, like somebody had dropped a brick. And then running water, groaning in the pipes.

Upstairs over the restaurant was a small apartment that hadn't been used for years. A set of rickety wooden stairs went up behind the Dumpster to a single room, a little tiny bathroom, and a corner that served as a kitchenette. I'd only been up there once, the day I rented the building. Marvin Beckstrom had taken great delight in showing it to me, suggesting that, considering my precarious financial situation, I might want to consider selling my house and moving up there permanently. The place was a pit, not fit for human habitation.

I heard another thump, which was a miracle in itself, since I ought not to have been able to hear a thing except the racing of my heart and the pounding in my ears. I grabbed a cast-iron skillet—the one I used for my cornbread—went out the back door, and peered up to the second floor.

It looked like a light was on up there, although it might've just been a reflection from the sign on the Sav-Mor Dollar

Store. I started up the stairs, skillet in hand, and about half-way up I stopped and grabbed hold of the railing.

What the hell did I think I was doing? It was pitch dark, practically the middle of the night. There could be anybody up there—an escaped convict, a serial killer, a drug dealer. I couldn't imagine why some mass murderer would hide out over the Heartbreak Cafe, but even in Chulahatchie we watched TV. We knew such people existed.

What I oughta do was go back down, lock the doors, and call the sheriff. What I did was go on up, one step at a time, until I got to the little landing at the top.

The door was closed but not quite latched. I raised the heavy skillet over my head, got ready to swing it, and pushed the door open.

There *was* a light on in there, just one bare bulb hanging from an overhead wire. Out of the corner of my eye I saw movement, and a shadow. I turned and swung the skillet. It flew out of my hand and crashed in the middle of the floor. An enormous gray cat jumped off the kitchenette counter and stood in the middle of the room with its back arched, all its fur on end, a mouse dangling from its mouth by the tail.

Relief flooded through me, and my legs turned to Jell-O. I held on to the wall for support.

"You scared the living daylights out of me," I said to the cat.

He—or she; I couldn't tell from the front—responded by tossing the mouse up into the air, catching it again, and then carrying it over to the corner and settling down to breakfast.

I retrieved the skillet and turned to address the cat again.

"Look, I appreciate you taking care of the mice up here, and all that," I said, "but you can't stay here. Now go on, shoo." I prodded at the cat with my foot. It didn't move.

I prodded once more, but the cat held its ground. And then something occurred to me, something my brain hadn't registered before. The place smelled different—like lemon cleaner and ammonia. The floors had been swept and scrubbed. There was a bucket over on the kitchen counter with a spray bottle sticking out, and a mop and broom propped against the far wall. And I realized the sound of running water had stopped.

"Cats don't turn on lights," I whispered to myself. "Cats don't run water or use Mr. Clean."

"No, ma'am, they don't."

The voice came from behind me, a low rumbling sound. I turned.

Filling up the narrow doorway to the bathroom stood the biggest, blackest man I had ever seen. He had a massive bare chest, a broad nose and large mouth, and biceps the size of rutabagas. His skin was damp and shiny, and drops of water clung to his close-cropped hair like the little seed pearls I had sewn all over my wedding dress.

He looked like he had just come out of the shower. Fortunately, he had his pants on, but no shoes, and a gray T-shirt hung on the bathroom doorknob.

I raised the skillet and tried to look threatening. "You stay put, now."

"Yes, ma'am." He raised his palms as if in surrender, and the pale skin underneath glowed pink in the glare of the overhead light.

The cat, who had finished its breakfast, strolled over and began to rub against the legs of his pants, purring loudly.

"I don't mean no harm," he said quietly.

I brandished the skillet at him. "What are you doing here?"

He shrugged. "Stayin'."

"Staying? You mean you're *living* here? Over my restaurant?"

"Yes'm."

"How long you been here?"

"'Bout a week, I reckon. I generally get myself gone before dawn and sneak back in after dark."

"So you're what, homeless? A bum? A hobo?"

He smiled briefly at the old-fashioned word. "I'm a . . . traveler."

"And you traveled yourself right into Chulahatchie and up the stairs to this abandoned apartment."

"Yes'm, that sounds about right."

"Using my water and electricity."

He raised a huge hand and scratched his head. "One bulb don't draw much power, ma'am. And I wash pretty quick."

I looked at him more closely. Who did he remind me of? The voice, the face, the enormous size of him . . .

Then I remembered. The convict in that Tom Hanks movie *The Green Mile*. The one on death row.

The recollection didn't comfort me none. "You got a name?" I asked.

He grinned. "Everybody's got a name. Mine's Scratch. You're Miz Dell, ain't you?"

"That's right."

He ducked his head in a little bow. "Mighty pleased to meetcha."

I gazed around. "You been cleaning up this place?"

"Yes'm."

"Why?"

He looked at me as if I'd lost my ever-loving mind. "It was dirty."

Something about the man touched me. He had a fierce, intelligent look in his eyes, a kind of fiery pride that, despite his circumstances, couldn't be quenched. He put me in mind of a warrior chief in Africa. I could almost see him with a headdress and spear and a necklace made of lion's teeth.

A hundred questions jumped to the front of my mind, but one of them won out. "How have you been living, Scratch?" I asked. "What you been eating?"

He shrugged again. "Leftovers."

"Leftovers? You mean the food I throw away? You're eating out of the Dumpster?"

"Leftovers," he repeated stubbornly. "You a mighty fine cook, Miz Dell, if you don't mind my sayin'."

I've always considered myself a good judge of character. Recent revelations about my husband should have proved otherwise, but I didn't think about that at the moment. All I knew was that this proud man, who called himself Scratch, might be homeless and jobless, but he was dignified, and decent enough not to live in squalor.

Chase woulda called him a bum, or worse. Much worse. I never use that word, the N word, but I was raised in the South and heard it plenty in the course of fifty years of living. Whether I'd use it out loud or not, it came to mind when I thought about Chase's reaction.

Folks in other parts of the country often look down on Southerners as redneck racists. I gotta admit that in the not-too-distant past, that reputation has been well deserved. I've seen a few white robes and hoods in my time—even knew which Baptist deacons were hidden underneath there, too. And some of our gun-totin', truck-drivin' good old boys mighta come straight out of *Deliverance*. But for the most part we've evolved enough to stand upright and walk on two legs, and we like to think we're a bit more civilized than people give us credit for.

Still, I won't lie; I felt just a little nervous, standing there in the apartment over the cafe with a huge, half-naked black man. I experienced a brief moment of fear, followed by a little twinge of attraction.

We stood there, eyeing at each other. And then I made a leap of faith. I decided I liked him. I decided I trusted him.

At least I didn't think he was gonna slit my throat with a butcher knife or rob me blind.

He must have seen the change come over my face. "I'm a real hard worker, Miz Dell," he said quickly, as if determined to plead his case before the moment passed. "I been kinda down on my luck lately, but I can do most anything. I can fix this place up. I can repair them stairs out back. I can short-order cook, or clean, or—"

I held up a hand to stop him. "Hold on. I can't afford to hire anybody."

"Don't need much," he said. "I know how to get by."

He wasn't begging. He was stating a fact.

I could hear Chase inside my head: *Dell, you must be out of your mind. You got no idea who this man is. For God's sake, woman, think! Think what you're doing; think what other people might say . . .*

And then, in the midst of my husband's rant, I heard Mama's voice cut across him. "Honey," she always told me, "when push comes to shove, you gotta trust your gut."

"All right," I said, half to Mama and half to Scratch. "If you're willing, you can work in exchange for a place to stay and two good meals a day—and whatever leftovers you want to take with you. You can bus tables, mop floors, clean the kitchen, run the dishwasher. We'll try it for two weeks. If I say go, you got to go, and no arguments. That sound okay to you?"

Scratch nodded. "Yes'm. Sounds about perfect."

"You need anything, you ask. If I catch you stealing, I'll call the sheriff, and he'll be all over you like white on rice."

He reached down and scooped the cat up to his broad chest. "What about Mouse?" The cat gazed at me with wide green eyes.

"Mouse?"

"Yes'm. When I found her she was just a bitty thing, about the size of a mouse. Her being gray like she is, the name just seemed to fit. She won't be no trouble."

"She can stay, but keep her out of the restaurant. It's against the health codes."

"Yes'm." He paused. "Miz Dell?"

"What?"

"You gonna hit me with that fryin' pan?"

Suddenly I realized I was still holding the cast-iron skillet up like a weapon, and he hadn't moved from the spot where I first found him.

I looked at the skillet. I looked at him. I looked at the tiny window, where the first gray light of dawn was beginning to seep in through the tattered curtain.

"No," I said. "I'm gonna go make some cornbread."

· 10 ·

Six-thirty rolled around, and I opened the doors to let in the truckers. Scratch had gotten himself some breakfast and was already in the kitchen wearing a clean white apron and slicing up the ham. In the back of my mind, as I flipped pancakes and poured coffee, I was making a plan.

The plan was not without its drawbacks. This man who called himself Scratch—this black man—was an unknown quantity. Maybe he was just down on his luck, as he had said. Or maybe he was a con artist who was biding his time before he made off with the cash drawer and put me in the poorhouse for good.

I didn't know. I had no way of knowing, not until he had a chance to prove himself. But while my mind stewed over the dire possibilities, another image rose up in the shadowy parts of my mind, one I liked a whole lot better. That old

Sally Field movie, where she's trying to make ends meet and get the cotton picked and sold after her husband's violent and untimely death. The way she trusted the black man who showed up on her doorstep because she didn't have any other choice. That turned out all right for her. Maybe it would turn out all right for me, too. Sure made me feel more noble than the other option, which was to call the sheriff and send him packing.

So here was the plan: Somewhere in that mess we called a guest bedroom was a double mattress and frame we hadn't used in fifteen years. I expected I could round up a table and lamp, too, and maybe a little chester drawers. And although Scratch was bigger across the shoulders and smaller in the waist, I thought some of Chase's clothes might fit all right.

Why I took it upon myself to feed, house, and clothe a man who was squatting in the upstairs of my restaurant, I have no idea. It just seemed like the right thing to do. It made me feel good about myself.

Until Marvin Beckstrom came into the Heartbreak Cafe that morning.

The place was buzzing, with only one empty table right in the middle. Toni was sitting in a booth with Boone Atkins, looking at some kid's book about wild things, with great illustrations of some very funny monsters.

Toni taught second grade at Chulahatchie Elementary, so she was always off in the summertime. We used to have great adventures in the summer, driving up through Aberdeen and Okolona and Pontotoc, going to flea markets and buying fresh vegetables at truck stands along the side of the road. But running the Heartbreak Cafe took up all my time and energy these days, and I rarely saw Toni unless she came into the restaurant, or occasionally on a Sunday afternoon.

I missed her, and I could tell she missed me. But she didn't complain; she understood I was only doing what I had to do. And she and Boone had gotten to be better friends. I guess they bonded over the argument about paint chips during the renovations. Whatever the case, it wasn't unusual to see the two of them together.

I missed Boone, too. Since the day the cafe opened, we never had a chance to go to lunch like we used to, just the two of us. Our only conversations had been a snatch here and a snatch there, in between serving customers and cleaning tables. Sometimes it felt like the Heartbreak Cafe owned me, and not the other way around.

Still, they were my two best friends, and I was awful glad to have them there that morning when Marvin Beckstrom made his appearance.

I'd avoided the Bug pretty successfully in the past few months, even though I was going in the bank a whole lot more often. I'd caught him peering out his office window a time or two when I was standing at Pansy Threadgood's cash counter. Probably wondering if I was depositing or withdrawing, and how soon it would be before his predictions of doom came true. It musta galled him something awful that I always paid my lease right on time and didn't give him any reason to meddle in my business.

Now he seemed determined to meddle whether he had reason or not.

The minute he edged his way through the front door, his weak little chin dropped to his chest. Obviously, he had not expected the place to be going like a house afire and was real disappointed that everybody seemed to be enjoying themselves so much.

He took the only vacant table, right in the middle of all the rowdy truckers, looking like a cockroach at an exterminator convention. The chatter died down and everybody turned to stare at him.

I went over to the table, fighting a strong temptation to dump hot coffee in his crotch. Instead I took the high road. "Mornin', Marvin," I said with all the pleasantness I could muster. "How 'bout some coffee?"

He nodded. I poured. "We got the pancake special this morning. Two cakes, two eggs, with bacon or sausage for four-ninety-five."

Marvin wasn't listening. His protruding eyes, magnified behind his Coke-bottle glasses, were fixed on Scratch, who had just cashed out two of the truckers and was now wiping down the counter.

"Who the bloody hell is that?" he said.

The room went even more silent, like the whole restaurant was holding its breath.

If circumstances had been different, it mighta been funny. The Chickenhead had a habit of putting on airs, and his most recent airs seemed to be of the British variety, saying things like "bloody hell" and "wicked" and "off you go, then." Toni reckoned he watched *American Idol* behind closed doors and had a crush on Simon Cowell.

But nobody laughed. The tension inside was thicker than the humidity outside, the kind of static you feel in the air when the clouds get that greenish tinge and the tornado sirens are just about to go off. You brace yourself, and you wait, but you know there's nothing you can do but ride it out and hope for the best.

Scratch looked up, laid down his cleaning rag, and came around the counter.

"Name's Scratch," he said, holding out a massive hand. "I'm Miz Dell's new—" He paused, and a hint of a grin passed over his face. "Associate."

Marvin didn't shake his hand, didn't meet his eyes, either, but looked at some middle point just beyond Scratch's left ear, as if Scratch wasn't worthy of his full attention. "You're not from around here, are you, b—"

He caught himself just before he said *boy*, but the word hung out there, unspoken, like the butt flap on a pair of dirty long johns. Nobody moved.

That tingly electric sensation increased, a thunderstorm on its way across the river. Scratch was big enough and strong enough to pound Marvin into mincemeat, and everybody knew it. Even Marvin.

Especially Marvin.

We all waited for the storm to break. Instead, Scratch looked down at him, and the smile flickered across his face once more. "Pleased to meetcha," he said. "I'd best get back to work."

As soon as Scratch was safely behind the counter again, Marvin jumped on me like fleas to a coonhound. "What are you thinking, Dell? Taking in that—that—"

"Don't say it," I warned. "Don't."

He didn't pay me any mind. "Here you are, a single woman, alone, vulnerable. What would Chase say?"

I knew exactly what Chase would say. I'd already heard it all inside my head. He'd call Scratch every vile name in the Southern Book of Bigotry, and then summon the sheriff and have him arrested for trespassing. And he'd feel perfectly justified in doing it.

Marvin was still ranting. "Why, that man could steal you blind! He could murder you in your sleep. Who knows what he might do? You gotta have more sense, Dell. Taking on a stranger? And one like . . . like *that*?"

He took a breath, and his eyes strayed to the back booth, where Boone was sitting. "Besides that, look around. What kind of people are you attracting here?"

I looked. For a small town in Mississippi, there was remarkable diversity. Mostly men at this time of day, but a few women as well. Suits and hard hats, wing tips and work boots. White faces, black faces, brown faces, jeans and dress pants and khakis and blue uniforms with name patches sewn over the pockets. And Boone, of course, who to Marvin's narrow little mind was in a different category altogether.

Everybody in the place was listening, waiting to hear what I was going to say.

And then my brain did something very, very strange. Everything slowed down, like one of those nature shows where you can see every beat of a hummingbird's wing. Marvin Beckstrom seemed to shrink, getting smaller and smaller until it felt like I was looking at him through the wrong end of a telescope. His mouth was still moving, but all I could hear was my own pulse roaring in my ears.

I tried with all my heart and soul to summon the spirit of Sally Field, to channel her energy and outrage and courage.

And for a second or two, I felt it—the horrible injustice of Marvin Beckstrom's prejudice, the better part of me that desperately longed to stand up to him.

In that moment, I wanted to turn his scrawny hide inside out and feed his liver to Scratch's cat. I wanted to pick him up bodily and throw his bony butt out on the street. I wanted to tell him that Chulahatchie Savings and Loan might own this building, but he didn't own me. I wanted to say he was a despicable little skinhead bigot, and that Scratch wasn't a stranger, he was my cousin. Twice removed.

I could just imagine the look on Marvin's face if I said *that*.

But I didn't. I couldn't.

The better part of me stuttered and died. Marvin's words had hit a nerve somewhere, and if I was gonna get honest with myself, deep down I wasn't sure I trusted Scratch either. Not because he was black, but because I was a woman alone.

Even as the thought went through my head, I knew it was a rationalization, knew it woulda been different if Scratch had been white. I tried to fight the feeling, tried to argue it away and push it below the surface, but it wouldn't stay down.

I just stood there, stiff and frozen as a side of beef, unable to move or speak.

"What would Chase say?" Marvin repeated, and his voice was an echo off in the distance, someplace far away.

I didn't want to think about Chase. Yes, he was my husband, and yes, I had loved him, but sometimes I didn't like him much at all. Sometimes he drove me crazy with his backward attitude toward blacks, toward women, toward people like Boone. Sometimes it was all I could do not to slap him silly and tell him to grow up and come into the twenty-first century like the rest of the world.

But here I was, harboring the same attitudes and feeling the same prejudice. I just wasn't as honest about it. I just wanted to look better on the outside.

What would Chase say? He'd say I'd lost my ever-loving mind, and that I ought to hightail it back to my own house and my own kitchen, where I belonged. He'd say I had no business opening the Heartbreak Cafe in the first place, and that I damn well oughta know better than to let somebody like Scratch get within spitting distance.

But Chase was dead, and he had left me with no choice but to figure out how to make ends meet without him. For the first time in my life, I was entirely on my own, and at the moment I was feeling more vulnerable than I'd ever felt in my life.

Take a risk, Toni and Boone had told me. Well, I had taken one. I had jumped in with both feet before I even bothered to test the waters. And now the fear, which I had pushed down, or ignored, or denied, came rushing to the surface like some prehistoric sea monster. I remembered something Boone had told me once, about the place where the oceans fell off the edge of the world: *There be dragons here.*

"I'm only looking out for your best interests, Dell," Marvin said. He put two crisp new dollar bills on the table to pay for the coffee, got up, and headed out the door.

I glanced back toward the kitchen. Behind the counter Scratch was making fresh coffee like nothing unusual had happened. Boone and Toni had gone back to looking at the wild things. Fart Unger and two of his Tenn-Tom buddies were waiting at the register to settle up.

Everything was back to normal. Everything except for me.

Because in that moment, when I coulda told Marvin Beckstrom off and didn't have the courage, I found out something about myself that I didn't like one bit. Not just the fear, although that was bad enough. But something else, layered over the fear, like scum on a pond.

Something I didn't have a name for. A shadow, a darkness I never knew was there.

I always thought I was a pretty good person.

Now I wasn't so sure.

· 11 ·

In the old house, Mama always had what she called a "possible drawer," full of string and glue and screwdrivers and batteries and such. Most folks would call it the junk drawer, but Mama liked to put a positive spin on things. "It's possible you might find just about anything you need," she said, "if you stir long enough."

I figure my guest room coulda been called the "possible room," but we had to stir real hard to find what we needed. And although it was just Boone and Scratch in there stirring with me, I couldn't help being embarrassed at the state of things, and hoped they'd both have the grace to keep their mouths shut about my dirty little secret.

Scratch had stayed, and worked hard, and gave me no reason not to have faith in him. But I watched him like a hawk anyway, as if I was just looking for an excuse to send him packing.

I've always been a trusting soul, trying to think the best of folks until they give me cause to do otherwise, and I gotta admit I didn't like this suspicious turn of mind one little bit. I tried to convince myself that if Scratch had been white, I woulda felt the very same way. But the rationalization didn't stick very well, and even when I believed it, the thought didn't comfort me much.

I reckon being a coward was better than being a racist; still, I wasn't too keen on the idea of wearing either one of those labels.

I went on with the original plan, helping Scratch set up housekeeping in the little apartment over the Heartbreak Cafe. With Boone's assistance, we shoveled out the guest room and came up with a bed, a rug, a three-drawer chest, a side table and lamp, and an easy chair Chase had been saving for twenty years, saying he was gonna reupholster it when he got around to it.

Boone brought Chase's truck back from the river camp, and we loaded up the furniture. I scared up sheets and blankets and pillows and an old Dove in the Window quilt, and pulled some clothes out of Chase's closet. Once we got everything up to the apartment and all set up, it looked right nice—not the lap of luxury, by any stretch of the imagination, but livable enough, considering that Scratch had spit-shined the place until it just about glowed.

Over and over again, he kept saying "Thank you, Miz Dell," "This is so nice, Miz Dell," "I sure do appreciate it, Miz Dell," until I wanted to tell him to shut up about it. Truth was, I was ashamed of what I was feeling and didn't know how to stop, and being thanked half to death didn't do nothing to make me feel any better about myself.

After we were done, Boone came back to the house with me for meatloaf sandwiches and potato salad, and that's when the trouble really started.

"What's going on with you, Dell?" he said before I'd gotten down the first bite of my sandwich.

I should have expected it. Boone and I had always been pretty direct with one another, and when I wasn't being totally honest with him, he'd spot it and nail me to the wall in a heartbeat. It was one of the things I loved most about him, and about our relationship.

Except for today.

I swallowed hard and finally got the meatloaf down. "What do you mean?"

He laid aside his fork and looked at me. "Something's bothering you. I can tell. You're not yourself lately."

I tried to laugh it off. "Who have I been, then? Somebody gorgeous and sexy, I hope. Like Marilyn Monroe."

Boone shook his head. "Don't try to joke your way out of this. Just tell me. Be honest."

I gave up. "All right. I'll tell you. The truth is I don't like myself very much right now." I poured it all out—my gut-level response to Marvin Beckstrom in the cafe, and the fact that I couldn't bring myself to tell him off. How I felt like a coward and a racist, and my ambivalence about trusting Scratch, even though he had been a model of trustworthiness so far. "God help me, Boone, it galls me to think that Beckstrom might be right for once in his sorry life, but I can't help wondering. Why, all of a sudden, am I feeling like this? I've never been the suspicious type. I always take people as they are—leastwise, I *think* I do—but here I am feeling nervous and anxious and afraid, and even worse, looking in the mirror and seeing this person I don't recognize half the time."

He sat back in his chair. "Makes perfect sense to me."

I gaped at him. "What?"

"Well, just think about it for a minute."

He ate his sandwich and finished his potato salad, watching me. The clock over the stove tick-tocked loudly in the silence, like a dripping faucet that gets on your nerves so bad it makes you want to scream.

I tried to ignore it, but it seemed to get louder with every passing second. And then the lightbulb clicked on. I'd been trying to ignore something else, too, something that kept nagging at me in the back of my mind, and even though I had tried to distract myself with busyness, it hadn't gone away. And wouldn't, until I fixed the drip.

"Chase," I said at last. "This isn't about Scratch at all. It's about Chase."

"Bingo." Boone grinned. "Go on."

"It's about living a whole lifetime with a man I trusted, and then finding out he wasn't worth the trust. He betrayed me. And somebody else betrayed me, too, although I don't know who she is. Maybe it's somebody I see every day, somebody I've known forever. Somebody who comes into the cafe, or passes me on the street and says hey, or sits next to me in the pew on Sunday. Maybe it's somebody I think of as a friend."

Boone nodded. "And if you can't trust a friend, how can

you trust someone who shows up out of nowhere in the middle of the night?"

I wouldn't exactly call it an epiphany—maybe more like an epiphanette. It did help me feel a little less guilty about being suspicious of Scratch. But it didn't address the deeper problem, the shadow side of my own self that had reared its ugly head.

I still didn't know who Chase had been with that day. Didn't know who I could trust—who was a friend, and who might be an enemy.

And I realized that on another level, I didn't really trust myself, either. If I could be such a bad judge of character as to live with a man for thirty years and not understand his true nature, then how could I think I understood anything at all? On my bad days I felt worthless, rejected, duped, and generally stupid. On my good days I felt as emotionally wrung out as a damp dishrag.

The epiphanette was worth something, I suppose. But there's a big difference between identifying the drip and fixing the leak.

· 12 ·

Once word got out about the Heartbreak Cafe, the days
started taking on an order of their own. Boone and I once
had a long and very interesting discussion about the body's
internal clock, based on something called circadian rhythms,
and although I don't recollect all the details about the evo-
lution of that biological clock and which part of the brain
controls it all, I could see it working in the folks who came
into the cafe.

The truckers and Fart's buddies from Tenn-Tom Plastics
showed up when I opened at six-thirty and usually stayed
until seven-thirty or quarter to eight. Boone came in for
breakfast just about the time the truckers were heading
out. There was a lull from about nine-thirty to eleven, and
then the old folks started wandering in for lunch. The place
would be full until early afternoon, when ladies doing their

shopping would come in for coffee and pie. A handful of folks would regularly show up for a late lunch and hang around until I ran them out at two-thirty.

It got to where I could just about guess, when the bell over the door rang, who was gonna be standing there and where they'd sit and what they were likely to order. We're all creatures of habit, and if you don't believe it, look around at church on a Sunday morning. Chances are you sit in the same spot so often that your buttprint is permanently embedded in the pew.

But I wouldn't have predicted that on a Friday morning early in September Purdy Overstreet would make the first of her visits to the Heartbreak Cafe.

Purdy was a girlhood friend of Mama's, eighty years old and living at the St. Agnes nursing home. I hadn't seen her since Mama's funeral nearly five years ago, but I knew she had Alzheimer's and kinda floated in and out of her right mind. I remembered her as tiny and frail, with a heart-shaped face framed by a halo of wispy white hair. A sweet soul with no children of her own, she used to invite me over to make sugar tea cakes when I was a little girl.

It was quarter to eleven, the slow time between breakfast and lunch. I was in the kitchen stirring up gravy to go with the roast beef. Scratch was clearing tables and serving coffee. The only customers left from breakfast were Hoot Everett, who was sitting in the first booth by the door mopping up fried eggs with a crust of his toast, and a couple of women from Alabama who'd stopped for gas on their way through to Tupelo.

The bell jingled and the door opened. I looked up. For a minute I didn't know who it was, but I had the fleeting sensation that I'd been caught up by the nape of the neck and set down in the middle of a circus.

It was Purdy Overstreet, all right, but not the Purdy I remembered. Not the Purdy with the sweet wrinkled face and the cotton-candy hair. This Purdy had flaming orange locks and a big red mouth painted on way past her ordinary lip line. She was wearing a black leather miniskirt, which showed legs that went practically up to her neck, with fish-net stockings and three-inch heels, a spangled electric-blue tank top, and a yellow feather boa.

Everybody stared. Purdy seemed to take this as her cue, and she began to sing: *"Her name was Lo-la, she was a show-girl . . ."* She cha-cha'ed her way into the restaurant, slapped a brightly manicured hand to her stomach, and began a se-ries of tottering twirls.

I pulled my gravy off the stove and hightailed it toward the door. But I was too late. Purdy slipped and began a slow-motion fall, still singing at the top of her lungs.

Scratch lurched toward her and caught her just as her feet went out from under her. I held my breath. In Purdy's day, a black man never touched a white woman. Never. But here she was, leaning back in Scratch's burly arms.

She looked up into his face, and then, remarkably, she laughed. "Dip me, baby!" she shouted, throwing her boa around his neck.

He smiled, and dipped her, and set her gently back on her feet.

By that time I was across the restaurant and at her side. "Thanks," I murmured under my breath to Scratch, and to Purdy I said, "Are you all right?"

She steadied herself, narrowed her eyes, and glared at me. "Who the hell are you?"

I guided her over to a booth and helped her slide in. "I'm Dell Haley, Purdy. Don't you remember? I'm Lillian's daughter."

"Lillian's daid!" she yelled. "Lillian's daid, and I don't know you!"

"It's all right, Purdy," I soothed, patting her hand. She jerked it back as if she'd been snake-bit. I sat down across the booth from her. "Do you want me to call somebody, Purdy? Somebody at St. Agnes?"

"What I want is for you to get me a drink!" She smacked her hand down flat on the tabletop. "Can't a girl get a drink around here?"

Scratch eased over, set a glass of sweet tea in front of her, and replaced the feather boa around her neck. She beamed up at him. "Thank you, baby."

"You're welcome," he said.

She winked at him. "I get off at five. Why don't you meet me at the stage door? We'll go out on the town and have ourselves some fun."

I looked past Purdy to the next booth, where Hoot Everett was gaping at us, egg yolk dribbling down his stubbly chin. "What are you staring at?" I said.

He came to his senses, blinked his rheumy eyes, and shook his head. "Hot damn," he said. "That's one fine mama."

"Keep your shirt on, Hoot. This is Purdy Overstreet, and she's eighty years old."

"What the hell difference does that make?" he demanded. "I'm eighty-three, and I ain't dead yet." He let out a wheezing little guffaw. "And you're right, Dell. She is purdy. 'Bout the purdiest thing I seen in a coon's age."

Purdy twisted in the booth and looked over her shoulder at Hoot, contorting her painted lips into a grotesque and exaggerated smile. "Sorry, honey, I've already got me a date. But you're right cute." She cut her eyes toward Scratch. "Not as cute as him, but you'll do in a pinch."

She turned back in my direction and twisted the boa in her clawlike fingers. "You still here?"

"I'm still here," I said. "You stay put and I'll get somebody from St. Agnes to come get you."

"Agnes?" she yelled. "Agnes was my mama, and she sure as hell weren't no saint!" She slurped at her tea. "Besides, she's daid, too."

Purdy was right. Her mama's name was Agnes, and she had died when I was in junior high. From all accounts around town, Agnes Overstreet was about as far from sainthood as you could get without actually doing a deal with the Devil.

Behind her, Hoot Everett had shifted to the other side of his booth and was now craning his neck to get a better look. "Lemme buy you lunch, Purdy," he crooned.

She snapped around. "Ain't I told you, I already got a date? Besides, I got money." She jerked open a small beaded evening bag and pawed through it, coming up with lipstick, a gold compact, various bits of string and balls of lint, a wad of rubber bands, a handful of assorted pills, and a twenty-dollar bill. "See there? Just like I said." She waved the twenty in my face. "So, is this a restaurant, or not? You gonna sit there like a stump, or you gonna get me something to eat?"

Scratch appeared again, this time with a pad and pen in

hand. "What would you like, Miss Purdy?" he asked in a tone befitting a tuxedoed maitre d'. "Would you like to hear our specials?"

Her demeanor changed instantly. Her face went all soft, and her eyes fixed on Scratch's face as if she'd never seen anything quite so beautiful. "Yes, please."

"For the soup we have chicken corn chowder. Our entrees are roast beef with mashed potatoes, or baked chicken with dressing. You also get your choice of three vegetables from the list on the board, and either biscuits or cornbread."

"Better give me the chicken and dressing," Purdy said. "Roast beef gives me gas."

While Purdy was eating her lunch under the watchful gaze of Hoot Everett, I made a quick call to Jane Lee Custer, the head honcho out at St. Agnes.

"Thank heavens," said Jane Lee with obvious relief. "We were about to call out the National Guard. Couldn't figure where she might have wandered off to."

"Well, I got her. I'll keep her here for the time being." I hesitated. "She's eating lunch. That's okay, isn't it? I mean, she's not on a special diet or anything?"

"Lord, no, she's healthy as a horse," Jane Lee said. "To tell the truth, she wouldn't have to be here at all if she had anybody to take care of her. She's not a danger to herself, she just drifts from time to time, that's all."

Hoot Everett seemed right disappointed when Jane Lee showed up to take Purdy home. "I coulda done it," he said. "Got my truck right outside."

I gave him one of my looks. "Hoot, anybody who'd get in a car with you would have to be off their rocker."

He shrugged and handed over a five spot for his breakfast. "Well then, I reckon maybe she's just about the perfect woman."

Purdy paid for her lunch and tucked everything back into her evening bag. "Thank you, Dell," she said, and reached up to pat my cheek. "You've grown into a fine young woman. You tell your mama I said hey."

I looked into her eyes, bright and blue and clear. She was still in there somewhere, rising to the surface now and again. The sweet old Purdy with her soft-spoken ways and her sugar tea cakes, never mind the orange hair and the fishnet hose.

"I'll tell her, Purdy."

When she reached the threshold, she turned and raised a hand, like Miss America waving to the crowds. "You be waiting for me backstage," she called to Scratch. "I'll be back in time for the second show."

I headed toward the kitchen, but apparently she wasn't done. Not quite yet. She slung the yellow feather boa across her shoulder and pointed a crooked, twiggy finger in my direction. "Dell!" she said. "We ought to have us a talk about Chase." She gave a quick nod and fixed me with a sharp, beady eye. "I know. I know it all."

The bottom dropped out of my stomach. And then she turned and left, clutching Jane Lee's arm, still waving, still dragging the feather boa behind her.

After that, Purdy showed up at the Heartbreak Cafe most every afternoon, but when she seemed to be in her right senses, I didn't get a chance to talk to her, and the other ninety percent of the time, it was no use.

Half the day every day, Hoot Everett laid claim to the second booth on the left, watching for her. Hoot had it bad, that much was clear. He mighta been half blind, but his vision took on some kind of miraculous recovery when she came through the door. Faith healing, maybe. Or the power of love. Whatever it was, he had that cocker-spaniel-puppy look on his face, which on a sappy seventeen-year-old boy is bad enough, but on a crusty eighty-year-old man is downright creepy.

Purdy, unfortunately, had eyes only for Scratch. She flirted shamelessly with him and tried to get him to dance with her so often that I finally got in the habit of turning the radio off as soon as I saw her coming.

But Scratch treated her with a gentle kindness that amazed me, because on her bad days Purdy could be downright nasty. I had to keep reminding myself of the other Purdy, the one who was Mama's good friend for all those years. Once, when she smashed her chicken and dumplings into the floor, I had to excuse myself and take refuge in the kitchen to keep from losing my composure completely.

"She's just old," Scratch reminded me. "Old and confused and probably scared, too. She don't mean no harm. It's just when people get old, they lose their ability to sort things out and know how to act. She's like a little child throwin' a temper tantrum right now. You'll see, she'll forget all about it in ten minutes."

"How do you do it, Scratch?" I asked, searching his dark eyes for an answer. "You're so good with her. It's like you see inside and know what's going on in that addled brain of hers."

He shrugged. "I had me a mama once. Had me a baby girl, too. Reckon I learned a few things along the way."

It was the closest Scratch had ever come to revealing anything personal about himself. But it got me thinking. Not about the mama part; everybody's got a mama. But about the little girl, and the wife, maybe, who hovered like a ghost in the background even if he didn't mention her. A whole life I knew nothing about.

I reckon everybody's got their shadows.

*   *   *

It was a Tuesday afternoon the last week of September; Purdy Overstreet had come and gone, and Hoot had left shortly after. Scratch was in the back room checking inventory, and there was only one customer in the place when Boone came in.

"I didn't expect to see you here," I said. "Late lunch?"

"No, the library business was kind of slow today, and I just decided to take half a day off. Jill's a good assistant; she can handle things."

I brought him coffee and pie and sat with him, glad for a chance to talk. I told him about Purdy's mysterious declaration—her claim that she "knew it all" about Chase.

"I wouldn't put too much credence in what Purdy says," Boone warned. "You know how she is."

"I know she's not there most of the time, if that's what you mean," I said. "But Boone, every now and then she comes back, and I get the feeling she really does know something."

"Look," he said, pushing aside his pie and taking my hand across the table, "I'm aware that Purdy was a good friend of your mama's, and I know you spent a lot of time with her when you were little—"

"You didn't know her, Boone," I interrupted. "Not the way I knew her. I remember listening to her talk. She knew everything that went on in this town. And she wasn't a gossip, either, she just . . . well, she understood. She saw things other people didn't see. Looking back, I guess I'd say she was wise. Maybe the wisest woman I ever knew."

"But most of that's gone," Boone said. "Besides, this isn't about what Purdy knows or doesn't know. It's about—"

I finished his sentence for him. "It's about my obsession with finding out who Chase was fooling around with." God knows I'd heard it often enough—from him, from Toni. Both of them were at me all the time to let it go, to get on with life as it was.

But letting it go was easier said than done. Maybe the two of them understood me better than anybody else, but there was a lot inside of me that they didn't understand, that no one else could even get close to. The dreams I had about Chase and the faceless bimbo, both of them laughing at me. The sense of feeling less-than, inferior, unworthy of love and faithfulness.

I'd already had me a talk with Chyna Lovett down at the sheriff's office, the one who took the 911 call the night Chase died. Chyna shrugged her shoulders and fiddled with her nose ring and told me that nobody was on the line— nobody at all.

Standard procedure, she said, when an emergency call came in: If no one responded, run a trace and send a team. Happened all the time. Usually it was a false alarm, but they couldn't take that risk. Once, Chyna told me, an elderly woman fell in the bathtub, and her Pomeranian dialed the phone and barked until the EMTs arrived.

Most likely Chase made the call himself, she said. Had the heart attack, called emergency, and then passed out and died before help could arrive.

Logical as that might be, I wasn't buying it. Someone else was there—I was sure of it. No matter what anyone said, I couldn't get past the suspicions. I even wondered briefly, during my last haircut, if it might be DeeDee Sturgis.

I knew for a fact Chase loathed DeeDee and thought she was an idiot. But that didn't matter. Every woman in town seemed to be fair game, and my stomach stayed in knots most of the time.

Boone was right, I'd be better off if I let it go. I'd sleep better, for sure, and I reckoned my digestion would improve if my gut wasn't all tied up with anxiety. But sometimes what you know you *oughta* do, and what you *can* do, are two different things.

I was just about to change the subject when Boone changed it for me.

"I think I recognize that woman in the back booth," he said. "Who is she?"

I craned my neck and looked. She'd been coming in for a couple of days now, always at the same time and sitting in the same place, but I'd been so busy I hadn't really had a chance to talk to her. Besides, she sent out signals that she didn't want to be disturbed—really big signals, like emergency flares or Fourth of July fireworks. Head down, writing in a brown leather notebook, some kind of a journal, looking up only to signal for more coffee.

"I believe that's Peach Rondell," Boone whispered.

"You gotta be kidding."

"No, I really do think it's her. I heard she came back to town a few months ago, but I hadn't seen her."

"I wouldn't have recognized her. She's—"

"Changed," Boone said quietly.

I woulda said *fat*. Boone's answer was kinder.

She had changed, all right. Peach Rondell, in her day, had been Chulahatchie's golden child—wealthy, privileged, beautiful. Miss Ole Miss, Soybean Queen at the county fair. Second runner-up for Miss Mississippi.

But that had been years ago. After high school she went to Mississippi University for Women, which shocked the heck out of just about everybody. Two years later she transferred up to Ole Miss. She didn't come home very often after that, and didn't stay long when she did. Soon as she graduated, she moved away and got married and nobody had seen hide nor hair of her in more than twenty years.

Her mama, Donna, still lived in the big mansion down at the end of Third Avenue, but since Donna ran with the antebellum/country club herd, I rarely laid eyes on her unless we passed on the street. She'd certainly never set foot in a place like the Heartbreak Cafe, where she might have to rub elbows with the working riff-raff.

Peach was younger than me—she'd be in her forties now—but I remembered her with long blonde hair and a perfect complexion, exactly the kind of Barbie clone who could win beauty pageants and marry a jock and go on to be a model or a game show hostess like Vanna White.

This, I thought, was definitely a peach gone bad. I wasn't proud of thinking it, but I couldn't help myself. Her face was round and puffy-looking, and if she was wearing makeup, it wasn't doing a very good job of covering up the blotchy, uneven skin tone. Her hair was still long and blonde, but I could see an inch or two of dark roots, and she had it pulled back in a ponytail at the nape of her neck. She was wearing jeans and an old blue sweatshirt with raggedy cutoff sleeves and a faded Colonel Rebel on the front.

"Dang," I said. "Wonder if her mama knows she's out in public looking like that."

Boone gave me *the look*—the reprimanding one that indicated I was being overly critical and borderline bitchy.

"Well, what?" I said. "You know as well as I do what Donna Rondell would say about that hair and that outfit."

I was right, and he knew it. Shoot, everybody in Chulahatchie knew it. That woman had raised her little girl to be Miss America, and anything less was pretty much gonna be a disappointment—even being the Bean Queen and Miss Ole Miss. From the time she could walk, that child had been primped and prodded, primed and painted until it was hard to tell whether she was a little girl or a big old china-faced baby doll.

And now here she sat in full view of the whole town, looking like something the cat dragged in, looking like Hulga-Joy Hopewell in that Flannery O'Connor story Boone had read me once. I reckoned Donna hadn't seen her, or we'd have heard the ambulance sirens on their way to get her after her coronary.

"We went to school together," Boone said. "I asked her out once, to the junior prom."

I gaped at him. "Peach Rondell was your date to the junior prom?"

He shrugged. "I didn't say she was my date. I said I asked her. As I recall, she ended up going with Cade Young."

"The football jock," I said. "Figures. There's a stereotype for you. The homecoming queen and the quarterback."

"He was a wide receiver," Boone corrected. Now and again he'd come up with something that shot the gay theory all to pieces.

100

"Doesn't matter. It was still Ken and Barbie."

"She wasn't really like that, you know. Looks can be deceiving. She was very smart, very creative."

I grinned at him. "Sounds like somebody's burning a torch."

He gave me *the look* again. "That'd set this whole town talking, now wouldn't it?"

I got up, retrieved a fresh pot of coffee, and went back to the booth where Peach sat, still writing furiously in her journal.

"Want a refill, Peach?"

Her head snapped up, and in the same motion she shut the book with a slap. "What?"

You didn't have to be a genius to know she didn't want anybody looking over her shoulder at what she was writing. She might as well have slung a chain around that book and padlocked it. I got the message loud and clear, and I took a step back.

"I asked if you'd like more coffee."

"Oh. Yes, thanks." She frowned up at me. "Do we know each other?"

I poured. "I'm Dell Haley. I own this place. And it's been a lotta years, but yes, we did know each other once. Not well—I was married by the time you started high school. But I reckon you remember Boone Atkins." I pointed toward Boone, who waved.

Peach waved back at him, and, apparently encouraged, he slid out of the booth and came to stand beside her table.

"Hey, Peach," he said. "Welcome home."

She was staring at him—people often did, when they

hadn't yet gotten used to how handsome he was. After a minute she came to and shook his hand. "You've got a Dorian Gray portrait hidden in your closet," she said to him. "I can't believe it—you look exactly the same."

"So do you, Peach," he lied. "I'm really glad to see you."

"So what brings you back to Chulahatchie?" I asked. "Just visiting?"

She exhaled a heavy sigh. "Actually, I'm going to be here awhile. Just some personal stuff. Since Daddy's death, Mama needs me to help out more."

To my way of thinking, Donna Rondell wasn't the type of woman who needed help of any kind, or would welcome it if it was offered. She might be seventy-something, but she was independent as an armadillo and twice as tough. Still, I didn't say so. And although I was mighty curious about the "personal stuff" that brought Peach home, I didn't ask that question either.

Instead, I said, "I'm sorry about your daddy's passing. I'm sure you'll be a comfort to your mama."

"Thanks," Peach said. "It's been a difficult year." Her eyes went a little watery, and I was sure there was something else going on back there, something that didn't have to do with her daddy's death. But I knew from hard experience that people have to work out their grief in their own way, and they don't always appreciate being pushed to open a vein in public.

Suddenly I felt ashamed of my catty remarks, that shadow side of me that kept rearing up when I least expected it. I oughta know by now that there's more to people than meets the eye. Every living soul's got something to hide, something to wrestle with.

Peach ran a hand over the brown leather cover of her writing book. "I hope you don't mind me taking up space in your booth," she said. "I know I've been here awhile."

"You're welcome to stay as long as you want. I quit serving at two, but I'll be cleaning up and prepping for tomorrow until two-thirty or three."

"Thanks," she said. "I just need a place to—" She paused, as if unwilling to finish the thought.

"To get away?" I nodded. "Well honey, you can get away to the Heartbreak Cafe any time you like. If you want to talk, I'll be here, and if you want to be left alone, we can do that, too."

An expression of relief came over her face, almost like wonder—like it had been a coon's age since anybody cared about what she felt or what she needed.

Boone chatted with her for a few minutes and then left, promising to take me out to dinner on Sunday. Tomorrow's entree was ham and scalloped potatoes, and I had a lot of peeling to do, but as I worked I kept an eye on Peach. She wrote in her book, cried a little, wrote some more.

Scratch came out of the storeroom with the inventory list and looked at her across the restaurant. "Pretty lady," he said.

Why was it, I wondered, that everybody else was quicker than me to see below the surface? "Yes she is," I said. "Very pretty."

"Friend of yours?"

I pondered this for a minute. "I hope so, Scratch. I truly do hope so."

I watched her awhile longer, and couldn't help wondering what she was writing—and why, when she left, she was clutching that book to her heart as if it was a lifeline, and without it she might sink and drown.

· 14 ·

When you're grieving, or in pain, or betrayed by life, folks always try to comfort you by saying that time heals all wounds. Nonsense. Time heals nothing. It's what you do with the time that counts.

The problem was, I had no clue what I ought to have been doing with the time. It had been six months since Chase died, and except for Purdy Overstreet's declaration that she knew something—something that was buried pretty dang deep inside that addled brain of hers—I was no closer to finding out who the woman was who had betrayed me with my husband.

Once in a while I'd go a whole day without thinking about it, without consciously wondering. But at night, when I was too exhausted to push it down anymore, it would rise up in my dreams—odd dreams like mixed-up puzzle pieces.

Sometimes it was pretty clear: Chase flashing his dimples at some faceless woman, a glimpse of his butt cheeks in those black silk bikini briefs. But other nights I wandered through a maze of hallways that looked like the corridors at the hospital, or through damp and dripping caverns that reminded me of the time we went to the Ozarks on vacation and toured the caves at Blanchard Springs. Either way, I couldn't get out; I just kept wandering around in circles, trapped. I'd hear a voice whispering, "This way, come this way," but when I followed it, I always came to a dead end.

One bright autumn morning when business was a little slow, I was puttering in the kitchen, debating about going to all the work of making fried apple pies, when Scratch came and stood in the doorway.

"There's a man out here asking after you," he said. "None too reputable-looking, if you don't mind me saying."

I almost laughed. When I found Scratch, he was squatting in the apartment upstairs and eating out of my Dumpster. Seemed to me he didn't have much ground to stand on when it came to being reputable.

But I didn't say so. Instead, I wiped my hands and went out into the restaurant.

Scratch might not have known him, but everybody else in Chulahatchie did. It was Jape Hanahan, standing just inside the door, looking scruffier than ever with a week's growth of dirty gray beard and wearing oily work pants and a ripped pullover hoodie with a skull and snake on the front.

"Mornin', Dell," he said. That was all. Just "mornin'."

I looked him over. Jape was what Mama used to call "no-count," and Mama wouldn't speak ill of the Devil unless you forced her to give an opinion point-blank. The man was sixty, maybe, thin and twisted as a string of barbed wire, and almost as dangerous if he'd been drinking. This morning his eyes were bleared and bloodshot, and he reeked to high heaven, but far as I could tell, he was more or less sober.

"What can I do for you, Jape?" I blocked the entrance with my body, tensed for fight or flight. No point in taking chances.

"Wondered if you might be able to help me out, Dell," he said. He craned his neck and peered over my shoulder, where Scratch towered like the not-so-Jolly Black Giant, fists clenched and hands on his hips.

Jape jerked his gaze back to me. "Had me some tough times of late," he said. "Got to have a operation—" He pulled up his pants leg to reveal a large lumpy tumor on his calf, full of greenish pus and oozing.

I'm not the squeamish type, but I turned my eyes away anyhow.

"So I's wondering if you might be able to lend me a twenty till my next gover'ment check comes in."

In the old days, when Mississippi was a dry state, Jape earned a substantial living running a bootleg operation out of his shack down on the river. Everybody knew about it—heck, the smell of corn liquor hung so strong in the air that it made the birds drunk just to fly over. The sheriff at the time, Mose Braden, didn't just turn a blind eye; he was down there almost every Saturday night, loading up the trunk of the squad car with moonshine in mason jars.

With the repeal of the liquor laws in the late sixties, Jape's income had dried up, but unfortunately he hadn't. For the last thirty years or so, he'd been begging and odd job-bing and (some thought) stealing his way through a hand-to-mouth existence while the liquor store at the county line happily cashed his disability check on the first of every month.

I glanced back to make sure Scratch was still standing guard. He was. "I don't have any money, Jape," I said. "But if you'll wait a minute, I'll get you a plate of food."

Mama believed that compassion was never wasted, even on the wasted. I'd grown up watching her fix up a plate for some poor migrant worker sitting on the back stoop, or a day laborer with an empty pail. And although it didn't come so natural to me, I reckoned I could follow Mama's example.

Scratch kept an eye on him while I went back to the kitchen and filled a to-go box with yesterday's leftover fried chicken and cornbread.

"Thanks," he muttered, but he wouldn't look me in the eye, and it was pretty obvious he'd rather have the twenty to spend on a day's ration of Thunderbird.

When Jape took off to hit up some other sucker for money, I left Scratch to tend to things at the Heartbreak Cafe and went to the Curl Up and Dye to get my hair done. I reck-oned I'd have to introduce myself to DeeDee Sturgis, it had been so long since I'd had a good cut.

DeeDee's beauty parlor was the kind of place where time

seems to stand still, no matter how fast the hands of the clock keep on moving. This particular morning Stella Knox was there, and Rita Yearwood, and Brenda Unger. Something inside me lurched and staggered, and suddenly I was flung back into last spring, into a rerun of the day I found out Chase was cheating on me.

"How you doing, honey?" DeeDee asked as she ran her fingers through my hair and scowled at me in the mirror.

"All right, I suppose," I said. "Hanging in there."

"Restaurant business is going like a house afire, from what I hear," Rita yelled above the noise of the hair dryer.

I turned my head toward her just as DeeDee snipped, and I heard a muttered curse behind my head. I looked down to see a huge chunk of hair—my hair, brown laced with gray—on the floor to one side of the swivel chair.

"Dang, DeeDee," I said. "What are you doing?"

"Well, *you* moved. Hold still; I gotta even it up. And don't jerk like that again less you want a notch taken out of your ear."

I forced myself to face the mirror and resumed my conversation with Rita. "We're doing pretty good," I said. "Making ends meet, anyway."

It wasn't the whole truth—not even half. Every single day I walked the razor's edge between solvency and bankruptcy, but I wasn't inclined to flaunt my financial dirty laundry at the Curl Up and Dye.

Stella Knox was sitting under the dryer hood next to Rita, still reading the tabloids and looking like she'd never moved an inch since the day Chase died. "Got yourself a new helper, too," she said. "I been told Purdy Overstreet's right sweet on him." She raised an eyebrow. "Course, Purdy can't be faulted; she's not playing with all her marbles."

"Purdy's just old," I said. "She forgets things."

"Forgotten where she left her mind, most likely," Stella said. "She ain't right."

"I'd have to agree with Stella." DeeDee flourished the scissors in midair. "If Purdy had all her faculties, she wouldn't be flouncing around in those miniskirts and dyeing her hair and throwing herself at a black man."

"Black or not, he's right easy on the eyes," Rita shouted.

"Rita, keep your voice down; you want the whole town to hear?" Stella picked up a copy of *Soap Opera Digest* and swatted Rita with it.

"I don't care who hears," Rita said. "He *is* good-looking. Like that Denzel Washington."

I bit my tongue and kept quiet. Scratch looked nothing in the world like Denzel Washington except that he was black.

"What's he like, Dell?" Rita said.

"Yeah, tell us," Stella said. "If I was a widow, I'd never in my life have the courage to hire somebody like that, right off the street. I'd be scared out of my wits. I'd never know if I could trust him not to bash my head in and steal my diamonds."

"Dell doesn't have any diamonds," DeeDee said, and smiled at my reflection as if she'd just uttered a helpful and supportive comment.

Rita waved a hand. "That's beside the point. The point is, Dell's sitting here getting a new haircut while he's over there at the cafe running things."

I hate it when people talk about me like I'm the Invisible Woman.

"Is he running things when you're not there?" Stella asked. "You trust him with the cash?"

"Yes, I trust him," I said. "He's a hard worker, and a very kind man, and he's never given me any reason to suspect him."

Even to my own ears this sounded like a canned speech, a pat defense. No matter what I said in public, I was still aware of a momentary hesitation inside me whenever I thought about Scratch, the kind of jerk that sends you off balance, like missing the last step on the staircase. Not enough to land you flat on your face, but enough to make you gasp a little and think about it twice the next time.

"Well, I'd keep an eye on him if I were you," Rita said. "Whatever else he is, he's still a man."

"You saying men can't be trusted?" DeeDee said.

Rita laughed. "Sure, you can trust 'em. About as far as you can throw 'em."

Everybody got real quiet, and nobody looked me in the eye. We were back to Chase, to the unfaithful husband, to the dead cheater who left his wife with no money and no answers.

And through it all, Brenda Unger sat leafing through a copy of *People* magazine with Denzel's picture on the cover, not saying a word.

DeeDee ran a hand through my hair. "All done, hon. Tell me what you think."

For the first time I looked in the mirror—really looked. The woman who stared back at me wasn't anybody I recognized. Her hair was cut short and chunky and spiked up all over the top. She looked like an aging punk rocker, minus the purple highlights. Goth meets AARP.

"Good Lord a-mercy, DeeDee, what have you *done?*"

"It's the style."

"It's insane. I'm fifty years old, DeeDee."

"Yeah, but you don't have to *look* fifty. Besides, once that big chunk was out of it, I had to do something. And consider it this way: You haven't changed your hairstyle in twenty years. It was about damn time for a new look. This will be so easy, perfect for working at the cafe. You get out of the shower, run a little spiking gel in there, mess it up, and bingo! You're finished."

"I look like I just got out of bed."

"Right," DeeDee said.

"I think it's cute," Rita said. "Maybe if you'd looked like that before—"

Stella punched her in the ribs to shut her up, but not in time. The rest of the sentence hovered low and threatening, like a storm cloud, like the ghost of unfinished business:

If you'd looked that cute before Chase died, maybe he wouldn't have cheated.

· 15 ·

That afternoon I managed to corner Purdy and tried to talk to her about what she knew, but it wasn't easy, between Hoot hanging over her shoulder like a vulture and Purdy turning on the charm every time Scratch got within spitting distance. The most I got out of her was a cryptic message that sounded like it came from a crystal ball session at Madame Celestine's Fortune-Telling Salon: *"Look to your friends, Dell Haley. Look to those you trust."*

Then she grinned at me, clacked her false teeth, and said, "I like your haircut, Dell. Reminds me of a dead porcupine I found once when I was a little girl."

I did my best to ignore the comment about the hair, but try as I might, I couldn't fathom how to interpret her words concerning trust. Did she mean I shouldn't trust the people

I *thought* were trustworthy? Or that I needed to trust them more than I did?

Besides that, I had no idea who I could trust. In six months my life had gone from simple and predictable, even boring, to impossibly complicated. I felt like I was crossing a ravine on a bridge paved with eggs, some of them hard-boiled and some of them raw, and not knowing from one second to the next when or where I was gonna break through. Or whether the breakthrough would turn out to be a blessing or a curse.

Fall sneaked up on Chulahatchie slowly, hesitantly, as it usually does in the South, like a cat stalking a bird and knowing it's got to stay invisible or it'll give itself away. Warm days, then a hint of a chill, and back up to the seventies again. Step, pause, step.

Some of my neighbors had already set out carved jack-o'-lanterns on the porch for Halloween, but in my experience those things were gonna stink to high heaven long before the trick-or-treaters arrived. You could almost see them rotting in the sun, caving in on their gruesome grins like toothless old men.

Most folks thought of fall as heavy and spicy and smelling of pumpkin and cinnamon, but this time of year always put me in mind of a soufflé, so delicate and fragile, rising high and yellow and fragrant. Somehow I wanted to tread softly, not peek too often, not shake things up, delaying the moment when autumn would collapse inward upon itself into a gray and rainy winter.

The collapse, of course, couldn't be avoided. I could keep quiet and hold my breath, hoping to delay the inevitable, but still I expected it, braced myself for it.

What I didn't expect was that the collapse would be an emotional one, or that it would come through Fart Unger.

The Heartbreak Cafe was empty. Hoot and Purdy had done their little ritual dance of advance and rejection and gone their separate ways; Peach Rondell had closed her secret journal and returned to her mama's house. Scratch was cleaning the kitchen. I'd already turned the sign on the door to read CLOSED, but hadn't yet locked it. When the bell jingled, I looked up to see Fart standing in the doorway, his bald head almost touching the lintel.

My inner circadian clock gave a jerky little spasm. Fart didn't come in the afternoon; he came early in the morning for breakfast with the other guys from Tenn-Tom Plastics. He was supposed to be at work, standing in the guardhouse at the front gate in his dark blue uniform with the plastic name badge clipped on the front. But here he was, in jeans and a blue sweatshirt that said *World's Greatest Dad* across the front, so tall and lanky and bowlegged that he looked like a pair of pliers sheathed in denim.

"Dell," he said. "I know you're supposed to be closed, but—"

"Come on in." I motioned him over, put down my wiping rag, and came out from behind the counter. "You want some coffee? There's still half a pot left."

"Yeah, that'd be great."

He dragged himself over to a booth, slid in, and waited while I retrieved two mugs and the last slice of pumpkin pie. Even with Hoot Everett's cataracts I coulda seen something was wrong. Shoot, I coulda seen it blindfolded at midnight.

I sat down opposite him and waited. I didn't have to wait long.

"I gotta talk to somebody, Dell, and you're the only person I could think of who might understand." Fart ran a hand over his shiny head, the way bald men often do. "It's Brenda."

A sudden fear clenched at my insides. I hadn't spent much time with Brenda since Chase died, even though as couples we'd always been close. But I'd been so tied up getting this restaurant off the ground, and besides that, things change when you suddenly become a widow. Even under the best of situations, married friends tend to drift away, not knowing what to do with half a couple, what to say, how to act. And God knows the circumstances of Chase's death didn't make anybody *more* comfortable.

Still, the four of us had been friends for years, and I loved them both. I reached across the table and touched Fart's hand. "What is it, Fart? Is she sick?"

He shook his head, and I could see his Adam's apple working in his neck as he tried to swallow. "She wants a divorce."

"What?"

This was the last thing I expected. Cancer, maybe. A lump in the breast. A shadow on the ultrasound, something borderline abnormal in the blood work that needed to be investigated further. All the things women our age dreaded whenever we went for an annual physical or a mammogram.

But not a divorce. And especially not Fart and Brenda.

They were the perfect couple, made for each other. She was outgoing and a tad flamboyant; he was solid and stable and absolutely adored her. They had two boys and a girl, all married and on their own now. A new grandbaby. Fart's sweatshirt told it all. *World's Greatest Dad. World's Greatest Mom. World's Greatest Marriage.*

He answered my first question before I had a chance to ask it.

"She had an *affair*, Dell," he said miserably. Right before my eyes his face aged with the pain of it, crumpled in on itself like a wad of paper. "She admitted it, only she wouldn't tell me details, who it was, or when, or even why. She just said she wasn't happy, and needed something. Something else."

"Well, good Lord," I blurted out. "Whatever happened to chocolate, or a new pair of shoes?"

That broke the tension a little bit, and he laughed, but the laughter quickly turned to a stifled sob, and his hand was shaking so bad that he sloshed coffee onto the table. He mopped it up with his napkin and avoided looking at me.

"Did you have any clue? Any signs?"

I could see a muscle working in his jaw. His Adam's apple bobbed again—once, twice. "Maybe I shoulda known. She ain't been the same for months now, maybe almost a year, since she started going through the change. Real grouchy, you know, always picking a fight about nothing. But I just thought that was . . . well, normal." He shrugged. "Then she just up and springs it on me that she wants a divorce, that she's realized how short life is, and the idea of living with me for the rest of it—"

He couldn't go on. Instead he attacked the pie, downed half of it in three bites, and struggled to swallow. "Good pie, Dell," he grunted.

I make a really excellent pumpkin pie—not the bland orange kind, but my grandmother's recipe, rich and firm and brown, spiced with cinnamon and cloves and nutmeg and ginger. It was one of Fart's favorites, but I was pretty sure his compliment was automatic; he hadn't tasted a bite. I sympathized. I could barely get the coffee down, and I was only drinking it to give myself something to do.

Fart was right. I *did* understand. I knew exactly what it felt like to be betrayed, to live with unanswered questions, to feel your whole world crash in around your head and come out of it dazed, like the survivor of a tornado when your house has been reduced to rubble. You can see the swath where the storm went through, but nothing you thought you knew looks even remotely familiar anymore. You can't think what to do or where to go or what your next step should be. All you can do is stand in the ruins and stare.

I knew all this, knew it intimately, like looking in the mirror, and yet I couldn't help the next question that came out of my mouth. "So what now?"

"I don't know."

It was the only answer he could give, and I didn't expect anything else. I also knew—or suspected—that this couldn't be fixed, but something inside me made me want to try anyway.

"Fart, we've been friends for a very long time. I'd like to go talk to Brenda. Would that be okay with you?"

His jaw dropped, and he gaped at me, flabbergasted that

I'd ask him such a question. "You don't need my permission to talk to anybody."

"Yeah, I do," I said. "You've told me this in confidence. If you want it to stay here, between the two of us, that's what I'll do. If I go talk to Brenda, she's going to know where it came from."

"You think she'll listen to you?"

"I don't know. I don't even know what I'm gonna say. I might make it worse by meddling in it."

"Can't get much worse, can it?" He gave a sarcastic little grunt of a laugh. "Go on, Dell. Meddle away. You're a woman. Maybe you can talk some sense into her."

He got up and fished in his back pocket for his wallet. I waved him off. "It's on the house."

"Thanks," he said. "And thanks for listening. Something tells me I'm gonna be in here a lot more often. No matter how bad things get, a man's gotta eat."

I left Scratch to close up the restaurant and went straight out to the Ungers' little brick bungalow on the south side of town. I had to ring the doorbell five times before Brenda finally opened up.

"Oh God, no, it's you."

"Nice to see you, too," I said.

She heaved an enormous sigh and stood aside. "Something tells me Fart came to see you. You might as well get on in here."

Their house was almost as familiar to me as my own: three bedrooms, two baths, a pine-paneled family room addition on the back. It wasn't fancy or modern, but it was always spotless. Brenda bordered on being obsessive about housework. You could eat banana pudding off her kitchen floor, all the way down to the very last vanilla wafer.

At the moment, however, the place was a holy wreck. Shoes in the middle of the living room floor, a basket overflowing with unfolded laundry on the couch, dust bunnies under the dining room chairs. She didn't even apologize for the state of things, just turned her back and headed toward the kitchen, expecting me to follow.

"Sit down," she said.

It was almost three in the afternoon, and the kitchen table still held the remains of breakfast: egg-crusted plates and leftover bacon congealing in its own grease. She stacked them up and set them in the sink, and didn't even bother to wipe the crumbs off the vinyl tabletop.

"You want something? I can make coffee."

I grew up in Mississippi, and knew the coffee code words as well as any Southern woman. *"I just made a fresh pot"* meant a long visit and cinnamon coffee cake to boot. *"I'll put some on; it's no trouble"* meant it was a bit of a bother and don't expect cake, but stay a little while and then let me get back to what I was doing. *"You want something?"* meant you're really not welcome, so state your business and be on your way.

"No thanks, I'm fine," I said. I plunked myself down at the table and proceeded to herd the crumbs into a pile with the edge of a used paper napkin. She could be as rude as she wanted, but I had no intention of leaving until I got some answers. Besides, two could play the rude game.

"What's going on, Brenda?"

She set herself down, took the napkin out of my hand, and started fiddling with the crumbs, arranging them into patterns the way you'd play with sand at the beach. "I guess you know what's going on if you talked to Fart. We've decided to separate."

"That's not what he says."

She snapped to attention. "Excuse me?"

"He says you've asked him for a divorce."

"Didn't I just say that?"

"No, you said, 'we've decided.' What Fart told me didn't exactly sound like a mutual decision."

"All right, have it your way," she said. "I just can't do this anymore. Life's too short to be unhappy."

"But I thought you and Fart *were* happy. You've always seemed like—"

"Like the perfect couple, yeah, I know." Her tone softened, and she looked at me with the same miserable expression I had seen on her husband's face. "Fart's a good man, a good provider. This isn't his fault. He's never done anything to hurt me. I suppose he loves me—"

"He's crazy about you."

"Okay, if you say so. He doesn't drink. He's not abusive. He doesn't gamble away his paycheck. He comes home every night. He's always been great with the kids—took them fishing, taught them how to play basketball. Even now that they're grown and gone, he's the one they come to when they need something. Like I said, he's a good man. For a long time I thought that could be enough, that there wasn't anything more. Until—"

She couldn't say it, so I said it for her. "Until you had an affair."

She put her face in her hands, her elbows planted in the toast crumbs. "Yes."

"Look, honey," I said. "I don't pretend to understand what would motivate you to go off with some other man, but I reckon I know a thing or two about being married for thirty years—some things Chase apparently didn't know. I know it's not always exciting, but at some point you choose between passion and promises. That doesn't mean that love isn't important anymore. It's always important. But somewhere along the line you realize that long-term loving is different from the temporary insanity of falling in love. You made a mistake, Brenda, but I know Fart loves you. And it doesn't have to change everything, if—"

"God, Dell, just leave it alone!" she shouted. "You're the last person I want to be talking to about this."

A faint little warning light flickered on in the back of my head, but I didn't pay it any mind. "Brenda, we've been friends for years—you, me, Chase, Fart. I was with you when your water broke with Bertie, took you to the hospital. Why on God's green earth wouldn't you tell me about it?"

Her head jerked up, and she fixed me with a look so fierce and fiery that I shoulda been scalded. "It's precisely *because* we're friends that I didn't tell you. You've been through enough. You don't need to be dealing with this, too. You've got plenty of pain of your own without me adding more."

She went back to playing with the toast crumbs. "It's over now," she said. "But it showed me what my life mighta been like, what it still could be like. I'm fifty years old, Dell.

I might live another thirty or forty. I don't know what's out there for me, but it's gotta be better than this."

We talked a little more, and after a while I left. But I couldn't shut out of my mind the things she'd said to me, and it gave me a funny feeling in the pit of my stomach. The same one Jesus got when Judas kissed him.

· 16 ·

I replayed the discussion over and over in my head, but the suspicions wouldn't go away. Was it even remotely possible that Brenda Unger would betray both me and Fart with my husband, Chase? The idea ate at me like poison, like a brown recluse spider bite working its way toward the bone.

She hadn't really *said* it, of course, and I wasn't at all sure that's what she meant. I kept trying to rationalize it away, put a different spin on it. But the idea haunted me anyway— a face to paste on that faceless woman in my dreams. All the feelings I thought I had resolved came rushing back in to drown me. Rage, confusion, worthlessness—pain so bad I thought it just might kill me, and sometimes wished it would. It'd be pure relief to be put out of my misery once and for all.

"You live long enough," Mama used to say, "and sooner

or later you come to realize there's a lotta things in life that hurt worse than death."

So while my heart ran off in one direction, my brain stayed home and worked overtime raising all sorts of questions it couldn't possibly answer. What was it about Brenda Unger that could possibly tempt Chase? I always imagined him with some young thing, blonde and brainless, hanging on his arm and flattering him with toothy smiles and fluttering eyelashes. Brenda was a sensible woman, my age, funny and outgoing, but nobody's fool.

Hell, she couldn't even cook.

But on second thought, I suspect Chase wasn't exactly looking for chicken and dumplings.

Maybe it wasn't about Brenda at all. Maybe it was just about something new, something exciting. Something forbidden.

Well, you couldn't get more forbidden than your best friend's wife.

The next day I went on about my business, trying to act normal, but when Fart came in, I avoided talking to him. I could see the hurt and confusion in his eyes, but I couldn't help myself. I felt like I had done something wrong, like I was the one who had betrayed him, and I knew if I got too close, I'd spill it all. He deserved better than hearing it from me like that.

I reckon emotional exhaustion takes more of a toll than physical tiredness, because I went home beat. And then that night, while I was asleep and my defenses were down, it all came crashing in.

*   *   *

The dream started out like a lot of dreams do, with people I knew in an environment that didn't fit them. In this case, it was me and Chase and Brenda and Fart at some kind of resort hotel, all fancy and luxurious.

I kept telling Chase he wasn't supposed to be there. He was dead. But he had come back again, assuming that everything was exactly as he had left it, and I would just be hanging around waiting for his return.

In real life, I don't wear glasses except for reading, but in the dream, I did. And they had broke—the little brass screw on the left side had come out, the lens was missing. Everything was all fuzzy and distorted.

I kept looking for the lens, looking for the screw, and all the while Chase kept moving from room to room and talking, expecting me to follow him. But he was mumbling and I couldn't understand what he was saying. It reminded me of trying to carry on a conversation with Toni on that blasted cell phone of hers. Every time I asked for clarification, for him to repeat himself, he got madder and madder, as if I didn't have the intelligence or the courtesy to pay attention.

The vividness, the detail of it, was unlike any dream I'd ever had. More like watching a movie, except that I was one of the actors. As we kept moving—Chase roaming through rooms, me following—everything around us became worn and shabby, like somebody's grandmother's house that needed a good scrubbing. The rugs were dingy and gray; the towels in the bathroom were thin and overused and cheap, like the kind people used to get for free when they bought twenty bucks worth of groceries.

I wanted to scream at him, "What are you doing here?" but my voice wouldn't work, as it never will in dreams.

There was no choice but to keep on following him, trying to talk to him, trying to figure out what he was saying. But the more I tried, the more garbled his speech became, and the more frustrated I was with not being able to understand.

And then I realized: He was morphing into something else—something human and yet not quite human, with gray skin and suspicious eyes and quick, jerky movements. Not at all the person I had once loved. And the change terrified me.

I woke up sweating, with my heart pounding so hard I thought it would jump straight on out of my chest. As I lay there in the darkness, trying to catch my breath, my mind scrambled to hold on to it, to make sense of it all.

Boone told me once that dreams are a person's subconscious sending a message to them, to let them know something the conscious mind has suppressed. I understood the part about not being able to see or hear clearly—I was pretty sure that had to do with Chase and his infidelity.

But it was the final transformation that disturbed me most. It seemed familiar, and yet foreign. And then I remembered, and it came into focus:

Gollum, from *Lord of the Rings*, clutching the magic ring and calling it his "precious." Refusing to let it go even though it was destroying him.

*   *   *

I cried so hard my ribs felt bruised, and my sinuses filled up until I thought my head was gonna explode. When the alarm went off at 4:30, I was shocked that I had fallen back to sleep, and the last thing I wanted to do was get out of bed and go to the Heartbreak Cafe, to cook breakfast and feed folks and listen to their troubles and their joys.

But I went anyway.

By the time I dragged myself into the cafe, Scratch was already there, prepping for breakfast and making coffee.

He gave me the once-over. "You all right, Miz Dell?" he said. "You don't look so good."

Why people think it's helpful to state the obvious is beyond me. "Bad night," I said.

He nodded. "Sometimes when folks get troubled, working helps," he said. "Hard work can be a pure salvation."

I glared at him but managed not to say what I was thinking—that he could keep his worthless drivel to himself. Besides that, maybe he was right. Maybe the Heartbreak Cafe was meant to save me. I don't know. I didn't feel saved, and if truth be told, it ain't all it's cracked up to be, this idea of getting rescued from your own sorry self. Sometimes you just wish God—or the universe, or whoever—would simply leave you alone to steep in your own despair.

It was closing time on Saturday afternoon. Scratch had cleaned the kitchen and gone on up to his little apartment, and since I didn't open on Sunday, I didn't have any baking or prep work to do. But Peach Rondell was still there, in the back booth that had become her second home, her head down, writing furiously in that familiar brown leather journal of hers.

I stood by the counter and watched her for a while. It must be nice, I thought, to be able to escape into another world like that, to shut everything out and just sink down into your own thoughts. For the hundredth time I wondered what she was writing, and why it was so important to her.

I waited until she got to a stopping place and went over to the table. She was staring off into the distance as if she saw something else altogether—not me, not the empty restaurant, not anything in this present universe. She didn't come to until I spoke to her, and then she jerked as if I'd materialized in front of her out of thin air, and slammed the book shut before I could get an upside-down peek at what was in it.

She was wearing beat-up jeans and a sweatshirt again— this time a frayed gray one with a huge blue W on the front, a relic of her time at Mississippi University for Women, more than twenty years ago. I thought about the first time she had come into the Heartbreak Cafe, and how bitchy I had been about the way she looked.

"Hey, Peach," I said.

She glanced down at her watch. "Sorry, Dell, I let the time get away from me. I didn't mean to keep you." She gathered up her stuff and made to slide out of the booth.

"Sit, sit," I said, motioning her back down. "I'm in no hurry. You got a minute to talk?"

"Sure," she said. "What about?"

"I don't know," I said. "Tell me about yourself. How is it for you, coming back to Chulahatchie after all this time?"

She ducked her head and rubbed her hands together. I noticed her fingernails were cut short, without so much as a dab of polish. "It's all right, I guess. Not the best of circumstances, but—" She gave a little shrug. "I didn't have much choice in coming home, you know."

I opened my mouth to say something, anything, but she cut me off.

"Don't bother denying it. I may have been gone for a long time, but some things don't ever change. This town still gossips, and I'm not deaf to it. After my divorce—well, separation, the divorce isn't final yet—I didn't know what to do. Daddy died, and Mama was alone here, and all things considered, it just seemed like the logical move."

"You don't sound so sure," I said.

"I'm not sure of anything," Peach said. "Staying with Mama is . . . well, a challenge."

"I can imagine."

"No offense, Dell, but you really can't. Mama puts on a good front, but I don't think anybody in three counties knows what she's really like. And I know what people are saying about me. Peach Rondell, the Bean Queen gone to pot. Broke, divorced, a failure." She picked at a loose cuticle and avoided meeting my eyes.

"So," I said, opting for a change in subject, "what are you writing in that book of yours?"

She laid a hand on the brown leather cover and pressed down, hard, as if she was afraid it might jump open and start spouting confidential information all on its own accord. "Just . . . stuff."

"Stuff," I repeated.

"Just thoughts. Ideas. Stories. Five hundred a month and a lock on the door."

Peach musta seen the confusion on my face.

"It's a quote from Virginia Woolf," she explained. "She said that every woman needs a room of her own, a place to think and write and discover herself. Five hundred a month—her own money to sustain her and set her free—and a lock on the door so she can create without interruption."

She gave a crooked little smile and shrugged. "Seems like this booth has become my room. Lord knows I can't get a moment's peace at the house, with Mama hanging over me nagging on me all the time." She waved a hand in front of her face, like she was swatting at gnats. "It's my soul's salvation, this restaurant, this booth. The only place I can seem to focus."

"Well, you're welcome to it anytime," I said. "Glad I can accommodate you."

"When I first came back to Chulahatchie, I was certain I had died and landed in the third circle of hell. But maybe one good thing has come out of it." She grinned. "This town sure has its share of characters."

I pushed down a twinge of apprehension, and wondered if Chulahatchie was about to become the new Peyton Place, with all our secrets revealed. It felt a little frightening, but exciting, too.

"You always wanted to be a writer?" I asked.

"Always," she said. "But life tends to get in the way. Expectations, you know."

I knew. Peach assumed I had no idea what her life was like, but I remembered how her mama was when Peach was a child. And I had a pretty good idea what Donna Rondell would think of her daughter now, all grown up and no longer a beauty queen.

"Things don't always pan out the way we hope," I said. "But maybe this turnaround in your life is giving you the chance to do what you've always wanted to do."

"I wish it was that easy."

"Oh, child, it's never easy," I said. "And it almost never looks the way you imagine it."

It sounded like something Mama woulda told me. And maybe something I needed to tell myself as well.

· 17 ·

The dream about Chase, with all its hidden meaning and significance, had begun to fade. I kept trying to recapture it, to replay it in my mind and figure it out, but it was like trying to hold sand in the palm of my hand. No matter how hard I clenched my fingers, it sifted away in the wind, leaving behind just a few grains, enough to settle in unreachable places and rub my heart raw.

When I was younger, and unafraid of what it would do to my spine or my heart rate, I used to love roller coasters. I was never scared, even of the rickety old wooden things they set up once a year at the county fair. You'd clink and clunk up and up and up, until you could see the river bend and half the county spread out below you. Then your stomach would lurch, and you'd plunge and scream down and down, into a hairpin turn that defied every law of physics I never learned.

I loved it, couldn't get enough. But in the back of my mind, I always knew I was safe, that in a couple of minutes everything would level out and jerk to a stop and be normal again.

Now there was no safe place, no leveling out. No normal world to come back to when the ride was done.

Boone insisted that this was grief, not depression. But it didn't much matter what label you used, it was a downward spiral without any brakes. You teeter for a second or two up on a rise where you think you just might be able to see the sun again and smell fresh air. Then gravity takes you, and the trip down is always a heck of a lot faster and more frightening than the tedious climb up.

Much as I tried to reassure myself that things would get better, my mind wouldn't stay there. It kept coming back to Chase, and the dream, and the images of deception and betrayal that writhed in my gut like a cutworm.

I was sinking fast. I needed my best friend.

"Well, call her then," Boone said curtly. He had come in for breakfast on Saturday morning and stayed right through lunch. It took me a while to figure out that he was waiting for me. Now it was almost closing time, and I had finally settled down with a glass of sweet tea and a bowl of apple crumb cobbler.

I pretended to be interested in the cobbler.

"Look," he said, leaning across the table, "I don't know what's going on, Dell, but something's eating at you. If you can't tell me, tell Toni. Talk to *somebody*, for God's sake."

Tears burned my eyes, a sudden stab in my stomach, a knot in my throat. I wasn't used to Boone being impatient with me, and I wished he wouldn't be. But there was something else in his voice, too, and in his eyes. Worry.

I hadn't told him about the dream. I hadn't told anybody. I had just kept it to myself, holding it close, picking at it like a scab.

"Maybe you're right," I said. "I'll call her."

But I didn't call her. Not right away, anyhow. I couldn't. I had to work up my nerve first.

Because the truth was, I was ashamed. Ashamed of being so caught up in my own narrow world that I had tunnel vision about anyone else's. Boone had tried to tell me that Toni missed me, that she was lonely. Every time, I vowed to myself that I'd get together with her. Soon.

And I meant to. She'd call me, and we'd talk on the phone for a while—mostly about me, now that I think about it. I'd complain about how much work it was to run a restaurant, and how tired I was, and she'd sympathize. We'd end up promising to have Sunday brunch or go shopping, just the two of us. But somehow it never happened.

Gradually the calls became less frequent, and shorter, and more like small talk. She came into the Heartbreak Cafe now and then, usually with Boone, and we'd hug each other and laugh and act like everything was fine.

But it wasn't fine. On top of all the other losses of this terrible year, I was losing my best friend. And it was my own damn fault.

Sunnyside Up was our favorite place for Sunday brunch—the only decent place, to tell the truth, within a fifty-mile radius of Chulahatchie. It was about twenty minutes out of town, on an unmarked dirt road back in the boonies. Right on the river, with a covered deck overlooking the water—the kind of place you'd never find if you didn't already know exactly where it was.

I couldn't for the life of me figure out how the owner, a huge cushy black woman named Netta Byrd, ever managed to make a living at it. But the woman worked magic with an egg, and baked wonderful yeasty caramel rolls, so locals came from all over the county. Especially on Sunday.

On weekdays Netta specialized in fresh fried catfish caught by her nephew Stub and brought up from the bank in a wheelbarrow full of river water. But on Sunday it was brunch, all day. And if you wanted those caramel rolls, you either had to skip church or hightail it out of there as soon as you heard the last *amen*. Otherwise you'd never beat the Baptists before they overran the place like a horde of swarming locusts.

Toni and I hadn't talked much on the ride over. The morning was warm and bright, one of those radiant November days you get now and then. We took a seat outside in the corner of the deck.

Netta spotted us at once and came rushing over. I braced myself. The woman's hugs were pretty overwhelming, but she didn't give them out to just anybody, so I figured I ought to count my blessings.

She embraced me and then Toni, and patted us into our seats. "Dell, baby," she said, "I's so glad to see you. You all right? I've had me some troubling dreams of late."

Netta's dreams were the stuff of legend around Chulahatchie. She had her own kind of religion—part Christian, part pagan, with a little voodoo thrown in for good measure. Boone suspected that if anyone on earth was truly psychic, it would be Netta Byrd.

"I'm fine, Netta," I lied. "Busy. You shoulda told me how much work it was to run a restaurant."

Netta raised her eyebrows. "You didn't ask me, now did you?"

Toni laughed, but I could hear an edge in the sound, just a hint of sharpness.

"I reckon I didn't," I conceded. "I'm just glad somebody else is cooking on Sunday."

Netta threw back her head and laughed, showing a multitude of gold crowns and caps. "The good Lawd's done give me a special dispensation to work on the Sabbath," she declared. "So's I can fatten up all these back-sliding Christians."

She waddled away, chuckling to herself. A skinny young girl, all knees and elbows and braids, sidled up to the table with a coffeepot in her hand. "Y'all want coffee?"

"Yes, please." Toni pushed her cup in the girl's direction. "And water, when you get time."

"Yes'm." The girl bobbed her head and vanished.

"She's just a child," Toni said, "not much older than my students."

"I expect she's one of Netta's grandchildren. Or a niece."

The conversation, such as it was, faltered. The granddaughter came back with water, refilled our coffee cups, and took orders. I chose a sausage and cheese omelet, biscuits and gravy, and hash browns. Toni ordered French toast and bacon. The caramel rolls would come later. We'd both be waddling like Netta by the time we were done.

We looked out over the river, watched the brown water oozing by like blackstrap molasses, commented on the nice Indian summer warm spell and the vibrant colors of the maple trees this year. I started squirming inside, uncomfortable with the small talk and the bigger talk I knew was coming, assuming I ever worked up the gumption to jump off that cliff.

Toni saved me the trouble.

"All right, Dell." She waved a forkful of French toast in my direction. "Out with it."

"Out with what?"

"Whatever it is that's on your mind. You're jumpy as a cat in heat. You won't look me in the eye, and there's obviously something you want to say but can't figure out a way to do it. For God's sake, woman, we've been best friends for a hundred years. Granted, you haven't been *acting* like a best friend in the past few months, but—" She stopped suddenly, shrugged, and put the wedge of French toast in her mouth.

I fiddled with my hash browns, picking off the crispy top part and scattering the rest. "You're right," I said. "I haven't been acting like a best friend. I've been preoccupied, and—"

"You think?"

I looked up at her. She was trying not to smile, but it wasn't working. I grinned at her.

"Yeah, I think. So, well, I wanted to apologize, and ask your forgiveness, and—"

"All right, all right, let's not make a federal case out of it," she interrupted. "But you're buying breakfast."

I felt that knot inside my chest loosen up a little and realized all of a sudden how long it had been since I had taken an easy breath. Since the day I went to see Brenda Unger? Since the night Chase died?

I thought it would be hard, but once I started talking everything just sorta gushed on out of me—all those months of wondering, obsessing about the identity of Chase's mistress, with no clues to go on. Then Fart telling me about the divorce, and my conversation with Brenda, and the dream where Chase became something else, something awful.

Lord help me, it was such a relief to get it off my chest, to share the burden with somebody I trusted. I didn't have the first idea what I was gonna do now, or what difference any of it would make, but at least I wouldn't be in it alone.

Finally I finished and looked up.

Toni was staring at me with her jaw gaping and her coffee cup halfway to her mouth. She put the cup down so hard the whole table rattled.

"Shit, Dell," she said.

"I know." I shook my head. "I never woulda guessed—"

"No. Listen to me. You're wrong."

"I wouldn't have believed it myself, Toni. But Brenda said—"

She propped her elbows on the tabletop. "Tell me exactly what Brenda said. Word for word."

I cast back in my mind, trying to bring up the conversation. "Well, she admitted she'd had an affair. When I tried to reason with her about leaving Fart, she got pretty agitated, said I was the last person she wanted to talk to about this, that we had been friends for a long time and she didn't want to cause me any more pain."

"But she didn't say, 'I was the one having an affair with Chase.'"

"Not in those words, no. Not right out. It was pretty clear, though, what she was trying to tell me."

"Was it?"

"Well, yeah. It was clear enough. I tried to second-guess it, but what else could she mean? Fart told me she hadn't been herself for some time—months, maybe a year. And then Brenda said it was over now, but she couldn't go back to the way things were with Fart, and she didn't want to tell me because I'd been through enough."

I narrowed my eyes and squinted at Toni. She had an odd expression on her face, one I couldn't quite read.

"We've been friends all our lives," she said at last. "And you know I love you. But I'm going to tell you something now that you need to hear. So pay attention."

She took a breath and exhaled heavily. "You don't *listen*, Dell. You *don't*. Especially in the last few months, you've been so caught up in your own pain and grief that you can't see anything else. Now, I know it's been a tough time for you, so I've cut you some slack. I've tried to be understanding. But you've got blinders on about this thing with Chase. You're jumping to conclusions, and you need to hear the truth."

She paused and pushed her plate away. I waited, watching that little vein throb just above her right eyebrow.

"It wasn't Brenda Unger."

"But she said—"

"What she *said* was that she didn't want to cause you any more pain, that you had been through enough. That's what

I mean about not listening, Dell. What she *said* was that she didn't tell you about her affair because she thought it would open up the wounds again. And that's exactly what she meant. That's all she meant."

"No, you're wrong," I said. "You weren't there."

"Trust me," Toni said. "Brenda didn't have an affair with Chase."

"How do you know?"

I had a dog once, a little spaniel mix, who would bite if she was scared or hurt or felt trapped. I learned to recognize the signs. She'd go rigid, just for a second, and her head would snap around. And she'd get this look in her eye, a glazed kind of look, as if she knew she'd regret it after it was all over, but she was going to bite anyway.

Toni had that look now. Instinct told me I ought to back off, but I couldn't help myself.

"How do you know?" I repeated.

She chewed on her bottom lip and stared out over the river.

"Because I know. Just leave it at that."

If I thought Brenda had given me the Judas kiss, here sat Toni with a big old sledgehammer, driving in the spikes. I could almost feel the vibration of the blows inside my head, running along my jawbone. Could almost hear the clang of iron against iron.

Netta tottered by with a coffeepot and refilled our cups while I struggled to swallow down the cannonball in my throat. Toni thanked her, and sat back in her chair, sipping her coffee, as if that was the end of the discussion. She watched me over the rim.

At last, when I managed to speak, my voice came out hoarse and creaky. "Just what, exactly, do you know?"

"I know it wasn't Brenda."

"Then who was it? And why the hell didn't you tell me? You know this has been eating me alive, Toni."

She reached across the table and tried to take my hand. I snatched it back. I didn't want her touching me, didn't want to have to look at her.

"I told Boone you'd respond like this," she muttered.

My heart dropped into my shoes. "Boone?" I said.

"Who else was I going to talk to? Let me explain."

"What is there to explain?" I shouted. "Another betrayal? Another twist of the knife?" I threw a twenty-dollar bill on the table and headed for the parking lot. Toni followed, running to keep up, still trying to talk.

"Just shut up, will you? Shut up and leave me the hell alone."

She shut up.

We drove back to town in silence. I don't know how we made it without ending up in a ditch, because I could barely see the road through my tears, and my hands kept shaking on the steering wheel. When we finally pulled up in front of Toni's house, she got out and I drove away.

Without even saying good-bye.

· 18 ·

I'd lived in Chulahatchie all my life and never once felt lonely.

Sad, sometimes, but it was the kind of sadness I reckon all women experience at one time or the other, when their husbands don't pay attention to them, or they're feeling put upon and unappreciated.

Never this block of ice in the pit of my stomach, this isolation. It made me feel like an alien set down off a spaceship, on a planet where people were saying words I understood but putting them together in sentences that didn't make a lick of sense.

It was like a bad dream I couldn't wake up from, like that movie, *Invasion of the Body Snatchers*. All the people I loved and counted on and thought I knew were morphing into terrifying strangers with familiar faces. Chase first, then

Brenda, and now Toni and even Boone. Nothing was solid enough to hold me up. The whole world had turned into sinkholes and quicksand.

The Monday afternoon lunch crowd had cleared out and the Heartbreak Cafe was closed, but here I sat in the corner booth, unable to force myself to get up and do. For fifteen solid minutes I'd been tracing a scar on the Formica tabletop with my thumbnail.

My stomach rumbled and my hand shook. Vaguely I thought I might be hungry, but it was hard to tell hunger from the emptiness inside.

I looked up to see Scratch standing over me with a plate in his hand.

"I know. I gotta get stuff ready for tomorrow morning," I said. "I just can't seem to . . ."

Can't seem to what? I thought. Can't seem to function? Can't seem to finish a sentence? Can't seem to come to grips with the fact that everybody I had ever loved turned out to be a liar and a cheat?

"It's all right," Scratch said. "Everything's done. I set all the food away and put a soup together for in the morning. Kitchen's clean and shut down." He motioned with the plate. "The vultures 'bout cleaned us out, but I made this for you. Thought you might be hungry, seein' as you hadn't eaten."

He set the plate in front of me. "Mind if I join you?"

I did mind. It felt wrong, somehow, sitting in a booth across from a black man, and although I wanted not to feel that way, I didn't have the energy to filter my own thoughts and make myself feel something else.

I liked Scratch, I really did. He was a hard worker, and kindhearted, and never gave me a minute's trouble. And yet I couldn't get over feeling a little tense around him, a kind of innate suspicion that to Southerners was bred in the bone.

Still, I said the right thing, even if I wasn't feeling it. "Have a seat." I peered at the plate he had brought me. "What is it?"

He sat down, slowly, like he was testing whether the seat would hold him. Seemed to me he wasn't exactly comfortable with the situation, either. "It's a sandwich."

"I can see that. What kind of sandwich?"

"Peanut butter and jelly and fried Spam."

"You can't be serious."

"Don't knock it if you ain't tried it. They say Elvis was partial to grilled peanut butter and bananas. Guess he never discovered Spam."

"Yeah, Elvis was forty-two when he died, too," I said. "Not the greatest recommendation."

Scratch motioned to me to eat up. "Go on, take a bite. Best comfort food in the world."

He had already cut the sandwich, on the diagonal the way I liked it. I picked one half up and took a bite out of the corner.

"Good, ain't it?"

It was more than good. The combination of flavors and textures was downright amazing—the smooth nuttiness of the peanut butter, the sweet tang of strawberry jam, the salty, slightly spicy flavor of the Spam.

I took two more bites and swallowed. "You win. It's delicious. But what makes you think I need comfort food?"

He drummed his fingers on the tabletop and then turned them palm side up. A simple movement, but it seemed so vulnerable, showing the pale underside of those strong black hands.

"Don't take a genius to recognize the signs." He shrugged. "You want to talk about it, I'm listening."

I opened my mouth to say no, I was fine. But then my heart betrayed me, and I couldn't hold back the tears.

"That's good. Let it out," he murmured. He pulled a handful of napkins out of the dispenser and handed them across to me.

I cried for a while, avoiding his eyes, and when I finally blew my nose and looked up again he was still there, gazing at me, waiting patiently. I'd never met a man except Boone who was comfortable with a woman's tears, but Scratch surprised me. The thought flitted briefly across my mind that he might surprise me in other ways, if I'd just give him a chance.

"I had brunch with Toni yesterday," I began.

He nodded.

"And, well . . ." I hesitated for a second and then plunged on in headfirst. Everything—about Chase, the dream, suspecting Brenda, and the fact that Toni and Boone both knew something they weren't telling me. About the depth of loneliness and isolation I had never felt before. Through it all he listened, not interrupting but obviously taking it all very seriously. When I finished, he had tears in his eyes.

Nobody had ever cried for me before.

"So what do I do?" I asked.

He didn't answer right off. He thought about it for a

minute, and then he said, "Sometimes people let us down. You hurt for a spell. Maybe a long spell. And then gradual-like, you start to forgive."

"I don't know how to forgive."

He looked into my eyes. "Nobody does. We just get up every morning and put one foot in front of the other. We take it one step at a time, let the healing come until we find the strength to let it go."

He spoke these words quietly, gently, as if he knew—really *knew*—what they meant. As if he'd been there himself.

I heard something in his voice then, saw something I'd been blind to before.

"So how, exactly, did you learn to forgive?" I asked.

He shrugged. "By getting up every morning," he said, "and putting one foot in front of the other."

· 19 ·

Monday night I sat down in front of the football game and started looking over my books to figure out how much I could afford to pay Scratch for the work he did at the Heartbreak Cafe. I'd done a little research, called over to the library when I was sure Boone wouldn't be there, and what I found out made me downright furious.

For one thing, I discovered that Mississippi did not have a minimum wage law. No protection for the working poor, no guidelines. I'd never thought about it, really. It never occurred to me what people did to make ends meet when they didn't have a salary and benefits to fall back on. Not until Chase left me high and dry, anyway.

Maybe it shouldn't have made a difference to me that I'd glimpsed a deeper side of Scratch—not just a black man, a drifter, a bum who needed a handout, but a *man*. Someone with a life beyond the Heartbreak Cafe, who knew about pain and loss and forgiveness. Someone who might, if I'd let him, turn out to be a friend.

After all these months, the beginnings of a personal connection. It made me think better of him, somehow.

And worse of myself.

When I looked in the mirror these days, I saw a shallow, self-absorbed middle-aged woman who hardly ever gave a second thought to anything besides her own needs. I could rationalize it, I reckon, make excuses for myself. Widowed, grieving, betrayed, struggling to run a restaurant all on my own. But however I boiled it down, it stunk to high heaven, like cabbage and broccoli burned to the bottom of the pot.

Toni was right about one thing: I hadn't been listening. I'd been sleepwalking through half my life, and it took losing just about everything to wake me up. Was that why Chase went elsewhere, I wonder? Was that why I didn't really respect Scratch until I was forced to acknowledge some wisdom or insight in him that I didn't have? Was that why I looked at Peach Rondell and saw a washed-up Bean Queen instead of the beauty who lurked inside?

Maybe I'd been asking the wrong questions all along. Maybe I'd focused too much on *what* and *who* and *when* and *how* but never got around to *why*.

"Why?" he said.

"Why what? Don't you *want* to get paid—you know, actual money, more than just tips? Cat food for that beast of yours, toothpaste." I forced a grin, trying to lighten things up. "Cleaning supplies. Don't bother denying it, I know you're obsessive."

Scratch narrowed his eyes and cocked his head. "Why now?"

I didn't want to answer that question, and I was pretty sure he knew it. "Let's just say you've proved yourself, and I've figured out I can afford it. Five dollars an hour isn't much, but it's something."

"Yes, ma'am," he said. "It sure is something."

"Then it's settled. Let's get back to work before I change my mind."

"Miz Dell?"

I turned.

"Thank you."

"You're welcome. And it's just plain Dell."

The afternoon wasn't just a rush, it was an all-out madhouse. It was a week before Thanksgiving, and maybe everybody was just bracing for the holiday onslaught and didn't feel like cooking. Or maybe the Heartbreak Cafe was trying to save me again, to keep me so busy I didn't have the time or energy to wallow in my misery.

By one o'clock I was out of roast pork and the chicken pot pie was running dangerously low. Scratch was in the freezer, scrounging for whatever we could cook real fast, when Purdy Overstreet waltzed in.

As usual, Purdy's theatrical entrance brought all conversation to a skidding stop. She bowed and waved to her audience and looked around vaguely.

Her regular booth was full of strangers, a family of four from Texarkana traveling over the river and through the woods to grandmother's house just south of Milledgeville, Georgia. They'd bent my ear for ten blessed minutes about Milldgeville and how their gran had known Flannery O'Connor personally and used to spend time at the farm feeding the peacocks. On a day like today I didn't really have time to listen and didn't give a flip about Flannery's birds, but I smiled and nodded and brought them their chicken pot pie.

Purdy fixed the evil eye on them and glared. They didn't get the message, just sat there sipping their iced tea and relaxing, in no apparent rush to get to grandma's. She stood in the doorway, shifting from one foot to the other like a clock pendulum. Tick . . . tock, tick . . . tock.

Then, from the booth nearest the kitchen, Hoot Everett looked up and spotted her. He lurched to his feet and upset two coffee cups and a glass of sweet tea cutting a mad swath through the crowd.

When he got to the door he extended a hand and gave an abbreviated, arthritic little bow. "Miss Purdy," he said, "I'd be pleasured to have your company for lunch today."

Hoot had spiffed himself up, as if he'd got a premonition that today might be his golden opportunity. He'd shaved off the bristly white stubble, except for one furry spot just under his left earlobe, and was all decked out in a clean white shirt and bright green suspenders. A jaunty bow tie, red with white polka dots, trembled like a nervous bird beneath his wattle.

I watched through the pass-through window as Purdy looked around, obviously searching for Scratch. But as her first love was nowhere to be found, second choice was better than none. She pooched out her painted-on lips and gave Hoot the smile of his life. "That would be mahvelous," she said, and extended her hand toward him.

He escorted her back to the booth, helped her into her seat, and settled in across from her, his wrinkled face shining with a look of absolute bliss, the expression of love at long last requited.

I snatched up my pad and headed over quick as my feet would take me. Purdy would want the chicken pie. I only had four servings left, and God help me, I wasn't about to give them away before Purdy got hers. Hell hath no fury like a woman denied her chicken.

I took her order, grabbed her tea, and scrambled around refilling cups and glasses while Scratch hid out in the kitchen. As it edged on toward two o'clock the place gradually began to clear out and I breathed a little sigh of relief. We'd made it through without having to resort to the fried chicken livers, which I was saving for a Saturday special.

I rang up the Milledgeville crowd and sent them on their way. Hoot and Purdy were huddled up with their heads together, laughing and obviously getting on like potatoes and gravy. Peach Rondell sat in her accustomed booth, watching them and writing furiously.

When I went over to Peach's table with a refill on decaf, she flicked her eyebrows and gave a wicked little grin. "There's a couple of characters for you," she said, motioning with her head in the direction of the two lovebirds.

"About time," I said. "I thought she'd never give up on Scratch."

"Maybe Hoot's got something Scratch doesn't."

"What do you mean?"

Peach nodded and pointed across the room. I looked just as Hoot, his mouth open in a mostly toothless smile, handed something across the table to Purdy.

A bottle. A green glass pint bottle.

"Dang," I said under my breath. "What is that?"

"I don't know," Peach said, "but they're liking it, I can tell you that much."

Just then the bell over the door jingled and Marvin Beckstrom entered, followed by the sheriff in full uniform with a pistol on his hip and handcuffs dangling from his belt.

"Oh, Lord," I said. "Peach, I gotta do something fast. I don't have a liquor license, and if what they're drinking is what I think it is, the sheriff could shut me down in two seconds. There's nothing that little turd Beckstrom would like better."

"Go," she said. "I'll distract them."

I headed toward Hoot's booth, plastering a smile on my face and trying to act normal. Behind me, I heard a crash of breaking china, a thud, and a groan. Marvin and the sheriff made a beeline for Peach's side of the room, and Scratch came out of the kitchen to see what was going on.

I shielded Hoot and Purdy with my body so that Marvin couldn't see them and Purdy couldn't see Scratch. "What do you think you're doing?" I hissed. "You can't drink that in here!"

"Shore we can," Hoot said. He was having trouble getting his mouth around the words. "We're both consenshual adults."

"Tha's right," Purdy chimed in. "We ain't chil'ren, and you ain't our mama. You're not the boss of me."

"What *is* that?" I jerked the bottle out of Hoot's hand and held it up to my nose. The tang of fruit and alcohol nearly knocked me over. "Whoo-ee, Hoot. That's some powerful stuff."

"Yep," he said, "thash my very own mushcadine wine, made special for Miz Purdy. I got me the best mushcadines in the county." He patted Purdy's clawlike hand. "And the best lady."

I threw a glance over my shoulder. Marvin and the sheriff were helping Peach to her feet, where she had pretended to slip and fall, and Scratch was cleaning up the mess of broken shards and iced tea. I could hear Marvin saying something to Peach about suing me for reckless endangerment.

"Y'all gotta settle down. Now," I said. "And I'll keep this." I corked the bottle and tucked it into my apron pocket, hoping I'd have a chance to dispose of it before the sheriff got wind of Hoot's muscadine wine.

"You give that back!" Hoot screeched. "It ain't yours."

"It's mine now. I'm confiscating it."

"Thief!" Purdy yelled. "I'm callin' the po-lice."

"The police are already here," I said. "And they'll most likely arrest *you* for being drunk and disorderly. So please, sit down and calm down, and I'll bring you some fresh coffee. On the house."

But Hoot had already struggled to his feet. He was getting redder in the face every second, and both the wattle and the bow tie were doing a quivering little dance. "We're leaving," he said. "C'mon, baby, let's get outta here." He held out his hand to Purdy, who staggered out of the booth and fell against him. "We'll go to my house, there's more where that came from."

I grabbed his arm. "Hoot Everett," I said, "you are not driving in that condition. You're a hazard on the road as it is. Give me your keys."

"Nope." He headed toward the door, one hand around Purdy's waist and the other steadying himself on the booths along the way. Purdy, barely able to walk in high heels when she was stone-cold sober, was now wobbling dangerously.

It all happened in slow-motion. Purdy caught a glimpse of Scratch, turned, and went down, arms flailing. She landed hard with one skinny leg tucked underneath her at an unnatural angle, and let out a howl of pain and rage.

All the commotion from the other side of the restaurant died abruptly. The fabricated distraction forgotten, Peach and Scratch rushed over, followed closely by Marvin Beckstrom and the sheriff.

Scratch knelt down and felt gently around Purdy's ankle and up the leg to her knee. Hoot stood watching like a drooling, overprotective bulldog, his clouded eyes daring Scratch to go any farther north.

"What did I tell you, Dell?" Marvin hissed from somewhere behind my head. "This place is a disaster waiting to happen. And do I smell *liquor*?"

"Shut up, Marvin," I said. "What do you think, Scratch? Anything broken?"

He shook his head. "I don't think so. It's probably just an ankle sprain. But at her age you can't be too careful. Better get her to the hospital."

Peach had already called 911 on her cell phone, and within a couple of minutes flashing lights appeared outside the door of the Heartbreak Cafe, accompanied by a growing crowd of rubberneckers. Dang, you couldn't pee in this town without five or six people congregating to comment on it.

The EMTs pushed their way inside, assessed the situation, put Purdy on a stretcher, and headed out the door for the three-minute ride to the emergency room. Hoot tried to climb in the back of the ambulance, but the paramedics refused. After a brief tussle, the sheriff stepped in and broke it up before it became an all-out slugfest.

"I'll take him," Peach said. "He ought not be driving."

The ambulance roared off with lights strobing and sirens wailing—a bit of overkill, if you ask me, but boys do like their toys. Peach herded Hoot into her little blue Honda and followed.

Only Marv and the sheriff were left, not counting me and Scratch. The sheriff was nosing around the booth Hoot and Purdy had occupied. Marvin was glaring at me, looking suspicious. I put my hand in the pocket of my apron and pushed the bottle down as far as it would go. It was still a big lump standing out against the fabric, but if I kept my hand in there and tried to act natural, maybe they wouldn't feel the need to frisk me.

Marvin narrowed his eyes and rubbed his hands together, a giant praying mantis about to consume a smaller, weaker insect. "I warned you," he said. "This was a bad idea from the beginning. I don't suppose you thought about how easily you could get sued, did you? And as the owner of record on this property, Chulahatchie Savings and Loan could be named in that litigation. If I could find some way to justify it—some legal way, I mean—I'd shut you down right now, today." He blurted all this out in a rush and then blinked, as if coming to his senses after a bout of temporary insanity. "For your own good, of course."

I wasn't about to give him the satisfaction of a response. I just stood there, staring him down, until he blinked again and swallowed. "But you have a lease."

"I do. And now I'll thank you for getting out of my way so I can finish up here."

Marvin motioned for the sheriff, a gesture that reminded me of a trainer calling to a dog. When the two of them finally sidled out, taking their own sweet time, I shut the door behind them, turned over the CLOSED sign, and pulled down the shade.

I sank into the nearest booth. "Good Lord A'mighty," I said.

"Amen to that." Scratch stood there with his huge fists on his hips. "What happened?"

I fished the bottle of muscadine wine out of my pocket and set it on the table. "Purdy and Hoot were having themselves a little party."

He gave a big bark of a laugh and set about cleaning the rest of the tables. I shoulda gotten up and helped, but my knees still felt like jelly, so I just sat there with my head propped in my hands. After a few minutes banging around in the kitchen, he came back out. "Everything's done," he said. "Guess I'll be getting on."

"Fine, Scratch. See you tomorrow."

"There's just one more thing."

I looked up. He was holding something, something that seemed strangely dwarfed in his massive hand. He laid it down in front of me.

I heard the bell over the door jingle as he left, but I didn't see him go. I couldn't drag my eyes away from the object on the table.

It was a book. A brown leather book.

Peach Rondell's journal.

· 20 ·

I knew I ought not do it. I *knew*.

It was an invasion of privacy, worse than spying on your neighbor with binoculars. Worse than sneaking through the bushes in the dark to peer into a bedroom window. Worse than picking up the extension and listening in.

But I couldn't help myself.

The restaurant was closed, the door locked, the shade pulled down, the lights off. No one could see me; no one would even know I was here unless they went around back by the Dumpster where my car was parked.

I coulda left and gone home, I reckon. Taken the journal with me and read it at my kitchen table. But that seemed worse, somehow—not just voyeurism, but kidnapping, too.

So I sat there for a while with the book shut in front of me, staring at it, considering.

"You can judge a person's character," Mama always said, "by what they do when nobody's looking." I expect she'd also say that God was *always* looking, but since I hadn't seen much evidence of the Almighty in the past few months, the notion of divine displeasure wasn't exactly uppermost in my mind.

I was curious, certainly, but it was more than curiosity that drove me. It was a kind of compulsion. My hand shook and my stomach churned and I heard Mama's warning in the back of my mind, but I couldn't seem to stop myself.

The journal fell open where Peach had quit writing, where her pen lay folded between the pages, about two-thirds of the way through the thick, bound book. The paper was smooth and heavy with faint narrow blue lines, the writing small and neat and even.

Hooch leaned over and gave Pansy a little kiss on the cheek. She never would have allowed it if she had been sober, he knew, but he had to take his opportunities when and where they came.

The blasted bow tie was about to choke him half to death. She smelled of homemade gin and face powder and a perfume so heavy it made his eyes water, and something else—Eau du Nursing Home, he thought. That peculiar smell you always got when a lot of old and dying people were herded together in constricted quarters.

My suspicions were right—Peach was writing about Chulahatchie, and the people in it. The people right here in the Heartbreak Cafe, in fact, and stuff that was happening here every blessed day.

And what else had she written?

I flipped the pages, scuttling backward like a crab. She'd written about everybody—Scratch, Fart, the boys from Tenn-Tom, the truckers, the little blue-haired ladies who came for coffee and pie. DeeDee Sturgis and Tansie Orr. Marvin Beckstrom, even.

Then a particular name caught my eye, and I stopped. Stopped and stared.

I should have said yes to Boone Atkins years ago when I had the chance. He was so sweet and smart and sensitive—not to mention damn good-looking—and we might have had something, if only I hadn't been a spineless wimp and given in to Mama like I always did. I hate the woman, honestly I do, and though I'm not proud of thinking it, my life would be infinitely easier if she'd just go ahead and die. But she's too hateful and too stubborn to give me the satisfaction. With my luck she'll probably live forever . . .

My heart hammered in my chest, and I shut the book, keeping my finger inside to hold the place. This was very private stuff, stuff I was sure Peach intended to keep to herself. I felt like a thief, stealing somebody else's precious possessions and then going on pretending to be a friend. But I couldn't quit. Not yet. Not if what I needed to know was in this book.

If I'd ever doubted it before, I was sure of one thing now. Peach Rondell understood people. She watched. She listened. It was all here, in her journal. All the quirks and eccentricities, the little details that made individuals stand out. The truth about Chulahatchie.

The things folks tried to hide, Peach saw.

Scratch, for example. She wrote about him with tenderness and compassion, characterizing him as a failed artist, a man with a painful hidden past. A love gone terribly wrong. A career in ruins. Reduced to waiting tables at a second-rate diner, never given the admiration he deserved.

How did she know anything about Scratch's deeper side, when all she'd seen of him was a short-order cook and busboy? And how did she understand about Fart? She painted him to perfection—a broken-down basketball star whose whole life and self-image was tied up in being a good provider, a good husband, a good father. A man who had buried his dreams of glory to make his wife happy, only to watch her walk away without a backward glance.

And Tansie Orr, whose husband, Tank (Peach called him Hank), played the adoring spouse in public but slapped her around behind closed doors. *Did he really?* I wondered. What had Peach seen that I had missed? Was she right, that Tansie's only recourse was to put on a front, to try to act as young and sexy as possible to bolster her flagging self-image? Was that why Tansie dressed so provocatively and dyed her hair and wore those outrageous acrylic fingernails?

It was all very interesting, very enlightening, but it wasn't what I was looking for. I was sure it was here, somewhere. I just had to find it.

And then my eye snagged on a word. A name. My name.

Dell Haley is an amazing woman. I sit here in this booth every day and watch her, and although I know some of what she's been through and can imagine, at least in part, the pain and grief she must be experiencing, she just keeps going. She smiles and talks and listens and makes people feel important and treats them with dignity. Even if they're idiots or assholes, like Marvin Beckstrom.

I've never seen that kind of strength in a woman. I was always taught, by precept if not by example, that a woman is the weaker vessel, and without a man to support and sustain her, she will crack and shatter into a thousand pieces.

When I came home to Chulahatchie I was cracked and on the verge of shattering. I didn't care if I lived or died. But Dell gives me an example of how to be strong, and thanks to her I have the will to go on. Maybe someday I'll work up the nerve to actually talk to her, to tell her that she's my hero and my inspiration.

Maybe someday we might actually be friends. Maybe—

The telephone rang, shrill in the silence of the empty restaurant. I jerked, slammed the journal shut, and pushed it away as if whoever was on the other end of the phone could see through the lines and know what I was doing. My heart thudded in my chest. Guilt smothered me so that I could barely breathe.

The phone continued to ring. I craned my neck to see the clock on the wall over the kitchen pass-through window. It was nearly four. I forced myself up and out of the booth, and answered the phone with a shaky voice.

"Dell, thank God," a voice said. "When I didn't get you at home, I was hoping you'd still be at the restaurant."

I swallowed vainly at the lump of cotton in my throat. The silence stretched on.

"Dell? Are you all right? It's Peach."

"Yes," I said. "Sorry. Yeah, I'm fine."

"I thought you'd want to know about Purdy Overstreet. She's okay. Like Scratch said, it's just a sprain, although the doctor says the ligaments are pulled a little, so he's put her in a walking cast for six weeks. One of those boot things you can take off to take a bath, and to sleep at night."

"That's good," I said.

"It just took a lot longer at the emergency room than we expected." Peach laughed. "And get this—Hoot Everett is determined to take care of her himself. He's got her set up in the spare room at his house."

"Are you kidding me?"

"Apparently she figures he'll be more interesting company than the folks at St. Agnes—she calls them the 'geriatric set.' Jane Lee Custer came down to the hospital while Purdy was being treated. Says she can't keep Purdy at the nursing home against her will, but she'll send somebody over to Hoot's every day to check on her."

"Guess I'll be delivering lunch to them, then," I said. "Purdy hates the food at St. Agnes."

"I think she'd like that," Peach said. "Although she'd like it better if Scratch did the delivering."

"Just what we need—a fistfight with Hoot defending Purdy's honor."

"Life's nothing if it isn't drama," Peach said. "Everywhere you go, there's a floor show."

I had no answer to this. Peach's journal sure reflected the drama she saw all around her.

"Listen," she said. "With all the commotion, I accidentally left my journal in the back booth."

I tried to keep my voice calm, to sound normal. "Yeah, I found it." I held my breath. She was going to suggest coming over to pick it up right now, I was sure of it. But I needed to buy myself some time. "Tell you what, I've got a few things to finish up here, but I can drop it by on my way home if you like."

"Thanks, Dell, but that's not necessary," Peach said. "I'll get it tomorrow. Just put it somewhere safe, will you?" She hesitated. "It's kind of important to me."

"I'll take care of it."

"I know you will. I trust you."

She signed off and hung up, and I dragged myself back to the booth and the journal feeling like pond scum.

I sat there for ten minutes or so, fingering the soft leather of the cover and battling inside my head. She trusted me. Well, I'd be worthy of that trust. I wouldn't read another word, and no harm done.

But I couldn't do it. It was like my hands belonged to somebody else, flipping those pages, and my eyes were out of my head and reading on their own. And then I found it, and I couldn't quit now, not if my soul would burn in hell for the sin.

He waited there, in the gathering darkness, looking out over the river and watching the snowy egrets that came in to fish in the shallows near the dock. The water had gone red from the reflected light of the sunset, bloodred like the rivers of Egypt under Moses's plague.

The cabin stood on pillars above flood level, although the waters had kept to their banks since the Army Corps of Engineers had built the dam and waterway. Below, underneath the back of the house, his truck stood hidden from prying eyes. An unnecessary precaution, probably. Only the egrets were fishing tonight, and the camp was situated at the end of a narrow dirt track, far off the beaten path on an isolated bend of the river.

He saw the reflected glow of headlights against the trees and crossed to the other side of the deck to watch the car bounce slowly into view. Behind him, in the cabin, the lights were off, candles lit, wine chilled, soft music playing. Everything was ready.

The car turned into the driveway. She got out and climbed the stairs, her long legs lithe and elegant in black jeans, her blonde hair swaying with every step.

She was beautiful and a little shy, and laughed easily, and made him feel attractive and sexy and desirable. He had felt that way once, long ago, when he was thirty and fit and still had his athlete's body and a bright future ahead of him. But time and reality had a way of flabbing muscles and dimming dreams, and it had been years since he had felt like anyone special.

And so he had kept his distance, plagued by self-doubt, questioning if he was interpreting the signals correctly. When she had finally made a move on him, he was so aroused he could have taken her right there, in the produce aisle of the Piggly Wiggly.

But this was better. Private, relaxed, secretive. The forbidden fruit, just waiting to be picked, and to hell with the consequences.

Mama used to say you should never condemn somebody without the testimony of two witnesses. It was somewhere in the Bible, I think, but wherever it came from, it was probably good advice.

A voice echoed in the back of my mind, my best friend's voice, telling me she knew for certain that Brenda Unger didn't have an affair with my husband—but not telling me how she knew. Now I stared at the journal, its pages spread out before me like a centerfold in all its obscene glory. My jaw ached from clenching my teeth, and my head throbbed with the strain of trying to read the words again in the fading afternoon light.

I reckon I just got my second witness.

Thanksgiving came and went, the worst Thanksgiving of my entire life.

The Heartbreak Cafe was closed for the day, and I sat alone in the house I had shared with Chase, eating a turkey sandwich and trying to distract myself with the Macy's parade and ten hours of nonstop football. I couldn't have told you who was playing to save my soul.

Toni. I couldn't believe it—my best friend and my husband. How could she have done such a thing? And how did Peach Rondell find out?

Besides that, who else knew, and wasn't telling? Boone, for sure.

I paced. I pounded the sofa pillows. I swore at the top of my lungs, yelled at the TV, cried until I thought I would drown in my own snot. Cried out to God, to the universe, to whoever the hell was listening: "No, dammit! No! I don't deserve this!"

But no one answered.

Friday, after three hours of sleep, I dragged myself out of bed and went to the restaurant. Scratch was already there, prepping for breakfast, making coffee. He gave me a look but didn't say anything other than, "Mornin', Miz Dell," and went on about his work. I let him do everything. I just sat in a booth and drank most of the first pot of coffee, and wondered what in blazes I was gonna do. How I was going to go on. How I could possibly survive.

Nobody showed up that morning. Nobody except Fart Unger.

He joined me in the booth and accepted Scratch's offer of coffee. For a while he just sat there with his hands cradling the mug, and then he said, "Dell, what's wrong? You look like you're on your last nerve."

I couldn't tell him. I just sat there with a fist-sized lump in my throat and shrugged.

"You've been working too hard," he said after a while. "Maybe you oughta take a few days off."

The kindness in his voice unraveled me, and I swiped at the tears. "Maybe you're right," I said. "I've been under a lot of stress lately."

He took a sip of his coffee. "I can listen, if you need to talk."

I gritted my teeth and determined to buck up. "I'll be okay," I said.

He reached out a callused hand and touched my fingers, just lightly, like a brush of sandpaper across my skin. "You don't need to be strong all the time," he said. "You got friends."

"I know."

That was all the response I could manage. If I said another word, I would start crying and not be able to stop. I changed the subject. "You want some breakfast?"

"You'll join me?"

I looked around the empty restaurant. "Why not?"

Scratch wouldn't hear of me getting in the kitchen. He made bacon and eggs and hash browns and banana pancakes and brought them to us like he was serving royalty. We small-talked our way through breakfast; Fart ate his and half of mine. If I didn't know better, I'd think he preferred Scratch's cooking. By the time he'd finished the last of the pancakes, I pretty much had him convinced that I was all right. Just tired. Just in need of a little break.

"Then take a break," he said. "The restaurant will still be here when you get back."

I musta been out of my ever-loving mind, taking off the way I did. The next morning I packed a bag, handed Scratch my keys, and put the CLOSED sign on the door of the Heartbreak Cafe.

"I'll be back in a few days," I said. "Folks can survive without my cooking until then."

He narrowed his eyes. "Shouldn't you call Toni? Or Boone? Somebody oughta know where you've gone to. They'll worry."

"Let 'em worry," I said. "It might be good for them."

Then, feeling a little bit like a rebellious teenager running away from home, I drove through the ATM at Chulahatchie Savings and Loan, withdrew the maximum—two hundred dollars—and headed for the Alabama line.

I had only a vague idea where I was going—Atlanta, maybe. Didn't much matter; I just wanted to get out of Mississippi, out of Chulahatchie in particular. As far away from Toni and Boone and the memory of Chase Haley as I could get on raging fury and a Visa card.

I might even drive all the way to Asheville—Tansie Orr couldn't stop raving about the place after she and Tank went last year. I remembered those mountains from long-ago trips to the Smokies, pristine and gentle and peaceful.

An hour into the trip, I was pretty sure I'd lost leave of my senses. Traffic through Tuscaloosa was a nightmare— apparently Ole Miss was playing Alabama. On both sides of me were cars full of honking, screaming college students and aging alumni flying flags out their windows and yelling at each other across the highway.

By the time I got past the university and out onto the Birmingham bypass, eastbound traffic was lighter, but my nerves were frayed to a ragged edge. Only then did it occur to me that I'd never done this before, taken a road trip by myself. Chase did the driving, and the few times we traveled over to East Tennessee and Western North Carolina, all I had to do was consult the map and enjoy the scenery.

Alabama didn't have much scenery to speak of, not that I coulda seen it anyway, sandwiched like I was between roaring semis. I almost missed the exit toward Atlanta. I caught a glimpse of the sign at the last minute, held my breath, floored it across three lanes, and swerved onto the exit ramp. Behind me, brakes squealed and horns blared, but at least I wasn't dead and didn't hear any sirens or crashing metal.

Thank God for small favors.

Three hours later, give or take a rest stop or two, the tall skyline of Atlanta emerged out of the mist. I came over a rise and there it stood, shimmering in the distance like the Emerald City in *The Wizard of Oz*.

But there was no magic, unless you count the miracle of surviving rush-hour traffic. I passed Six Flags, closed for the season, with its empty roller coaster hulking like a dinosaur skeleton in the rain. It took me another hour and a half to get to the far side of the city. By the time I pulled off at the Days Inn and rented a crummy room for the obscene price of sixty-four dollars a night, I was exhausted, depressed, and almost ready to turn around and go back to Chulahatchie.

But going back wasn't an option. This trip might have been crazy and impulsive and totally unlike the Dell Haley everybody thought they knew, but it was instinct, survival. I took myself back out again, went scouting, and ended up at an Italian cafe nearby, a place called Macaroni Grill.

How you grilled macaroni, I had no clue, but it turned out to be a Tuscan-style, overpriced restaurant that offered a mind-numbing assortment of pasta dishes, served with huge wheels of warm, crusty bread. I opted for the maximum dose of fat, cholesterol, and garlic, and chose the shrimp scampi Alfredo with Caesar salad and half a carafe of a white wine I'd never heard of.

Chulahatchie is the kind of place where wine comes with a screw-off top, or if you're a big drinker, in a box that will fit in the fridge. According to my waiter, a handsome young man worthy of Chippendale's, this was an Italian Pino, whatever that meant. I didn't much care—I just liked the idea of having somebody else cook, serve, and clean up.

Being served by a gorgeous hunk who flirted shamelessly was an unexpected plus.

The gorgeous hunk, of course, talked me into having dessert—a wedge of cheesecake half the size of my head, with hot fudge dolloped over the top and running down the sides into a small pond on the plate. After wine, shrimp, pasta, bread, and chocolate fudge cheesecake, I felt a little more cheerful, although if I'm going to be perfectly honest, the attention didn't hurt, either. I paid the tab with two crisp new twenty-dollar bills, patted my little Chippendale on the cheek, and told him to keep the change.

The next morning my body was heavier, my pocketbook lighter, and my head pounding from the excesses of the previous evening. But hey, you only go around once. God knows, Chase's untimely demise and Toni's betrayal demonstrated that we get no guarantees in life.

After several cups of strong black coffee, courtesy of the Days Inn desk clerk, I got back on the road and aimed my car toward North Carolina. Destination: Asheville.

The rain had ended overnight. The morning dawned chilly and fresh and bright, and I had the sense that I had driven through some invisible barrier into another world. The air had lost that fishy smell that hung along the banks of the Tennessee-Tombigbee. Sluggish brown creeks gave way to clear streams that burbled over rocks and tumbled downhill in a flash of white water. Long before I anticipated it, I crested a rise just outside a little town called Travelers Rest and got my first glimpse of the mountains.

I pulled off on the shoulder and sat there staring, my hands gripping the wheel and my breath coming in shaky gasps. People talk about the majesty of the Rockies, but there's no beauty on earth like the Blue Ridge. The Rockies are young mountains, high and hard and angular and bare. These are soft with age, dusted with snow like powdered sugar, and wreathed in mist. Trustworthy mountains, unchanged and unchangeable. Blue and purple and dark green and gray, folded together in layers. I could feel their steadiness, a comfort like old flannel, as if they were embracing me, drawing me in and welcoming me home.

I knew better, at least in my mind. Home was back there, four hundred miles behind me, where I'd lived all my life, where my husband was buried and my restaurant sat waiting and everybody knew my name.

Where I'd have to go back to, eventually.

The thought gave me no pleasure. So for now, for just a little while, I'd let the mountains enclose me, let myself pretend I belonged. Pretend I was coming home.

All the tourist brochures used words like "artsy" and "diverse" to describe Asheville, and I reckon they were right. The city seemed to be populated with aging hippies in blue jeans, young musicians who serenaded on downtown street corners, middle-aged women with tattoos who played African drums in the square. It was a little bit like being in a foreign country, except that everybody spoke English. Not a blessed thing like Chulahatchie, that much was certain.

But since my goal at the moment was to get as far away from Chulahatchie as possible, I determined just to relax and enjoy the diversity. I found an available room at a bed-and-breakfast on Montford Avenue, near downtown, and signed the charge slip without even looking at the price.

Map in hand, I found my way down to Biltmore Village and spent the afternoon wandering around the shops. At five I ate a chicken quesadilla at a restaurant called La Paz, and at six went across the street to the Biltmore Estate, which was already lit up for Christmas. I whipped out my Visa card again and joined a gaggle of other out-of-towners for the candlelight tour. We all gaped and oohed and ahhed at the sheer size and opulence of the place, while a string quartet and a Victorian caroling group entertained us in the background.

The Biltmore *was* impressive, especially when you consider it used to be a private home, but I sure as heck wouldn't have wanted to clean it. And I couldn't help thinking about Boone, who undoubtedly would have had a thing or two to say about the flocked wallpaper in the bedrooms.

A couple of days later I went up to the Grove Park Inn, where they were having their annual gingerbread house contest. The Grove Park, now *that* was amazing, with its huge lobby and two fireplaces big enough to park a Volkswagen in. Much more to my taste—lots of stonework and simple arts-and-crafts designs.

I wandered through the hallways, looking at the gingerbread house displays and wondering if I could have done that. These weren't your basic gingerbread houses, with four walls and a roof—they were gingerbread mansions, edible castles, large as the most elaborate dollhouse. I discovered a white-frosted antebellum with a wide front verandah that reminded me of Peach Rondell's house in Chulahatchie. A three-story Queen Anne with a tiny, intricate balcony under the eaves. There was even a gingerbread version of the Biltmore, complete with all the towers and turrets and a little gingerbread greenhouse off to one side.

After the gingerbread display, I took a glass of wine out to the Sunset Terrace. Chilly as it was, I stayed and stayed, watching the play of light and color over the western mountains. The tangerine ball of the sun hovered just at the top of the ridge, scattering gold and pink and purple into the clouds. Then it slipped behind the peaks, and the sky deepened to plum and navy blue, and a single star came out, a pinprick of light against the darkness.

Peace seeped into me along with the cold, and I found myself praying once more, wishing on that star, calling out to the universe. Not yelling this time, but whispering, a single word: "Help." As before, no answer came, but at least I felt a little more comfortable with the silence.

I stayed until the cold worked its way down to my bones, then went back inside and warmed up in front of the huge fireplace. At last I retrieved my car from the valet, tipped him five dollars, and headed back down the mountain toward my B&B.

*   *   *

I was sitting next to the fire in the parlor, eating a toasted turkey sub, when my landlady—or innkeeper, or whatever she's called—slipped in behind me and cleared her throat. "Oh!" I jerked, and spilled crumbs down my front onto her Oriental carpet. "Sorry. I guess I ought not be eating in here."

"You're fine. Nothing a quick vacuuming won't fix." She settled into the chair opposite me and smiled. "So how's your visit to Asheville? Having a good time?"

I looked at her, for the first time, really looked. I had only seen her twice—once when I checked in and then this morning at breakfast. She was younger than I initially thought—early forties, maybe. Wildish auburn hair, Irish eyes, very little makeup. She wore a sweeping kind of blue-green floral skirt with a matching T-shirt and an oatmeal-colored cable-knit cardigan. Her name, I thought I remembered, was Nell.

No, that wasn't right. *Neal*. Neal McLellan.

I roused myself to answer her question. "I've been to Biltmore, and shopping, and to the Grove Park. Think I'm going to go over to Wall Street and the Grove Arcade tomorrow, and just kind of wander around downtown."

"And how is it for you, traveling alone?"

The innocent question was a punch in the gut, and before I could stop them, tears welled up to choke me. Much to my surprise, Neal didn't seem the least bit uncomfortable when I began to cry, nor did she apologize. She simply waited.

There was something about her—something welcoming, like the mountains themselves. Ageless, eternal. As if she had nothing better in the world to do than sit there forever, being available to me, listening to whatever I chose to say.

"It's been a hard year," I said. And then, without planning it, without even giving it permission to come out, I began to tell her about Chulahatchie, and about Chase, about Toni and Boone and Scratch and Tansie Orr and Marvin Beckstrom. I confessed everything, sure as if I'd suddenly turned Catholic and she was a priest: my shadow side, my anger, my depression, my best friend's betrayal.

At last it had all been told, and I was empty as a sucked-out frog.

"Maybe you need to work some of those emotions out," Neal said.

"Isn't that what I just did?" In spite of the gravity of the moment, I found myself laughing. "Sorry. I didn't mean to dump on you."

"I'm glad you felt comfortable talking," she said. "But I might have something else that would help as well."

She got up, went to a small desk in the corner, and pulled a trifold brochure out of a drawer. When she came back she was smiling.

"Take it," she said. "It's this Saturday. I've been signed up for months. You can have my place."

I looked down at the brightly colored brochure. *The Painting Experience*, it read. *An unprecedented journey into the wild territory of painting directly from intuition. It's a leap beyond the predicted and expected—a venture into color, form, and image, where no rules apply.*

"I've never done anything like this before," I said. "I'm not an artist."

"That's the whole point," Neal said.

I wasn't sure what she meant, *the whole point*, and I couldn't figure out how it would help, to save my life. But I thought, why not? Asheville was an artsy place. I could be artsy for one Saturday.

"All right," I said at last. "Thanks. It should be fun."

· 22 ·

The painting studio was on the fourth floor of a building adjacent to the Pack Place art gallery, with tall windows overlooking Pack Square. All the walls were covered with heavy cardboard, and in the center of the room were tall triangular stations created from what looked like refrigerator boxes. People—mostly women—were milling about, getting name tags, laying claim to a painting station, settling themselves in a circle of chairs at the back of the hall.

Lots of people.

Strange people.

Not like people from Chulahatchie.

I swear, I'd never come across the likes. I might as well have been picked up by the scruff of the neck and set down in some kind of circus. There were three women with crew cuts, two with dreadlocks, one with a purple Mohawk. More tattoos than I'd ever seen in all my born days. One woman was a dwarf who barely came up to my waist.

I slapped my name tag on a station near the window, went to the circle of chairs, and chose a seat next to the most normal-looking person I could find. "I'm Dell," I said, holding out my hand.

"Suzanne," she said. She turned and smiled, and I saw the nose ring. "This your first time?"

I nodded.

"Me, too. My husband, Tad, thinks it's a waste of time and money, but a friend of mine did it and said it changed her life." She laughed. "Maybe that's what Tad's afraid of."

How, I wondered, *could a weekend painting workshop change somebody's life?*

"I'm not expecting anything quite that radical," I said. "I'm just here to have fun."

Suzanne opened her mouth to say something, but was interrupted by a shushing from the woman next to us.

"Welcome," someone said. "My name is Annie, and I'll be one of the facilitators for this weekend's workshop."

I turned my attention to the far end of the circle. It was the dwarf—or maybe they prefer to be called little people, I don't know. She had curly blonde hair and sparkly blue eyes and a wide, easy smile that showed a mouthful of white teeth bracketed by deep dimples. From the waist up, she was more or less normally proportioned, but her legs were short and bowed, and she carried a little plastic step stool around to stand on.

"Our other facilitators are Betsy, over there—" A tall woman in faded blue jeans raised a hand.

"And Evonne—" She pointed behind me, and I turned to look. The woman with the purple Mohawk. Of course.

"How many of you have attended a Painting Experience workshop before?" Annie asked. A few hands went up. "For the rest of you, let me fill you in a bit. This workshop is not about technique. It's not about learning to paint a pretty picture. It's not about the product at all. This is called process painting, and it is exactly what it sounds like. It's about entering into the process, and letting intuition and emotion guide you."

A murmur went around the circle, and Annie gave a little laugh. "You may not like what you paint. You may not like the emotions it brings up in you. Some of you may find the process painful, but it can also be immensely healing. So I encourage you to set aside your strategic mind and let flow what needs to come out onto the paper."

This all sounded a little bizarre and New Agey to me, and I wondered briefly when they were going to break out the crystals and incense. But I kept my seat, determined to see it through, and listened while Annie laid out the guidelines: the importance of silence in the studio, how to use the paints, what the schedule for the day would be, how the facilitators would help. "Now," she said at last, "let's go over to the paint table and see what we have to work with."

Within minutes we were all at our stations, and the studio had gone so quiet you could hear brush strokes. I stared at the blank paper in front of me without the faintest idea where to begin.

This wasn't about art, Annie said. It was about process. It was about tapping into something inside.

My gaze fixed on the bright whiteness of the untouched paper, and my eyes began to water. I had three colors in my palette: bright green, bright blue, and bright yellow. Happy colors—sky and grass and sunlight.

I wet a brush, dipped it in the sky, and moved toward the upper third of the paper. But I couldn't do it. I *couldn't.* My hand began to tremble, my knees buckled. I retrieved a chair from the circle and sank into it, still staring at my untouched white page.

My life. Brittle, blank, and empty.

My throat closed in on itself, and I couldn't swallow. I wanted to run for it, make a mad dash for the door before the walls closed in.

I felt a nudge at my elbow. Annie stood there, watching me closely. With her standing and me sitting, we were just about eye to eye.

"Having trouble getting started?"

I didn't trust my voice to speak. Instead, I nodded.

"What are you feeling?" she asked.

I thought about it for a minute. "Like I'm going to throw up."

This didn't faze her. "So you've got some unwelcome emotions churning in your stomach?"

I wouldn't have put it quite that way, but then in Chulahatchie people didn't talk much about emotions. "I don't know the right way to do this."

She laid a hand gently on my shoulder. "There is no right way. You're feeling something, and you don't like it."

It wasn't a question. I shrugged and nodded again.

"What's your first instinct? What do you want to do?"

I raised an eyebrow at her. "Run like hell."

To my surprise, she laughed. "Lots of people feel that way when they first get started. But let's assume you're going to stay. What color is this emotion?"

My rational mind could not wrap around that question. She might as well have asked, *What did your last alien visitor look like?*

Without thinking, I said. "Black. Kind of a sickly greenish black."

Annie went over to the paint table, brought back a cup of black paint, and tipped some of it onto my palette next to the green. I jabbed the brush into the paint and mixed the two together until it felt right, a dark slimy green like toxic mold. Then I looked back at the pristine white paper.

"Don't think," she said. "Just paint."

I slashed at the paper with my brush—hard, violent cuts angling down from the top and then across again, sideways. I'd never experienced anything like it, this white-hot rage I felt with every stroke. Like I had a huge butcher knife in my hand instead of a paintbrush, and had set out to kill some midnight intruder into my ordered and peaceful world. I could almost hear that screeching *Psycho* music in my head, the scene where Janet Leigh gets stabbed in the shower. When I came to a stopping place, I was breathing heavily, and tears streaked down my cheeks.

Annie had disappeared.

I sank back down into the chair and looked at what I'd painted. It was ugly, wounded, gashed open, gangrened.

It was me.

But it was something else, as well. Two dark rails of

paint, wider at the bottom and narrower at the top, bisected by horizontal bars.

A ladder, reaching heavenward.

No.

Not a ladder. A railroad track, climbing up a mountain pass, heading straight toward . . . a black hole, a blotch of paint at the top of my paper.

A tunnel. A threatening dark cave that could harbor all kinds of dangers.

Annie was back, standing behind me, looking over my shoulder.

"I hate it," I said. "It's hideous and disturbing, and I don't like the way it makes me feel."

"Maybe it doesn't *make* you feel anything," Annie said quietly. "Maybe it simply *reflects* what you already feel." She pointed toward the top, where the rails merged into darkness. "Tell me about this."

"It's . . . I don't know what it is," I said, even though I was pretty sure I did. "A cave, a tunnel."

"Where does it lead? What's inside?"

I gritted my teeth and resisted the urge to slap her silly. She was watching me with eyes as blue and deep as the Caribbean Sea, and as I met her gaze, something came out of her and into me. Peace. Courage. Willingness.

Whatever it was, it broke my resistance into about a million pieces.

"I have no idea what's inside," I said. "But I reckon I need to find out."

*   *   *

I never had therapy myself, but Toni had told me about hers after Champ died. This was a lot like what she described— becoming aware of dark places inside you where you didn't want to go. But you had to, if you were going to get better. Had to bring the light in there and see what was lurking in the corners. Had to lance the boil, even if it stunk to high heaven. Had to make friends with your shadow side.

Shoot. What I'd already seen of my shadow side, I didn't like the first little bit. If I'd had my druthers, I woulda preferred to just seal it up and let it rot and never think about it again.

A memory came back to me, the time Boone read me Flannery O'Connor's story about Hulga-Joy Hopewell with her Ph.D. and her wooden leg. I don't recollect the whole thing, but I still remember that description of Hulga-Joy like it was etched on my brain: *The look of someone who has achieved blindness by an act of will, and means to keep it.*

I guess we all understand what it's like to will ourselves blind. The problem is, once you *know* there's something in that dark place waiting for you, it'll haunt you 'til you turn around and look it in the eye.

So I went into the tunnel.

Reluctantly, dreading every minute of it, terrified of what I might find, I inhaled as much of Annie's courage and peace and willingness as I could hold, and forced myself to step into the black void.

· 23 ·

I painted—or at least tried to paint—everything I saw
and smelled and heard and tasted and felt. More than once
I wished I had some skill at this, some training that would
give me the ability to translate to paper what was up in
my head, and lower down in my churning gut. But I kept
on reminding myself that it didn't matter whether the
painting itself was any good or not. What mattered was
the process.

The studio was quiet except for the soft shuffling of people
moving back and forth to the paint tables and the occasional
whispered conversations of the facilitators. In a back corner
near the window, someone was crying—a primal moan, an
animal in agony. I knew how she felt.

Gradually, all sound and movement slipped away, into
some place of limbo, and became nothing more than white

noise. As if it had a mind and a will of its own, my hand moved the brush from palette to paper, choosing its colors, its images. It was like being inside a waking dream.

The inside of the cave was dark and dank and mildewy. Somewhere down in the distance echoed the faint drip, drip, drip of water. At first I could see nothing, but as my eyes adjusted I realized there was writing on the walls. Graffiti. Written in red, flowing like blood.

Bastard. Faithless. Liar. Deceiver.

The blood seeped into my pores. I inhaled its mist on the putrid air, tasted its metallic tang, knew—without knowing how I knew—that I would be poisoned by it if I didn't get away.

And I also knew, instinctively, that there was no going back. The tracks led in, not out. I had no choice but to press on.

I kept moving my brush, and the painting took me one step forward, then another. Something was crunching under my feet—gravel, I thought, but not hard enough. More like . . .

Bones.

I looked down. Thousands of them, tiny bones, big ones, some bleached white, others slimed with mold.

The bones of dreams that had died.

I stayed there for a long while, trying not to move so I wouldn't break any more of them. I closed my eyes and honored them, prayed for them, wished them peace. Gave them a decent burial, or at least the best that I could manage. And then at last, moved on.

The tunnel wound its way through the mountain, and I

followed. At last I rounded a bend into a huge, high cavern, so vast that I could not see the top.

Or the bottom.

I was standing on a narrow ledge of rock, and below me the floor dropped away into a deep chasm, an abyss that stopped my breath and made my head swim. I teetered for a moment, then got my bearings and looked.

On the far side of the cavern was another tunnel. At the very end of it, I could see light—just barely, just a hint of day, but enough to give me hope. And directly in front of the tunnel, a ledge like the one where I stood.

I kept painting, frantically now, hurrying. There was no way to get across. No bridge, no rope.

And besides, there were people blocking the way.

Where had they come from? A brushstroke here, one there, and they had appeared, faint as ghosts, lined up like tiny soldiers across the entrance to the tunnel.

I peered at them through the darkness, and my stomach lurched.

Boone. Toni, holding the hand of a small towheaded figure who had to be Champ. Fart Unger and Brenda. Scratch. Tansie Orr. Mama and Daddy, and Purdy Overstreet in younger days. Hoot Everett. Peach Rondell.

And Chase.

Not Chase. God, I thought, anybody but Chase.

I filled my brush with paint and leaned forward, intending to scrub him out of the picture. But just as I poised my paintbrush, a hand settled lightly on my shoulder.

"How are you doing?" Annie said.

I turned my head and blinked, totally disoriented, the

way you get when you come out into the daylight after a movie matinee. I stared at her for a minute as my mind struggled to comprehend the reality of a smiling dwarf standing beside me.

"Oh," I said. "Fine. I'm fine."

It was the kind of "fine" that really meant, *Go away and leave me alone*, and although I was pretty sure Annie didn't miss the message, she didn't respond to it, either. She just stood there, waiting.

"Looks like you were about to paint something *out* of your picture instead of *into* it," she said. "Would you like to tell me about that?"

I wanted to say, *Not really*, but that would be rude, and Mama always said that the only excuse for rudeness was bad character. So instead I bit my tongue, shrugged, and said, "I made a mistake, and I was about to correct it."

"Did you?"

I frowned. "Did I what?"

"Did you make a mistake?"

When I didn't answer, she went on. "In process painting there are no mistakes, Dell. Even if you don't like something, even if you want to change it, even if you want to tear the picture off the wall and rip it into a thousand pieces, it's still not a mistake. It represents something about you, something that came from inside you. So rather than destroying it, maybe you could sit with it for a while. See how it fits into your overall vision. See what that so-called mistake might say to you."

She squeezed my shoulder gently and was gone.

Dang, I thought, for somebody with such short stubby legs, she sure got around.

At the lunch break, I joined a small group of women leaving the studio; we walked across the street to Bistro 1896 and sat on the patio. It was a little chilly, but none of us wanted to go inside, so we kept our jackets on and ate our Reubens and salads in the early-afternoon sunshine.

My table consisted of Suzanne of the Nose Ring, one Dreadlocks, a Crew Cut, and three Tattoos. Our server sported her own body art, something I assumed to be a Native American totem marking above her left eyebrow.

Other than the obvious—which was obvious to me at least, though it seemed invisible to everyone else—my lunch companions turned out to be remarkably normal women. They talked about ordinary stuff, jobs and dogs and kids and husbands and partners, as well as experiences I knew nothing about, like therapy and spiritual direction and meditation and the healing arts. Most were, like me, newcomers to the Painting Experience, but the consensus was that everybody found the process immensely valuable and would do it again in a heartbeat.

"When I first started this morning, I didn't know if I was going to make it," said Beck, the woman with dreadlocks. "It brought up so many painful memories, issues I thought I'd already dealt with."

"Was that you crying in the corner?" Crew Cut asked.

Beck shrugged her shoulders and ducked her head. "Yeah.

But it got better. It's been a rough year—I've been through a divorce and the death of my father, and although I thought I had grieved, it's obvious there's still a lot of pain inside. Somehow this painting process is releasing stuff I haven't gotten to in counseling or journaling."

I didn't say much, but I was glad to know I wasn't the only one. And by the time lunch was over and we were heading back to the studio, I found myself barely even noticing the tattoos.

I returned to the bottomless cavern and sat with it for a while, just looking. Somehow, after lunch with the tattooed women, the line of little people on the other side of the chasm did not seem quite so threatening anymore.

I waited. I stared. And just when I thought I was done with the painting and nothing else was going to come to me, it happened. I picked up a small, slender brush, filled it with a ghostly blue-white, and began to paint. One by one they moved—first Scratch, then Boone, then Toni and Champ, and all the rest, right down to Chase, who came last. Stretching themselves out across the open blackness of the cavern, linking hands and feet.

Forming a human chain to span the gulf. A bridge of friends and loved ones, leading from the darkness toward the light.

I painted until the bridge was complete.

And then I wept.

· 24 ·

Early Sunday morning I packed my bag, paid my bill, and headed back to Chulahatchie. On the seat beside me lay my paintings from the workshop, the last one on top, that dark abyss bridged by the spectral figures of my friends.

Traffic was light; even through Atlanta, I-85 was nearly deserted. I tried to listen to the radio, to distract myself, but most of the stations were already playing Christmas carols. The realization that it was almost December hit me like a punch in the gut. My first Christmas without Chase.

I fiddled with the dials and came across a preacher who tried to convince me that Jesus was the answer. Evidently he subscribed to the theory that the louder he yelled, the truer his words would be—a philosophy I was pretty familiar with, since I grew up attending small-town revivals every summer.

I listened for a bit, and then turned him off. Dang if I knew how Jesus was the answer, when I couldn't even figure out the questions.

If only I could shut up the voices inside that easy.

In the silence of the empty car, loneliness descended like a fog, and every little noise seemed magnified. The heater whirred as it pumped out warm air, tires thumped across the expansion joints in the highway, wind whistled past the window. A giant heart beating, blood rushing through veins.

The rhythms took me back, and the memories spooled out like old family movies, jerky and scratchy and indistinct . . .

It was a Saturday morning in early June, bright and washed yellow with sunshine. The day would warm up later on, but at least it wouldn't be the stifling humid heat of a Mississippi midsummer.

Mama stood behind me, fiddling with my hair, trying to tuck a strand of seed pearls in so they wouldn't shift. I looked in the mirror and didn't hardly recognize the person staring back. I still felt like a girl, unsteady as a newborn foal, but the reflection in the mirror was a woman.

A woman about to be married.

An imposter, I thought. A fraud. A little girl playing dress up, who suddenly found herself in a grown-up body with grown-up responsibilities.

I desperately wanted to go back, to rewind my life to childhood. To say, *This is all a huge mistake,* and get a do-over.

I wanted my daddy.

I tried to blink away the tears so the mascara wouldn't run. Mama noticed, and peered at me in the mirror. "You all right, hon?"

I swallowed at the boulder in my throat. "I'm . . . scared."

She laughed. "Why, there ain't nothin' to be scared about, honey. Chase Haley's a good man, even if he is a tad rough around the edges. It'll be all right, you'll see. You just relax and let him take the lead, and—"

A red flush crept up her neck, the way it did whenever she tried to talk about anything embarrassing. She ducked her head and busied herself with the pearls again.

Then it hit me. She was talking about sex. About the wedding night.

Lord a-mercy, how dense could this woman be? I'd charmed that snake a long time ago, and not with Chase, either. If truth be told, I'd lost my virginity on the eighth hole of the Riverbend golf course the night of my senior prom, with a bony basketball player named Gant Yarborough.

Gant's daddy was a maintenance supervisor at the junior college, and they moved away from Chulahatchie shortly after graduation. It was a good thing, too, because although Gant wasn't a screw-and-tell kind of guy, in a small town it's not easy to keep a secret like that for very long. The only other person who knew was Toni.

Besides that, Chase and I had been doing the dirty deed for more than a year—in his car, in a secluded cove down on the riverbank, even once in Mama's bed when she was gone for a couple of nights tending to Purdy Overstreet after her hysterectomy.

But I couldn't tell Mama any of that—especially not the part about sex in her bed. Let her think that I was nervous about the wedding night. What she didn't know wouldn't hurt her, and I couldn't have told her what I was feeling, anyway.

The best I could explain it, even to myself, was a sense of loss. A grief deep as the ocean. A wave had come up behind me, and lifted me off my feet, and carried me out to sea. I couldn't feel the bottom of it. And I didn't even know what had died.

I just couldn't shake the conviction that I was missing something, that as soon as I stepped foot through this door, all the other doors and windows would seal up tight behind me. All the other possibilities would vanish, and the walls would begin to close in.

It wasn't about getting married in general, or even about marrying Chase in particular. It was about me, about leaving behind a childhood filled with what-ifs and grand imaginings, and settling into an adult world where today looked just like yesterday and tomorrow would look just like today.

I gazed at my unfamiliar reflection again, the imposter in the glass. Mama had drug the big cheval mirror over behind me, so I could get the full effect of the wedding dress. And there I was, reflected front and back. An image of an image of an image, on and on into eternity.

"I don't think I can do this," I said, mostly to myself.

"Don't be ridiculous," Mama said. "Just remember, there's two things in life a man can't get enough of: good cookin' and good lovin'." She smiled at me and patted my cheek. "I taught you everything I know about good cookin'," she said. "The rest you'll have to figure out on your own."

It was a good thing I hadn't been waiting for the wedding night as the culmination of all my girlhood dreams. I'd've been bitterly disappointed.

The day dragged on, what with the preparations, the ceremony itself, and then the receptions. Receptions, plural. We couldn't have dancing or drinking at the Chulahatchie Baptist Church, of course, so we ended up with a teetotalers' party in the fellowship hall, with punch and petit fours and a lot of boring conversation, and then later in the evening, a bigger blowout at the Knights of Columbus, with barbecued ribs, a rock 'n' roll band, and a whole lot of beer and champagne.

Mama didn't much approve of the drinking, being as she was a Sunday school teacher and all, but she did some selective interpretation when it came to Baptist doctrine, and she could cut a rug with the best of them. By the time the second reception wound down to a reluctant close, Mama had jitterbugged with half the men in Chulahatchie, including the new Methodist minister and the old Episcopal rector, and I suspect she had indulged in a glass or two of bubbly on the sly.

With one thing and the other, Chase and I made it to the hotel suite in Tuscaloosa exhausted, a little drunk, and not the least bit interested in sex. We fell into the massive king-size bed, slept comatose until noon the next day, and as a result had to pay for two nights and lost half a day of travel toward our final destination of Tybee Island, off the coast of Savannah.

Hung over and grumpy, Chase mumbled and grumbled about having to drive eight hours for a three-day honeymoon. I had suggested New Orleans, which would have been half the distance, but he wouldn't hear of it.

It was dark when we got there, another day lost, and too late to go scouting for one of Tybee's famous seafood restaurants. We settled for a burger and a walk on the beach, but it wasn't quite like the scene in my imagination. Moonlight on the ocean is only romantic if you're in a good mood to begin with.

Day two wasn't much better. I wanted to take the historic tour of Savannah. Chase wanted to play golf. I wanted to take the Pirate Cruise and see the lighthouse. Chase wanted to go deep-sea fishing. I wanted to explore the shops. Chase wanted to lie on the beach.

In the end our honeymoon was, as Boone would say, "a harbinger of things to come." Chase went his way and I went mine, and at the end of the day we came back together over dinner and sometimes a roll in the hay.

The pattern was set. He didn't seem to mind. Shoot, he didn't even seem to notice.

But I looked in the mirror and saw those images reflecting themselves, back and forth, back and forth. All the way to a point of no return.

· 25 ·

Chase wasn't a bad husband. He always worked hard, provided well, brought home a paycheck every week, and didn't give me cause to suspect he was up to no good, at least not until the very end. He just wasn't—what's the word? *Attentive.*

I musta caught something rubbing elbows with the artists and hippies in Asheville, because I can't remember ever thinking such a thing before. Where I come from, most women didn't concern themselves with whether their husbands were *attentive*. They were just grateful if he didn't drink or gamble or beat up on them or bang the new church organist in the choir room on Wednesday nights.

But wasn't that what Brenda Unger said about Fart? She might not have used the word *attentive*, but seems to me that was what she meant. He was a good husband, a good father, a good provider, but she wanted more. Or maybe she needed more, just to survive without losing her soul in the process.

I reckon Chase was pretty much like everybody else's husband, his mind on man stuff. A woman's dreams or needs or longings simply weren't on his radar screen. He worked and brought home a paycheck and grunted his thanks for a good meal and then fell asleep in his La-Z-Boy in front of the TV.

Lord, I hated that ratty old chair. Toni always called it his "Bubba chair," and when he was alive, I couldn'ta pried him out of it with a crowbar and a stick of dynamite. Now it was out of my living room once and for all, moved up to Scratch's little apartment over the restaurant, probably covered with cat hair and weighed down by the books he was always reading. Chase'd have a cow if he knew I'd given it to Scratch.

But Chase was gone.

Grief and rage sneaked up behind me and smacked me upside the head, and suddenly the landscape of highway and berm and trees outside the windshield swam and wavered in the shimmer of unshed tears. Dang. When was I gonna get over this? When was it gonna go away for good?

I was sick and tired of hurting. Sick and tired of feeling the pain and anger surge up without warning or permission. Sick and tired of being sick and tired.

My mind drifted back again, to the years with Chase and the memories that stuck out. The time he took me hunting—once. I shot a deer and then made the mistake of watching it die. Its eyes, liquid brown like melted chocolate or strong coffee, looked up at me as if to ask why, and then its head sank to the ground and the life drained out of its gaze. I went into the bushes and threw up my breakfast, and after that I couldn't stop crying, sobbing as if I'd murdered my own child.

Chase, of course, didn't have a clue. He acted like I ought to be proud of myself, like I ought to stuff the head and hang it on the wall. He field dressed the deer and took me home. I stayed in the shower scrubbing the guilt off until the water went cold, and never ate venison again.

Other adventures—the few we shared in thirty years of marriage—turned out a little better, at least for Chase. He planned our twentieth anniversary cruise all by himself, and I give him credit for trying. He just couldn't keep his eyes off the bikini-clad beauties on the beach at Cozumel. I wasn't much interested in being a substitute for his fantasy, and the trip back was pretty icy, despite the warmth of the Caribbean sunshine.

Had I been a good wife? I couldn't help wondering. Maybe I was guilty of the same accusation I made against Chase. Maybe I just went my own way, lived in my own world, did my duty, and maintained the status quo.

But I wish it had been different. I wish I had been valued and appreciated. I wish I had spent more effort in loving the man I claimed to be in love with. I wish I had felt more loved.

I was so caught up in my own thoughts that it was a miracle I didn't run the car into a ditch or end up in Podunk, Arkansas. When I pulled off at the exit to Chulahatchie and saw the Pump 'n Run, it was like swimming up to consciousness out of a deep dream.

Lord, it felt like I'd been gone for years, and like the last thing I ever intended to do was come back. But Chulahatchie looked just the same, the streets deserted on a Sunday afternoon. Christmas lights had gone up around the square in the week I'd been in Asheville; they looked pale and faded and sorry rather than festive. Somebody had put a Santa hat on the statue of the Confederate soldier and stuck a plastic poinsettia in the muzzle of his rifle.

I swung on around the circle and headed down toward the cafe. I oughta tell Scratch I was back, and see what kind of supplies we needed for breakfast tomorrow morning. Just thinking about it turned my heart to a lead weight in my chest.

And then, something I'd never expected.

The Heartbreak Cafe—*my* cafe—surrounded by yellow crime tape. The glass busted in, the door hanging off its hinges. The sheriff's squad car parked out in front with its red and blue lights flashing.

In the doorway stood the sheriff himself, with both hands on his hips.

26

"Where the hell have you been?" the sheriff said.

I got out of the car and moved in a daze across the sidewalk to the doorway. "What happened?"

"Ain't it obvious? There's been a break-in."

"A break-in?" I looked up at him, all grown up and big and bulky, nothing like the skinny little kid everybody called Runt in elementary school. His real name was Warren— Warren Potts—but when he'd become a law enforcement officer, he'd left that name behind. Now he was a bully with a badge, and everybody just called him Sheriff.

I entertained a brief, slightly hysterical image of his wife calling out, "Sheriff! Oh yes, Sheriff!" in the throes of passion, and couldn't suppress a giggle.

He stared at me as if I'd lost my ever-lovin' mind. "Answer me, Dell. Where you been?"

The question rankled me. "I went out of town for a few days, if it's any of your business."

"Well, you ought to have told somebody," the sheriff said. "You just up and leave without a word, folks are gonna get upset. You coulda been kidnapped."

Lord, I'd never heard anything so absurd. "Kidnapped? Who'd want to kidnap a middle-aged woman with nothing to her name but the Heartbreak Cafe? Look around, Sheriff. I'm not exactly ransom material. And if I want to pick up and go out of town without telling anyone, it's nobody's concern but my own. Besides that, Scratch knew I was gone. I gave him the keys to the place in case of emergency."

"Scratch? The, uh, fella who works for you?"

"Yeah. He lives in the apartment upstairs." I got a sinking feeling in my gut. "Where is he?" I said. "Have you talked to him?"

"Well now, that's the other thing," the sheriff said. "He's gone."

"What do you mean, gone?"

"No sign of him. Apartment upstairs is empty. I reckon he took the money and ran." He gave me a condescending, pitying look.

"That's the most ridiculous thing I've ever heard," I said. "I'm sure he'd never steal from me."

But the truth was, I *wasn't* sure. I wasn't sure of anything anymore. How well did I know Scratch, anyway? How well did I know anybody—-Toni, Boone, Chase, anyone?

Purdy Overstreet's words echoed ominously in the back of my mind. *"Look to your friends, Dell Haley. Look to those you trust."*

"I trust him," I repeated, willing myself to believe it. Yet even as I said the words, I felt my stomach cave in, felt the emptiness, the aloneness, overtake me.

"Doesn't matter. We're pretty sure he's our perp, and we'll get him collared sooner or later."

Under ordinary circumstances I would have laughed in his face. He sounded like a bad stereotype from a B-grade detective movie. *Redneck Gumshoe.*

I scrambled for a foothold, something to believe in. "Scratch had the keys," I said. "Why would he break the door down when he's got a key? And for that matter, why would anybody come through the front door, in full view of the square, when they could be totally secluded if they broke in from the back alley?"

"We figure he did it that way deliberately, to throw off suspicion. But we didn't just fall off the turnip truck."

I mighta taken issue with that, but something else was nagging at me. "Sheriff, why do you keep saying 'we'?"

A movement just past the broken doorway caught my eye. "Somebody's in there!" I said.

"Yeah." He turned slightly. "Come on out. Miz Dell wants to talk to you."

A large buggy head appeared behind the shattered windowpane. Marvin Beckstrom.

"What's he doing in my restaurant?" I said. "What's he got to do with this?"

Marvin stuck his hands in his pockets and jingled his keys. He took a breath and thrust out his chest. "In case you've forgotten, Dell, you're a renter, not the owner of this building."

"So?"

"So what happens here is my business, too. A crime has been committed on my property."

"Your property? Don't you mean the property of Chulahatchie Savings and Loan?"

""Not for long," he said. "The property's going up for sale the first of the year, and I plan to buy it. I'll be your landlord then. Me, personally."

"Yeah, well, I've got a lease," I said.

He smirked. "So you do. For the time being."

"Dell," the sheriff interrupted, "you need to cooperate here. Where would Scratch have gone?"

"How should I know?" I said. "I'm not his mama. Besides, you're treeing the wrong possum. Scratch didn't . . . wouldn't—"

"You don't sound so sure," the sheriff said. "How much do you really know about this man, Dell? Did you know his real name is John Michael Greer? Or that he has an outstanding warrant against him?"

"A warrant?"

The sheriff nodded. "Parole violation. He was convicted of assault. Served five years. This parole violation sends him back to lockup."

Marvin gave a smug grin and jingled his pockets again.

"He's run once," the sheriff went on. "Now looks like he's on the lam again."

I couldn't take it all in, couldn't think. I still felt like I was in a bad B-movie, but the urge to laugh at it all had vanished. Assault. An arrest. A prison record. A whole secret life I knew nothing about.

And then in the midst of my shock, the truth about my own situation sank in. Cash register empty. Money gone. I had left in such a hurry on Saturday morning that I hadn't gotten around to making the deposit from Thanksgiving week. No big deal, I thought. It would wait until I got back.

But it was more than a big deal. It was a disaster. I ran the cafe on a margin about as thin as a potato peeling, always right on the edge where a couple hundred dollars would make the difference between red ink or black. If the big deposit from last week was gone, I'd be digging those peelings out of the Dumpster.

"I'm gonna go now," the sheriff said. "You hear from Greer, you need to call me, understand?"

"I understand."

"Rent's due next week; don't forget." Marvin gave me a superior twitch of his eyebrows. "And you better get that door replaced right away."

I shot daggers at him but didn't say all the rude things I was thinking. "I'm gonna call Fart Unger. He'll fix it."

They left, and I went inside. The lights were off, and the room was dim and chilly in the weak November light.

I slid into the booth at the back, the one where Peach Rondell always sat, and put my head in my hands. I thought about Peach, and about the forbidden journal entry I had read. I thought about Chase, and how he had betrayed me after thirty years. I thought about Toni and Boone, my best friends, who had deceived me. I thought about Fart and Brenda and their perfect marriage gone to pot. I thought about Scratch, and how gentle and good he had seemed, and

I wondered where he was, and how a man like that could be a convicted criminal.

None of it seemed real. None of it seemed consistent with the people I thought I knew.

But none of that mattered right now.

I got up, went to the kitchen, and dialed the phone. But I didn't call Fart Unger. The door could wait. I dialed Toni's number, and held my breath.

27

Toni came through the door at a run, a hard, blazing expression on her face. She caught me up in a fierce hug, and held on for a long, long time. She didn't seem to notice I wasn't hugging back.

Over her shoulder I could see other faces—Boone, and Peach Rondell. Both looked worried and wounded.

"Are you okay?" Boone said when Toni released me.

"I think so."

Toni smacked me on the shoulder. "God, woman, we were so worried about you. Why'd you go off like that, without telling anybody?"

"I needed to get away. To think."

"Well, think about this: We're your friends. We care about you. Don't do it again, all right?"

"What happened here?" Boone said.

"Just what it looks like. Somebody broke in, took all the cash in the drawer, and maybe the whole till from last week, I don't know yet." I shut my eyes and gritted my teeth. "Scratch is missing. The sheriff thinks he's the one who did it. And to top it all off, Marvin Beckstrom—himself, personally—is gonna be my landlord. He's buying the place."

Toni started muttering curses under her breath, but Boone ignored her. "What do we need to do, Dell?" he asked.

Think, I told myself. *Think.* But my brain wasn't working. I hated the feeling of being helpless, some simpering Southern girl with an attack of the vapors. I was a fifty-year-old woman, for God's sake, and ought to be able to take care of myself.

Peach Rondell rescued me from the spiral into despair. "Maybe the first thing we should do is try to find Scratch."

"The police are looking for Scratch," I said. "What makes you think we could find him first?"

"I don't know, but we have to try," she said. "Come on, Boone."

And without further explanation, she grabbed Boone by the hand and hauled him out the door.

The door closed behind Peach and Boone—or rather, tried to close, because it was still hanging off its hinges like a broken bone—and suddenly I was left alone with Toni.

My best friend.

My betrayer.

She put an arm around me and led me to a booth. "I'll make us some coffee. Do you want anything to eat?" She looked around. "There's no pie, since you've been gone for a week, but I could probably scrounge up something from the pantry."

I shook my head. "Couldn't stomach a thing."

What I couldn't stomach was having to face her alone, not knowing what to say after a lifetime of telling her all my secrets. Acid roiled in my gut, and a terrifying sense of loss and loneliness overwhelmed me until I could barely breathe.

I was back there, in that dark and bottomless cavern, with no way to get out. Silence pressed in on me, a claustrophobic blackness from all my old nightmares.

I sat with my head in my hands until Toni slid in opposite me and pushed a mug of coffee in my direction.

"This must be awful for you," she said. "A break-in is such a violation—"

Something inside me snapped, that internal censor that keeps you from saying something you'll regret later. I couldn't help myself. "Well, it's sure not the worst violation I've ever endured."

Toni stared at me. She seemed to be considering whether or not to speak what was really on her mind. The struggle was etched in the lines of her face, a pain that ordinarily would have elicited compassion from me.

But I didn't care. I didn't give a damn about anything she had to say to me.

And yet I had called her. When crisis struck, her face was the first one that rose to mind.

"We have some things to talk about," she said at last.

"No, we don't."

"We sure as hell do," she said, and her cheeks flushed with anger. "We're stuck here, you and me, just like we've been stuck together since we were kids. We're not going to sit here and glare at each other."

"You don't like it, there's the door." I pointed.

She looked around at the broken glass and the door hanging from a single hinge. "So to speak," she muttered. "But not much of one anymore."

Against my will, I laughed. It shattered the tension the way somebody's fist or hammer or wrench had shattered the glass.

"That's better." Toni leaned forward and cradled her coffee mug in both hands. "Talk to me, Dell. Why are you doing this? Why, all of a sudden, are you shutting me out?"

I couldn't believe she had the nerve to ask the question. "You know why. I know the truth."

"I was going to tell you, Dell. I just couldn't bring myself to do it." She cleared her throat and took a drink of her coffee. "How'd you find out?"

I was too full of righteous indignation to admit that I had violated Peach Rondell's privacy and read her journal. "Never mind. Just tell me what happened."

She shrugged. "You don't want to hear this."

"Damn!" I shouted. I pounded my fist on the table until half my coffee had sloshed onto the Formica. I came out with every blessed cuss word I could think of, and some that had never passed my lips in my fifty long years of life. Words my mama woulda scrubbed off my tongue with lye soap. "Shit, Toni. How can you be so . . . so . . . *casual* about it? You betrayed me with Chase. You slept with my husband!"

I railed on at her for a while until I ran out of words, and then I became aware of the fact that she wasn't saying anything back. I looked up. She was smiling.

"Is that what you think? That I slept with Chase? That I was the one he was having an affair with?" Toni began to laugh—a low chuckle at first, and then a belly laugh so intense that tears streamed down her cheeks. "Oh my God, Dell," she said when she could catch her breath enough to speak. "We were talking about Chase, right, and you said you were sure Brenda Unger was the one."

"Yeah. And you said Brenda wasn't having an affair with Chase. You knew it for certain."

Toni leaned forward and looked me straight in the eye. "Yes, I knew it for certain. But not because I had an affair with Chase."

Like a flashbulb popping, the light went on. "You?" I said. "You and—"

"Yeah." She ducked her head. "Me and Brenda."

Unforgiveness is like hugging a cactus and wondering why you can't quit bleeding.

I still had a few nettles sticking here and there, but that didn't matter so much now that I had my best friend back.

The table between us was littered with the remains of sandwiches—Scratch's famous comfort food of peanut butter, jelly, and Spam. We'd eaten a sandwich apiece and most of a bag of ripple chips, and now we were starting on some leftover chocolate pie Toni found in the freezer.

"So tell me more," I said. I felt wickedly scandalous, being privy to the juicy details. "How did it happen?"

"It was nuts," Toni said. "I ran into Brenda one evening at the Pump 'n Run. She seemed upset, and so naturally I tried to comfort her. We ended up driving over to Tuscaloosa, and drinking a whole bottle of wine while she spilled her guts about the feelings she was having and how as much as she loved Fart, she couldn't stand the idea of going on with this charade. That was her word, *charade*. Seems she'd always felt like this—being attracted to women, I mean, but of course when we were growing up it was totally taboo."

"No kidding," I said. "All we ever heard were stupid fag jokes and preachers railing about how people 'like that' were going to hell."

"Well, anyway," Toni went on, "we'd had too much to drink to drive back to Chulahatchie, so we got a motel room, and . . ." She raised her eyebrows.

"So what was it like?" I said. "Details. Give me all the details."

"Let's just say things got real interesting real fast."

"And you enjoyed it? But you're not a . . . a—"

"A lesbian?" Toni laughed. "It's okay to say the word, Dell. You don't get cooties by saying the word."

"Well, are you?"

"No. But Brenda is. She told me she has felt this way all her life, and even though she loved Fart—still does—she married him because in our generation, that's what you did. It didn't ever seem natural to her."

"Then why—"

"Why did it happen—Brenda and me? I don't know. I

214

care about her, of course. I was lonely. It felt good to have someone touch me. None of them very healthy reasons."

She shrugged. "Brenda and I talked about it, and she understands. She actually thanked me for giving her a safe place to find herself."

I looked at Toni and felt like I was seeing her for the first time. For one thing, I didn't think my best friend capable of something like this, but it wasn't judgment or disappointment in her. The way she explained it, it actually seemed like an act of friendship, a kindness. I was just amazed that you can know somebody so long and so well, and they'll still surprise you now and again.

"Besides," Toni said, "I don't think it's all that cut and dried. I think most of us, given the right circumstances, could be attracted to a person of the same gender."

I lodged a protest at this, but it was a halfhearted argument, and I felt strangely and unexpectedly titillated.

"Brenda made me promise I'd keep her secret," Toni said. "I think for a while she was a little bit in love with me—or at least had an enormous crush. So I didn't tell anybody, not even you, until I absolutely had to."

"Except Boone."

"Well, yes. I knew he'd understand. And I knew he'd keep his mouth shut."

"You know I will, too," I said. "I won't tell anyone."

"Yeah, I know." Toni grinned. "You haven't spoken to me in weeks."

I remember once when I went to the doctor for X-rays, they made me wear a lead cape to protect the other organs from the radiation. It didn't feel that heavy at first, but as I carried it around for a while, it seemed to weigh me down until I could barely stand.

I'd borne this burden far too long, and it felt a pure relief to set it aside and go back to being friends with Toni. I'd missed her, and I was glad in that moment that she wasn't the kind to hold a grudge or dangle forgiveness over my head like a guillotine.

I'd almost forgotten about the break-in and the theft until I heard the honk of a car horn. I looked through the window and saw Peach's little blue Honda pull up to the curb.

Toni and I went to the doorway and waited. Peach and Boone got out and came in our direction.

"No luck," I said.

"Don't be so sure." Toni pointed.

A black-and-white pulled up behind the Honda, its red and blue lights flashing. It slowed down, honked again, and then headed toward the square. In the back seat, staring at me through the window, was a big muscular black man.

Scratch had been found.

· 28 ·

"I didn't do it, Dell," he said. He dropped into a chair and put his head in his hands.

We stared at each other. His face was a scruff of coarse black stubble, and his eyes were bloodshot and weary. The pain and disappointment in his expression cut me to the quick, but I couldn't bring myself to utter a single word of reassurance. Part of me wanted to reach out and comfort him, and another part of me recoiled, sensing danger and wanting to flee.

"Why are they arresting you, then?"

Silence stretched between us, broken only by the scrape of chair legs on the floor as the others drew up around the table in the interrogation room of the jail.

The sheriff had allowed me and Boone and Toni to talk to Scratch, even though, as he reminded us twice, it was "against protocol." I reckon he thought we'd have a bet-ter chance of getting a confession out of him, which would make the process of locking him up and throwing away the key that much easier.

To my relief, Boone took over the conversation, because I had gone blank, and could think of nothing except the pain on Scratch's face, the defeated angle of his shoulders, and my own suspicion, which ate at my insides like drain cleaner.

"You got any idea what happened at the cafe?" Boone asked.

Scratch shook his head.

I gritted my teeth. "Then why'd you run away?"

"I didn't run. I was just away. Thinking."

I turned to the sheriff. "Where'd you find him?"

"Why don't you ask me?" he said, his voice full of re-proach. "I hitched a ride out to the river camp. I didn't think you'd mind. I didn't go in the house, didn't steal anything, if that's what you're worried about." His eyes cut away. "I just sat on the dock."

"That's where we caught up with him." The sheriff nodded.

"I wasn't exactly trying to escape," Scratch said. "And you didn't find any money on me, did you?"

At the mention of the money, my gut twisted. "Did you, by any chance, deposit last week's till?" I asked.

Scratch shook his head. "No, ma'am. I thought you'd done it before you left town."

I took in a deep breath and exhaled slowly, trying to fend off panic. At the Heartbreak Cafe, a week's income could make the difference between staying afloat and sinking.

"The sheriff said you had outstanding warrants," Boone

said, trying to get us back on track. "Something about a parole violation?"

"No," he said. "I mean, yes, I was on parole, but I'm done with it. There's no violation, and the sheriff ought to damn well know that." He blinked and looked around. "'Scuse my language."

The apology was so incongruous that everybody laughed. The sheriff cleared his throat as if to say, *Get on with it.*

"I think maybe we ought to know what this parole violation thing is about," Boone said. "I don't want to pry into your life, Scratch, but we've got to be prepared if we're going to help you."

As Scratch gathered his thoughts, my mind cast back to other conversations I'd had with him, particularly the one where we talked about forgiveness, and how to go on after your life has fallen apart. I wondered how he had come to learn those lessons, but I hadn't taken the time to ask, to find out.

I had a feeling I was about to get the missing pieces of the puzzle.

"I was married, once," Scratch began quietly. "Had a baby girl. But I also had a controlling and manipulative father-in-law who didn't think I was good enough for his daughter.

"We didn't come from much," he went on. "Daddy was a sharecropper on a peanut farm in south Georgia. We always had enough to eat because we had the land, and Mama kept a big garden. But there was never much money. Not money for college, anyway. I played football, but I wasn't good enough to get a scholarship, and in those days there weren't many options.

"Anyway, I joined the Navy right out of high school, and when my time was up, they paid for my tuition to More-house. Then during my senior year, I met Alyssa. She was a junior at Spelman. Prelaw."

He gave me a sidelong look. "Morehouse and Spelman are both historically black colleges in the Atlanta area. More-house is all male; Spelman's female."

I nodded as if I already knew this, and he continued.

"I was in premed and had been accepted at Emory medi-cal school—"

"Medical school?" The sheriff said with a sneer.

"Yeah, med school. But plans got changed when Alyssa turned up pregnant."

A child, I thought. The little girl he'd referred to.

"Alyssa was ready to get married right away. And I *wanted* to marry her; I had known it since the day we met. But her parents were dead set against it. Especially her father."

I couldn't keep my mouth shut any longer. "Why?" I said. "If the two of you were in love—"

"He was a high-powered lawyer in Atlanta. A high-powered *black* lawyer with a gorgeous blonde wife. He didn't reckon I was good enough for his baby girl."

"But surely a doctor—"

Scratch waved the objection away as if he was swatting at gnats. "He never believed I'd make it. I was a sharecropper's son, that's all he could see. All I'd ever be. And, well, I guess I proved him right."

He let out a long sigh. "We eloped, took up residence in a cheap one-bedroom apartment. Not what Alyssa was accustomed to, that's for sure. I went to work nights so I could finish my senior year and graduate, but med school was pretty much out of the question. Alyssa tried, she really did, but in the end she couldn't handle the pressure. Once the baby was born it got worse, and then one night I came home from work and she was gone."

He ran a hand over his hair. "I did everything in my power, but her father's hold on her was just too strong. She couldn't stand up to him."

Scratch clenched his fist on the table. "He was a man accustomed to getting what he wanted, and he rarely settled for less than everything. He was determined to split us up, and he put so much pressure on my wife that in the end she caved in and went back home with our baby."

Scratch paused and looked around. Even the sheriff was listening intently, although the expression of derision and disbelief hadn't left his face.

"Anyway," he continued, "I mighta been raised poor, but I was raised proud, and I wasn't about to lay down and roll over like a dog under his command. I went to the house, demanded to see her. The police were called. I was arrested for disturbing the peace and aggravated assault."

"Holy shit," Toni said, and didn't bother apologizing to anybody.

"Yeah," Scratch agreed. "Alyssa's father had a lot of influence. It only took a word from him to ensure a slam-dunk conviction. I went to prison. My life as I knew it was over. Not much call for a young black surgeon with a felony conviction."

"Do you really believe this load of bullcrap?" the sheriff interrupted. "This boy, in medical school? Married to a lawyer's daughter?"

A glance ricocheted around the table, but no one commented.

"You got no reason to hold him," Boone told the sheriff. "No evidence."

"Yeah, and since when did you become a defense attorney?" The sheriff said. "He stays right here till we sort this parole thing out and find where he's hidden the money."

Everybody looked at me like they were expecting me to protest, to say I wasn't pressing charges about the robbery, that I believed in Scratch's innocence . . . something. But I didn't. I couldn't. I still had a potful of questions swirling in my mind like Wednesday's stew, and didn't know how to ask any of them. And I sure as heck didn't have any answers.

"Get your boy a lawyer," the sheriff said when he escorted us out. "He's gonna need one."

The coffeepot was empty and we were all still sitting around a table in the cafe. We'd been over it and over it, and hadn't gotten anywhere. And they were all staring at me, trying to figure out what had got into me, and why I wasn't participating in the plans to save Scratch's hide.

I couldn't explain, even to myself. My whole head was full of what-ifs. I'd trust him, and then I'd get nervous and suspicious again. Advance, withdraw. Advance, withdraw. I didn't like myself one bit for doing it, but I couldn't seem to stop.

At last Peach spoke up. "What'd the sheriff say Scratch's full name was?"

"John Michael Greer," I said.

"And his wife?"

"Alyssa, I think."

She fished a pen out of her pocket and wrote it down on a paper napkin.

Odd, I thought. But I didn't have the energy to ask her why.

· 29 ·

The sheriff kept Scratch on ice for three days.

Three very long and stressful days.

On Monday morning, Fart Unger showed up with a new front door in the bed of his pickup. As he puttered around, removing the old door and resetting the new one, I watched him. Those long skinny blue-jeaned legs, the sloped crown of his bald head, the look of resignation in his eyes.

I was glad he was there. For some reason I couldn't put my finger on, he brought a calming presence into the place. A deep cleansing breath of sanity amid all this craziness.

Boone, Toni, and Peach came and went at various times, discussing how they were going to help Scratch, and who might have committed the break-in, who they could find to represent him, and what was likely to happen next. The same unanswered questions they'd been batting around for days, with no answers in sight.

For my part, I couldn't seem to break the downward spiral of confusion. On the one hand, I wanted to believe that Scratch was innocent. On the other hand, he was a convicted criminal, and how much did I really know about him, anyway? The story of his past—a rich lawyer wife, a future as a surgeon—seemed about as likely as me finding Ed McMahon on my doorstep with a bouquet of balloons and a giant check for ten million dollars. And yet I remembered, with a good deal of uneasiness, the way he tended to Purdy Overstreet when she sprained her ankle.

But if Scratch hadn't done it, then who did?

And then the other question, the one that twisted my gut into a knot: How on earth was I going to make up that stolen till?

Seemed like folks in Chulahatchie musta missed my cooking, or else they were just caught up in the pre-Christmas rush of planning and shopping, because Wednesday lunch went nonstop from eleven to one-thirty. The place was packed, every table full and people waiting three deep at the doorway, craning their necks like vultures, trying to hurry the stragglers along.

Scratch's absence throbbed at me like a toothache. I worried it with half my mind, the way you'll absently probe your tongue into that broken molar, never mind the pain.

I was running my tail off trying to keep up. I missed him on that count, the way I had come to depend on him for cooking and serving and keeping the kitchen going. But it was more than that. I didn't just miss what he did; I missed who he was. His sense of humor and funny quips. His gentleness and tolerance with folks like Hoot Everett and Purdy Overstreet. The way he had of making me feel safe, and not quite so alone.

I oughta trust him. I oughta be able to make myself turn off the doubts and believe. But I couldn't. And the conflict was ripping me right down the middle.

Finally the last of the lunch crowd cleared out, and I bussed the final table and went back into the kitchen. Fart Unger stood at the dish-washing station in one of Scratch's white aprons, running the sprayer over a full rack of glasses.

"You don't have to do that, Fart."

He shrugged his bony shoulders. "Just helping out." He said it real casual, but I heard something else in his voice.

"You want to talk?"

He looked down at me and his huge Adam's apple bobbed up and down in his long skinny neck. "Yeah," he said after a minute. "I reckon I do, if you don't mind."

The cafe was empty and quiet, with a watery December sun shining through the streaky glass of the new door. I made a mental note that I needed to clean it, and get the name painted back on. I forced my attention back to Fart.

He sat down across from me and clenched his long fingers together until the knuckles turned white. "I figure you know pretty much everything about me and Brenda and . . . and all," he said.

It was on the tip of my tongue to say, *Yes, Toni told me everything,* but something stopped me. I don't know what— the look in his eyes, maybe, or the way he was chewing on his right thumbnail, or the way the sun picked out the silver

226

hairs in a day's growth of stubble. Instead, I said, "Why don't you tell me?"

"When Brenda said she wanted a divorce, I never saw it coming," he said. "I thought we were happy. I thought I was being a good husband. I thought—" He hesitated. "Well, I thought a lotta things. But what I didn't think was that the woman I'd loved and married and had kids with and shared my life with could turn out to be somebody I didn't recognize."

A muscle worked against his jawbone, and he exhaled heavily. "I still don't really understand it, this thing of hers, this—well, you know. But I gotta accept it. It's like you can't make somebody be something they're just not. What's that old saying? *A bird may love a fish, but where do they make their home?*" He attempted a pathetic little smile. "I just gotta accept it, that's all. But, Dell—"

His eyes met mine, and the expression of raw agony almost took my breath away. "She says she still loves me, and every time she says it, she gives me hope. But how can she love me, and do this?"

He lapsed into silence, and I waited until I knew he was finished.

"Fart, I'm not claiming to understand it any better than you," I said. "But I believe Brenda does still love you, and always will. It's just a different kind of love, that's all. Like the love I have for Boone, or Toni. Or—" I hesitated for just a beat, then forged ahead. "Or you."

He looked up, startled.

"We're friends," I hastened to add. "We care about each other. We stand by each other. We're family."

He nodded miserably, as if this was cold comfort on a winter's night.

"Anyway," I said, "Brenda's come to an awareness about herself that has nothing to do with you, or how good a husband you've been, or what your character is like." Without thinking, I put my hand over his clenched fists. He flinched a little, but I held on.

"I feel . . . I don't know. Rejected," he whispered. "Like something inside me isn't good enough."

I squeezed his hands. "Trust me, I know the feeling."

"So what do we do?" he asked. His eyes scanned my face like he thought he'd see the answer written there. But if he did, it was in a language he'd never learned.

I thought about Boone, and Toni, and Peach—and even Scratch—that line of ghostly figures stretching themselves into the darkness so I could have a bridge into the light. Friends. People who loved you, no matter what stupid thing you said or thought or did. People who wouldn't turn their backs, even when you deserved it. People who would lay themselves down for the sake of that friendship.

"We stick together," I said at last. "We care about each other. We get out of bed every morning and put one foot in front of the other." I patted his arm. "We give it time, and we help each other get through."

Fart and I sat there for the longest time, not talking much, just drinking the last of the coffee and shifting in our seats. Finally I got up and went into the kitchen to finish getting stuff ready for the next day. There wasn't much in the way of leftovers—the locusts had pretty much cleaned me out—but there was enough roast beef left to make stew, and plenty of vegetables.

As I cut up the butt end of the beef and peeled potatoes, I let my mind drift back to Scratch, locked up in the jail-house, probably pacing the cell like a big black panther.

Wasn't a blessed thing anybody could do about it. Boone and Toni kept talking about bail money, but it wouldn't do any good. The sheriff was still holding out on releasing him, claiming he hadn't got word from the authorities in Atlanta yet.

For God's sake, I thought. *This is the twenty-first century. What kinda communications technology is that idiot sheriff using, anyway? Pony Express?*

But I knew, of course, that it wasn't about any communications breakdown. It was about power. Using it, flaunting it, proving it.

A pissing contest.

I'd finished the potatoes and moved on to the onions—big red Vidalias, from over in Toombs County, Georgia. Sweetest onions in the whole wide world.

But this afternoon they didn't seem so sweet. Soon as my knife blade sliced into the first one, tears came to my eyes. I blinked and sniffed. Usually Vidalias didn't do this to me. My eyes burned, but I didn't dare raise a hand to wipe them away.

Somehow I knew, even if I tried to deny it, that these tears weren't about the onions. How many times, I wondered, could you get your heart broken before it was shattered beyond all hope of repair?

Everything blurred. The knife came down, slipped, and glanced across my finger. Blood splattered the worn wood of the cutting board.

I musta yelled, because in a flash Fart Unger was standing beside me, holding my hand, gripping my cut finger to put pressure on the wound. He had his other arm around me, and a good thing it was, too, because my head went fuzzy and I woulda fallen if he hadn't been there holding me up.

"It's okay, Dell," he said. "Just hang on; I'll take care of it."

And he did.

He took me over to the sink, washed out the cut, and then went into the pantry to get the first-aid kit. With a gentleness I'd never felt in a man's touch, he applied antibiotic ointment and bandaged it. And then, in an instinctive gesture undoubtedly traced to his years as a daddy and granddaddy, he lifted my finger to his lips and kissed it.

"All better now," he said.

I looked up into his face. And though I'd known him all my life, it was the first time I'd ever noticed how blue his eyes were.

We stood there, frozen, looking at each other, while a strange unnamed awareness flooded through me. He felt it, too. I could tell by the sudden tension in his hands and the way his breath caught and stuttered.

I didn't know what it was, but it terrified me. His face, so familiar—and so close—suddenly transformed into something else, a stranger's face. It was like that horrible midnight moment when you wake up and look at the person lying next to you in the moonlight and think you're in bed with someone you've never met.

I couldn't breathe. Couldn't swallow. Couldn't move, even though everything inside me wanted to bolt and run.

If the bell over the door hadn't rung, we mighta just stayed that way.

But the bell did ring, and we jumped apart like two guilty teenagers. I ran a hand through my hair and stepped out into the cafe.

In the doorway stood a woman—the most beautiful woman I had ever seen up close and personal. She looked like a movie star, like a cross between Halle Berry and Queen Latifah. Tall and curvy with skin the color of caramel, and black, black hair, and wide brown eyes and high cheekbones. Pressed close to her side, as if needing protection, was an equally stunning little girl. A daughter, obviously, the spittin' image of her mama except that the child's skin was a dark rich chocolate brown.

"Excuse me," the woman said in a voice like velvet. "I realize you're probably closed, but—"

"Come in," I said. "Please, have a seat."

"Thank you. We've been driving for hours."

The little girl tugged at her mother's arm and whispered something in her ear.

"Would it be all right if my daughter used the restroom?"

"Of course," I said. "Come on, I'll show you."

The child shrank back a bit. "It's okay, honey. Go with the nice lady." The woman looked up at me. "Her name is Imani. It means *faith*."

"Well, I'm pleased to meet you, Imani," I said. I held out a hand and the child shook it solemnly. "My name is Dell. I own this place. And believe me, we can use a little more faith around here."

Imani smiled shyly. I took her back to the restroom, and then returned to find the mother slumped in a booth with her head in her hands. I watched her for a moment. The body language spoke of despair and frustration, and it did not fit the image she projected when she first walked in the door.

Here was a woman, I thought, accustomed to putting on a good front. But inside, she was crumbling.

I went over to her, and without thinking if it might be an intrusion, laid a hand on her shoulder. She didn't pull back. Instead, she leaned into it as if she hadn't felt a comforting touch in a long, long time.

"What can I get for you?" I said. "Sweet tea? Coffee? I'll need to make a fresh pot, but it won't take a sec."

"Coffee would be nice. And orange juice for Imani, if you've got it."

"Coming right up."

I went back to the kitchen to get the OJ and start the coffee. Fart had disappeared.

When the coffee was done, I took it out to her, steaming fresh and fragrant. She had settled Imani at an adjacent booth, where the little girl had pulled crayons and paper out of her backpack and was busy coloring.

"Do you have time to sit for a minute?" the woman asked.

I got myself a cup of coffee and joined her. "Would you care for something to eat?"

"No, we're fine." The woman hesitated. "My name's Alyssa. Alyssa Greer."

I had known it, of course, from the instant she walked through the door. It couldn't have been anyone else but Scratch's family. Scratch's estranged wife. Scratch's baby girl.

This woman was cultured, refined, obviously educated.

He had been telling the truth.

How she found her way to Chulahatchie, I couldn't for the life of me imagine. But here she was, and ready or not, Scratch was about to have to deal with the unexpected meeting of his past and his present, the collision of two vastly different lives.

· 30 ·

Seeing Scratch in that jail cell is a picture I wish I could erase from my mind forever. When he was first arrested, and I had gone with Boone to talk to him, he had been in a room with a table and a few chairs. It was bleak, for sure, but not like this. Not bars and locks. Not a cage for an animal.

Peach was back at the restaurant, coloring with Imani and playing hangman. She had come immediately when I called, and didn't seem the least bit surprised that Scratch's estranged wife and daughter had shown up without warning on my doorstep.

The look on Scratch's face when he caught his first glimpse of Alyssa revealed everything. No matter what had happened between them, he loved her, and to have her see him here, cooped up like a dangerous animal, was almost more than he could bear.

Alyssa, on the other hand, was all business.

"Oh, so you're the little woman." The sheriff leered at her.

She raked him with an appraising glance. "I'm the lawyer," she said. "And you will release my client. Now."

"Hold on there, missy," he said. "He's a convicted felon who's violated his parole. He ain't going nowhere until I get the paperwork—"

She retrieved a manila folder from her bag and slapped it against his chest. "There's your paperwork. He's completed his parole, as you very well know, and you don't have a shred of evidence to hold him on the robbery. I've also got cause to bring charges against you, and against this office, for false arrest and unlawful detainment. And maybe even racial profiling. But I'm guessing you'd rather not go there."

The sheriff gaped at her and tried to respond, but apparently his mouth had gone dry and he couldn't speak. Without a word he fished out his keys, opened the cell door, and stood aside.

"Thank you," Alyssa said.

Scratch edged out of the cell and stood there shifting from one foot to the other. "Alyssa," he said. That was all, just "Alyssa." He choked up and couldn't go on.

"Let's get back to the cafe," I said. "There's a beautiful little girl waiting there who might like to meet her daddy."

It was nearly dusk by the time Scratch came down from the apartment, showered, shaved, and looking more like himself. Alyssa was sitting in a booth alone, clenching her fists and gnawing on her knuckle. Imani and Peach were drawing on the paper place mats. Boone and Toni had gone home, and I was in the kitchen seeing what kind of makeshift meal I could put together for the five of us. Folks gotta eat, no matter what else is going on.

I figured mac and cheese might be good comfort food, and God knows we were gonna need it. I put a pot of pasta on to boil and started grating Parmesan and Romano. Scratch and Alyssa were in the corner booth closest to the kitchen door, and I could hear most of their conversation. I wasn't trying to eavesdrop, but I listened anyhow.

"Why did you come?" he said. "And how did you know where I was?"

"I got a call," Alyssa said. "Apparently your Peach Rondell is an extremely resourceful woman and a good researcher. I should hire her as my assistant."

"So Peach found you, and interfered—"

"She didn't interfere, John. She was concerned about you. You ought to be thankful to have such good friends."

"I *am* thankful. These people have been like family to me. They believe in me, unlike—" He stopped suddenly, and I could imagine him gritting his teeth like he did sometimes, that big muscle in his jaw popping out.

"Unlike me."

"Yes."

"John, I was young. I was stupid. I was afraid. Daddy had controlled me all my life, and he wasn't about to let me go that easily. He was convinced you were going to ruin my life."

"So he framed me and ruined *my* life."

She let out a deep sigh. "Yes."

"And you did nothing to stop it."

"I was barely twenty years old, John. I couldn't stand up to him."

"And now that you're nearly thirty, and he's put you through law school, and you've passed the bar, you've suddenly grown a backbone?"

A long silence stretched between them, disturbed only by the gurgle of the pasta bubbling at my elbow. After a while he said, "Answer me, Alyssa. Why are you here? Aren't you afraid your daddy's going to find out and come haul you back to Atlanta?"

"Daddy's dead," she said. "He died two years ago."

Scratch made a small strangling sound in his throat. "I'm sorry."

"I'm not!" she fired back, her words hard and fierce. "I'm glad he's gone!" She let out a little sob. "No, that's not completely true. He was my father. I loved him, no matter what his faults. But what he did to you—"

"All right," he interrupted. "I guess I can accept that you were young and didn't know how to handle the situation. And I'm sure you were scared, too. You'd never lived on your own, without your daddy's support. But why now, Alyssa? Why come looking for me now?"

"I've been looking for you for a long time," she said. "Until that Peach woman called me, I had no idea where you were. What on earth made you choose a place like this, anyway?"

He chuckled, that deep, rumbling laugh that started way down in his chest. "I reckon I didn't choose it at all," he said. "Feels more like it chose me."

A pause, the length of a heartbeat or two. "I still love you, John," she said. "I've always loved you."

The homemade mac and cheese went down easier than I'd anticipated. By the time the meal was done and I had served the last of the lemon meringue pie from lunch, Imani was sitting on her daddy's lap and eating from his plate.

She kept looking up at him, as if amazed that this mountain of a man was somehow connected to her and her mother. Alyssa sat close to the two of them, her eyes fixed on his face, her hand straying now and then to brush against his fingers.

Something happened to me as I watched them. Something I didn't expect. My doubts about Scratch thinned like a cloud in the wind until I could barely see it anymore, just a haze, a thin veil between me and the sun. And then it was gone.

Scratch shot glances at me over the top of Imani's head, like he was trying to read my mind, figure out what I was thinking. And I couldn't have told him to save my soul. All I knew was that the knot in the pit of my stomach was gone, and I could look him in the eye. He seemed to understand, and when I smiled at him, he just nodded and let it go.

"We oughta get out of here, Dell, and let you get on home," he said at last. "I'll help you clean up."

"You'll do nothing of the sort," I said. "You'll go and spend time with your wife and daughter. And if you even think about coming in to work tomorrow, I'll fire you."

Scratch laughed, but the unspoken question hung out

there in space. Where would they go? Not to the dingy little apartment above the restaurant, surely.

And then I knew. Knew as surely as I'd ever known anything.

Chase had mortgaged our future for that damned river camp. I hadn't been back there since he died; swore I would never set foot on that ground again. Every time I thought about it, rage and pain rose up in me. Bitter disappointment, like hot bile in my throat.

And now, for the first time, I was glad I owned it. It felt like Somebody had a different plan for that cabin—not my husband's little love nest for his affair, but a safe place for the healing of a relationship that had been broken for a long, long time.

I got up, retrieved Chase's keys from the nail next to the kitchen door, and handed them to him. "It's not exactly the Hilton," I said. "And I can't guarantee how clean it is. But it's yours for as long as you want it."

"Thanks, Dell," he said.

And by the way he said it, and the look in his eyes, I knew he wasn't just talking about the cabin.

· 31 ·

Now that Scratch and his family were staying out at the river camp, I couldn't get the place out of my mind. I kept thinking about it, sometimes even dreaming about it—those forbidden images from Peach's journal, the lithe blonde woman walking into the cabin, into my husband's arms.

Mama always advocated facing a problem head on—taking the bull by the horns. "You might get gored," she said, "but it sure as heck beats grabbing the other end."

I'd been grabbing the other end for months—suspecting every woman in town, including my best friend, stressing, obsessing, twisting my gut into knots, turning circles like a rabid dog.

So when Peach Rondell came into the Heartbreak Cafe on Friday, that third week of December, I decided it was time to let go of the back end and face this thing head-on.

Lunch was over and Peach was the only one left. As usual, she was writing in her journal, oblivious to her surroundings. I edged over to the table, coffeepot in hand.

I refilled her cup and poured a mug for myself. "You got a minute, Peach?" I said.

She finished her sentence, stuck her pen between the pages, and closed the book. My eyes gravitated to the cover. She was stroking the brown leather, absentmindedly, the way you'd pet a beloved dog. I knew what the leather felt like, could almost see the imprint of my own fingers against the spine.

I sat down, afraid my jelly legs wouldn't hold me up much longer. Confession might be good for the soul, but it wreaks havoc on the rest of you, at least until it's done.

She was looking at me, curious, waiting. *Get on with it,* I told myself. *Bull. Horns. Spit it out. Now.*

"I need to talk to you about something," I said. My voice cracked and shook.

She leaned forward. "Sure, Dell. Is anything wrong?"

"It's about—well, about your journal."

Her hand clenched protectively around the book. "What about it?"

"Remember the day Purdy Overstreet sprained her ankle? You left your journal in the cafe, and came to get it the next day?"

"I remember." Her eyes narrowed. I was pretty darn sure she knew what was coming.

"Well—"

"Did you read it?" she said. Her voice was even and steady, which was worse than yelling.

"Yes. I'm sorry, Peach. I shouldn't have done it."

"No, you shouldn't have," she said. "I trusted you."

"I know." I ducked my head and let her anger and disappointment flow into me. "I'm sorry. But—"

"But what?"

"But there's something I've got to know about what you wrote in there. And the only way I can know it is to ask."

Peach shrugged. "Might as well. The damage is done."

I looked up at her. She had gone eerily calm, stony, like a statue made of ice. If I'd held that gaze a second longer, it would have frozen me from the inside out.

I stared down at my hands, clenched so hard around my coffee cup that it was a wonder the thing didn't shatter. "You wrote about my husband, Chase, and the woman he was having an affair with. The river camp. The meeting between the two of them. Who was she, Peach? And how did you know?"

I kept my eyes trained on the coffee in my cup. It was vibrating in circles, shaken by my trembling fingers. An earthquake in miniature. A shifting of the world.

She didn't answer. I didn't look at her. The silence between us stretched thin as taffy, pulled to the breaking point. And then I heard a sound. A gasp. A little croaking noise.

"Oh my God," she said.

I raised my head. Tears were streaming down her cheeks. Her shoulders rose and fell with her sobs. She put her face in her hands and cried so hard I thought she might wrench her soul out of her body.

She fought for air like a woman drowning. I knew the feeling; I'd cried like that many a night since Chase had died. I pulled a handful of napkins out of the dispenser and pressed them into her hand.

My touch seemed to burn her skin. She jerked away, and I could see her withdrawing into herself, collapsing. "No," she said. "Please, no."

I didn't move, but I didn't touch her again, either. After a while the weeping subsided. She sat up and blew her nose, and at last she spoke.

"Dell, I'm so, so sorry."

"Sorry for what? I'm the one who needs to apologize."

"No, you don't understand." She took in a ragged, pain-racked breath. "It was me."

She was right; I didn't understand. "What are you talking about?"

"The man. The river camp. The woman. It was me."

"You wrote about it, yes. I shouldn't have read it, but I did. And—"

"Dell!" she said, her voice sharp. "I wrote it from the man's viewpoint, wrote it as a fictional scene, like in a novel. But it was me."

"It wasn't you. It was a tall, thin blonde woman, it was—"

And then the truth sank in, all the way down to the pit of my stomach. She had been writing about herself, as she saw herself, as she used to be, or as she wished she could be again. Thin, beautiful, attractive. Desirable.

"But Chase—"

"I didn't know you at the time, Dell, and I sure didn't know he was your husband. I didn't know he was *anybody's* husband, not until the very end. He told me—" She stopped. "Well, never mind what he told me."

"I can guess," I said. "Probably the same thing every married man tells a woman he's trying to seduce."

"Probably." She looked up at me, her eyes full of misery and despair. "I was an easy target, I suppose. Lonely, hurting, feeling abandoned. New in town, for all practical purposes. He told me his name was Charles."

"It is," I said. "Chase was a nickname, but nobody ever called him anything else." I felt as if I might unravel at any second, but I pulled myself together and forged ahead. "Did anyone else know?"

When she answered, her voice came out a whisper. "We only met at the river camp, and once or twice at a restaurant in Tuscaloosa. Hardly anybody was aware that I was back in town, or would have recognized me even if they'd known. People might have suspected him, I'm not sure."

"They suspected, all right," I said. "But y'all must have been pretty discreet, because nobody knew for sure, or at least if they did they kept quiet about it, and that's not very likely in this town."

She offered no comment on this. I waited, and then finally asked the question I had to know. "Were you there the night he died?"

Peach shook her head. "No. I had been there earlier in the day. He was alone, as far as I know."

She didn't say what I expect we both were thinking, that maybe she was to blame for his heart attack, that maybe the exertion was too much for him, or the stress of keeping such a secret. An image shouldered its way into my head, of Peach and Chase together—not the imaginary Peach with the long legs and flowing blonde hair, but the real Peach, with her dark roots and puffy eyes and faded Ole Miss sweat-shirt. What did he see in her that I didn't see?

Then a strange sensation came over me. A door shutting in my mind. Or maybe it was a coffin. I had my truth at last. Maybe in time the pain would subside and the wounds would heal, but right now that truth wrapped around my senses like razor-sharp barbed wire. There was no solace in Peach's confession, but at least there was resolution. At least there was relief.

And oddly enough, I didn't blame her. Like the rest of us, she sought comfort where she found it. Like the rest of us, she went in blind, feeling her way through the darkness.

"Dell," Peach said, "that last day, the day he died, he told me he couldn't see me anymore. He told me he was married, and that he had to try to make things right." She paused. "He loved you, Dell. He always loved you."

I didn't believe she was telling the truth. But it was a compassionate lie, all the same.

· 32 ·

I never revealed to anyone what Peach Rondell had told me.

Not Toni. Not Boone. Not anybody. I just kept it shut tight between the pages of my heart, hidden away. Some things are too precious or too painful to be spoken.

It's a lesson I've been slow in learning. Certain gifts, certain heartaches, certain memories, lie too deep for words, too close for tears.

I had my answer. There was no reason for anyone to think less of Peach because she was the one who supplied it.

After Peach left, I locked the door, turned off the lights, and sat there while the early dusk of December closed in on me. It was almost Christmas, and I couldn't think of a single damn reason to celebrate.

Boone, who had grown up Catholic while I was getting born again over and over at the Baptist Church, had tried to educate me about the season of Advent. The liminal time, he called it—the threshold moment between darkness and daylight, between *now* and *not yet*. The transition, the waiting time.

I'd never quite gotten it. Baptists didn't do Advent—we just went straight to Christmas, to the baby in the manger, to shepherds and wise men and starlight shining overhead and angel choruses. I reckon we didn't like waiting much, and sure as heck weren't sophisticated enough to appreciate what Boone called "the gifts of the darkness." Baptists are all about light, and come hell or high water, we're gonna switch the power on.

Now I was beginning to understand. I thought about Mary, too young and too naive, pregnant and afraid and shamed— because who would believe such an outrageous story, anyway? An angel visitation, a virgin birth? At best, it had been a dream or a vision. At worst, a psychotic breakdown. Either way, a pretty lame excuse for a sin that could get her stoned.

I could imagine the reality of it now; for the first time in my life I got past the tinsel and the presents and the glad tidings. I saw an exhausted teenage girl, pregnant as a beach ball, riding into Bethlehem on an uncomfortable and stubborn ass. Standing in line for hours, while her ankles swelled, to pay taxes they couldn't afford. Going into labor in a barn because all the hotels were overcrowded and they didn't have money for a room, anyway. No midwife around, just a burly, rough-handed carpenter who didn't know nothing about birthin' no babies.

Mary didn't have a clue about the hallelujahs ringing over the fields, spooking the sheep and scaring the bejeebers out of the shepherds, or about rich kings making their way from the Orient with expensive gifts. All she knew was the night and the cold and the pain. All she felt was the blood and the mess and the terror of childbirth. All she heard echoing around her was the shuffling of animals pushed out of their stalls, and Joseph's desperate prayer that she wouldn't die, that the baby wouldn't die, that somehow they'd all live to see the sunrise.

The waiting time. The darkness. The fear. The trembling, feeble hope that somehow hung on, persistent, in the face of all odds—

Someone was knocking on the door.

I jerked back to reality, turned to look. It was Marvin Beckstrom, peering in through the glass, with the fresh new lettering, HEARTBREAK, reflected backward over his big buggy head. Behind him stood the sheriff, motioning for me to unlock the door and let them in.

I was pretty darn sure they weren't here to say they'd caught the thief and return my stolen money.

The eviction notice was clear, even to me: I had until January 1. Alyssa looked it over and said that, unfortunately, it was legal and there was nothing I could do about it. Pretty quick work, to my way of thinking, but my lease specified thirty days' grace in the event of nonpayment. After the robbery, I hadn't been able to make the December rent.

It was over. The Heartbreak Cafe was history.

Back in April, I had set my sights on still being solvent by the end of the year. A pretty modest aspiration, all things considered. Nine months. But it wasn't going to happen. This baby was going to die.

The day after the papers were served, Scratch came into work bringing a small fir tree from the riverbank. He set it up in the corner near the door, where it stood looking bare and forlorn. A Charlie Brown tree.

He stood back and surveyed it. "Reckon I'd better get some decorations before it depresses everybody who walks through the door."

"I've got plenty," I said. "I'll bring some in tomorrow."

I wasn't putting up a Christmas tree at home this year, and didn't really want one in the cafe, either. There didn't seem to be much point. There would be no presents, no lights, no celebration. Chase was gone; the cafe was gone; life as I knew it was gone. At the moment the only blessed thing I could do was hang on and try to survive the holidays, waiting for the axe to fall.

When you're part of a family—a wife or husband, brothers and sisters, aunts and uncles and cousins and friends— you don't think about how hard those special days are for folks who don't have anybody. You don't think about the lonely widower rambling around his empty house, eating a turkey sandwich and trying to distract himself with Thanksgiving football. You don't think about the divorcee whose life is in shambles and who fights every single day to keep from giving in to despair. You don't think about the old woman down the street living on Social Security and trying to decide whether to buy food or medicine. You don't consider the folks who have no one to kiss on New Year's Eve at midnight, no one to bake a birthday cake for, no one who's waiting for a phone call. You don't think about the homeless, the loveless, the lonely.

Now I was thinking about all that, and more. Feeling it. Trying unsuccessfully to push it down below the surface of my consciousness. Trying not to panic.

"Oh, there's something else," Scratch said. "Hang on a minute."

He went outside and came back in cradling an enormous turkey in his arms. "I stopped by the Piggly Wiggly this morning. Seems like you won the raffle." He held out the bird, a twenty-pound monster encased in thick plastic and yellow netting.

I stared at him. "What the heck am I supposed to do with that?"

"Cook it," he said.

The man did have a way of cutting right to the heart of the matter. In spite of myself, I started to laugh.

"Scratch," I said, "what are you and Alyssa and Imani doing for Christmas?"

He shrugged. "I reckoned we'd just spend the day at the river camp. Alyssa took off work until after the first, so we're in no rush to go anywhere."

"How about if we serve Christmas dinner here, for folks who got no family and no place else to go?" I said. "You know, turkey and dressing and all the trimmings? Fix it up real nice, like a banquet?"

"You feel like doing that?"

"What else am I gonna do?" I said. "Besides, the worst

has already happened. I've lost the cafe. Might as well go out with a bang."

And so we did.

Christmas Day dawned bright and chilly. I was up before dawn with all the lights blazing in the Heartbreak Cafe, baking pumpkin pies and stirring up a huge vat of cornbread dressing while the turkey began to cook. Everybody was bringing something—mashed potatoes and sweet potatoes and green bean casserole. Boone promised to put together his famous oyster casserole, and Toni was making her aunt Madge's homemade yeast rolls.

Scratch had pushed four tables together in the center of the room to create a kind of long banquet table, and we'd covered it with a dark green tablecloth and red cotton napkins. The effect was remarkably festive, for a dumpy little diner on the verge of bankruptcy.

By the time everybody started to arrive, the cafe was filling up with all those nostalgic smells. Toni had brought a CD player and set it up in the corner, and the sounds of Mannheim Steamroller's *Christmas* album threaded in and out among the buzz of conversation. Every now and then the bell over the door would jingle, another friend coming to join the party. It reminded me of my favorite Christmas movie, *It's a Wonderful Life*. Another angel gets its wings.

I was just stirring up the gravy, and Scratch was slicing the turkey, when the door opened and Hoot and Purdy waltzed in. Hoot looked downright spiffy, in red suspenders and a matching bow tie. Purdy was wearing an ill-fitting wraparound skirt poofed out with crinolines and sparkling with glitter and sequins.

Her ankle was completely healed, it seemed, for she twirled around like a ballerina and only stumbled once. Hoot caught her in his arms, and she planted a big old red-lipstick kiss sideways across his mouth. Glitter scattered around her as she righted herself.

"Guess what ever'body?" she yelled above the music. "Hoot and me are getting married!"

All conversation skidded to an abrupt halt. "Well, ah, congratulations," I said. "But isn't this kinda sudden?"

Purdy snorted. "When you're eighty-something, you ain't got time to mess around." She cackled and gave a wicked little grin. "Besides, we gotta get married. We already done the dirty deed."

Hoot blushed. "More than once," he muttered.

This was way more information than I was comfortable with, and a mental image I desperately wanted to erase. I was thankful when Scratch came to the rescue. "Congratulations, Miss Purdy." He gave her a kiss on the cheek and shook Hoot's hand. "I reckon the best man won."

"That's all right, honey," Purdy said in a whisper everybody could hear. "You're still second on my list, and if this thing with Hoot doesn't work out, I'll be parking my bony little ass right on your doorstep."

"I'd be honored," Scratch said. "But in the meantime, there's somebody you need to meet. Purdy, this is my wife, Alyssa, and my daughter, Imani. Alyssa, Miss Purdy Overstreet."

"You got a wife?" Purdy shrieked with laughter. "You

bad, bad boy!" She thumped him on the chest with her purse and turned toward Alyssa. "You treat him right, now. You got competition waiting in the wings."

Imani was staring wide-eyed at Purdy and Hoot. "Is that a Christmas tree skirt you're wearing?"

Alyssa prodded her in the arm. "Imani! It's not polite to comment on people's wardrobes."

"Yeah, but—"

Purdy was unfazed. "You bet it is. I got the idea from that show *Designing Women*. Those ladies got real good taste, and they're funny as hell, too."

Dinner was ready, the makeshift banquet table loaded down with a dozen steaming dishes and that huge golden-brown bird. Peach Rondell appeared, having escaped her mother's house at the earliest opportunity, and squeezed in between Imani and Fart Unger.

Peach glanced at me, as if to ask if it was okay for her to be here. I smiled and discovered it wasn't really an effort, either. I'd quit hugging the cactus, I guess, and the wounds had begun to heal up. She smiled back.

Imani gazed up at Peach. "When I grow up," she whispered, "I want to be a beauty queen, just like you."

Peach patted her cheek, then reached down and took something out of her purse. Something bright and sparkly.

She leaned over and placed the tiara on Imani's head. "I crown you Queen of Corn Casserole," she said. "Duchess of Dressing. Princess of Pumpkin. Monarch of Muffins."

Imani started to giggle and ducked her head as everyone clapped and cheered.

When the applause died down, we all sat there, a little

awkward, waiting for someone to start. At last Scratch said, "If nobody has any objections, I'd like to give thanks."

We held hands and waited for him to speak. As silence descended over us, a certain slant of winter sunlight came in through the window and glinted off the tinsel on the pitiful little Christmas tree.

"Thank you," he said in a quiet voice, "not only for this food, but for all the ways you feed us. For love and friends and family reunited. For acceptance and trust and honesty. For giving us each other. For healing our wounds and making us whole again. Fill our hearts with gratitude, and fill our lives with grace. Amen."

Murmured "amens" circled around the table. It was a hushed and holy moment, a moment filled with truth and significance.

I knew. We all knew. No one here was alone anymore.

We were family.

It was the best Christmas dinner ever. Purdy and Hoot held hands under the table like giddy teenagers. Scratch couldn't keep his eyes off Alyssa, and he held Imani on his lap for most of the meal. Toni, Boone, and Peach carried on an animated conversation about some new novel that had just been released. Fart was subdued, but seemed content to take it all in.

And then, just as I was about to suggest another round of pie, Purdy spoke up—not in her usual fantasy-land voice, but in a clear, straightforward manner. "Dell," she said, "what are you going to do about Marvin Beckstrom's plan to sell this place out from under you?"

I choked on my coffee and set the cup down with a trembling hand. "What did you say?"

Purdy gave me the eagle eye. "I overheard him in the bank the other day. Folks talk around me like I'm not there, but I heard him plain as day. On the phone with somebody, telling them you were broke, and the Heartbreak Cafe would be empty by the first of the year, and then the sale could go forward as planned."

Boone leaned forward. "Purdy, are you *sure* that's what he said?"

"I'm old, I ain't deaf," she said. "I heard him clear as water. He's planning to buy this place come January, so he can resell it and make himself a bundle. Got a buyer all lined up."

I looked into her eyes, clear and bright and lucid. And then, in the space of a breath, a shade fell over them again, and she said, "Why isn't your mama here, Dell? She'd enjoy this little get-together."

No one seemed to want to leave. The afternoon shadows stretched across the floor and faded into an early dusk. I went back into the kitchen to put away the leftovers and make another pot of coffee.

Fart Unger followed me. While I stacked plates in the dishwasher, he deboned the turkey and transferred the remaining dressing into a smaller container to go in the fridge. We chatted about nothing, barely avoiding grazing the subject of Brenda a time or two.

And then he stepped around me to reach for a towel, and

our hands met. "Sorry," I said. I pulled back, but he didn't let go.

"How's the finger?" he asked, raising my hand to eye level.

"All better." As soon as the words were out of my mouth, I was flooded with the memory of that moment when he kissed the bandage. I flushed and turned away, but he wouldn't let me.

"Dell," he said. "Thank you for including me."

"Of course." The words came out curt and dismissive, not the way I intended it at all. "I mean, of course you would be invited. There was never any question. I wanted you to be here."

"And I wanted to be here. Without you—and, ah, everybody—this would have been a miserable Christmas."

"For me, too," I said. "It was probably selfish, actually. I did it so I wouldn't feel so lonely."

"There wasn't a thing selfish about it," he said. "And you know it."

Our Christmas gathering of the odd and the outcast had brought a welcome, if temporary, respite from the stress and panic. But once the turkey was demolished and the little Charlie Brown tree stripped of its ornaments and flung in the Dumpster, anxiety overwhelmed me like a drowning wave.

Six days until eviction. Five. Four.

I decided not to reopen the restaurant for this final week. I had too much to do, and what was the point, anyway? A few hundred dollars of profit wasn't going to make any difference. A partial payment wouldn't bail me out; besides, Marvin Beckstrom obviously had other plans for the Heartbreak Cafe, much more profitable plans.

Marvin. Even the thought of him galled me and set my teeth on edge. I'd seen him on two or three occasions since he'd served papers on me—in the bank, on the square. Every single time, he'd been wearing that smug *gotcha!* expression.

"You think it's possible Marvin's behind the break-in?" I asked Scratch and Alyssa for the hundredth time.

"I don't know as I'd go that far," Scratch said. "But he's gonna profit from it, that's for sure."

I had to agree with Scratch. Marvin had an agenda in shutting me down, and whether or not he orchestrated the whole thing, he was set to cash in big-time from the sale of this building. Meanwhile, the sheriff was so far up Marvin's butt he couldn't see daylight, and I had lost all hope of ever finding out who stole from me, much less getting my money back.

"The problem is," Alyssa said, "it's not illegal for him to buy a rental property from the bank and then resell it."

When you're stuck with your foot in the rails and a train coming down the track, your mind goes to crazy places. My brain was full of old television shows. I fantasized about Magnum, P.I., breaking into the bank at night with a little flashlight clenched between his teeth, finding a paper trail, written evidence of the Chickenhead's crime. *Memo to self: Hire someone to break into HBCafe, ASAP.* With a canceled check for final payment stapled to the top.

All right, maybe there wasn't a paper trail. But Perry Mason could trick the truth out of him. He did it all the time, every week, at least he did twenty-five years ago. Got the perp on the stand as a witness—*"Permission to treat the witness as hostile, Your Honor"*—and then proceeded to weasel the truth out of him, making him so guilty and antsy that he'd stand up and yell, "Yes, all right! I confess! It was me!" And the bailiff would take him away in handcuffs.

But some folks don't cave in so easy, and I suspected that Marvin Beckstrom had been born without a conscience, just as he had been born without a chin. So the last resort was *Mission: Impossible*. And this one had to work.

It was a complicated plan, involving an elaborate setup with an exact replica of Marvin's office at the bank. Martin Landau, in disguise as the sheriff, would manipulate him into admitting, on tape, that he was the mastermind behind the whole caper. All to get his hands on the cafe and sell it for an obscene profit.

I was deep in fantasy about the creation of Martin Landau's latex mask from a bust of the sheriff when Scratch broke into my daydream.

"You wanta take these?" He held out a cardboard box filled with miscellaneous utensils—stainless steel spatulas and large slotted serving spoons, graters and paring knives and all the paraphernalia that went into equipping a restaurant kitchen.

"I don't know. I don't really have room for them at home." I shrugged. "Never mind. Just set them on the backseat of my car, if you don't mind."

Scratch shouldered his way through the door.

In a minute he came back with a strange look on his face. "Come outside. There's something you gotta see."

I followed him out and stood on the sidewalk shivering in the December wind. He pointed down West Main Street, to the liquor store on the other side of Sav-Mor discount.

"What are we looking at?"

"See that old red F-150 in front of the liquor store? Just wait."

An "F-150" meant nothing to me, but I gathered he was talking about the battered pickup parked at the curb. I waited, and within a couple of minutes a man came out of the store with a case of Old Grand-Dad, loaded it in the truck, and went back for more. Three trips. Then he got into the truck and drove away.

There was something familiar about him. Something that made my stomach jerk into a knot.

Lean and sharp as barbed wire, with that peculiar sloping walk.

Jape Hanahan.

"What the—"

"Yeah," Scratch said. "Last time we saw him, he was drunk as a skunk and looking for a handout."

"He was drunk?"

Scratch ignored this. "Question is, where'd he get the money for all that liquor?"

December 29. Three days until eviction.

"We got it," Alyssa said. She slapped a manila folder down on the table and grinned at me. Scratch stood behind her wearing an equally broad grin.

"He confessed?" I said.

"Spilled his guts." Alyssa sat down, took off her pumps, and rubbed her feet. "I've got the notes right here." She sighed. "You got any fresh coffee?"

"Sure, hang on." I brought the pot and three mugs. "How did you do it?"

"My wife's a pretty intimidating lawyer," Scratch said.

"You wish. The intimidation didn't come from me."

I looked at Scratch. "You didn't beat him up. Tell me you didn't hit him."

"He didn't have to," Alyssa said. "Just one threatening glance from John is enough to make a coward like Jape Hanahan give up his own grandmother."

Scratch shot me a humble little *aw-shucks* look. "That nice young deputy met us out there—sheriff himself wouldn't come. Didn't take long for Jape to cave in, and get himself arrested."

"Apparently he was watching the place while you were gone," Alyssa said, "and as soon as John left the premises, he saw his chance and broke the door in. If the cases of booze in his cabin are any indication, he spent the whole wad on whiskey—much of which is already gone."

I had to ask the question, even though I already knew the answer. "Will I get my money back?"

Alyssa bit her lip. "The money's gone, Dell."

"I figured. It was too much to hope for, I guess, to save the cafe."

"I'm so sorry," she said. "Wish it could have turned out different."

"Oh well," I said in a vain attempt to be stoic. "It was fun while it lasted."

At 4:30 the next morning I woke up to a shrieking alarm clock, jerked out of a dream about the cafe going up in flames, and all of us—me, Toni, Boone, Fart, everybody—standing helpless on the sidewalk as the volunteer firefighters joked and laughed and refused to do anything to stop it.

It wasn't my alarm clock. It was sirens—lots of them, shattering the early-morning silence with their high-pitched Doppler screams. I listened. Cop cars, fire trucks, an ambulance or two. Years of living in a small town had taught me the difference. In Chulahatchie, you take your entertainment where you can get it.

The dream still lingered around the edges of my mind. I could almost smell the smoke. I stumbled out of bed, pulled on a pair of jeans and an old Falcons sweatshirt of Chase's, and reached for the phone.

Toni answered on the first ring. "Good, you're awake," I said. "What the heck is going on?"

"I don't know, but every light in the neighborhood is on. It sounds like it's coming from the square. I'll meet you down there."

She hung up. I called Boone, who was also awake, and then dialed the river camp and got a very sleepy Alyssa on the line. "Tell Scratch to get down to the cafe," I said without bothering to explain or even apologize for waking her. "Something's happened, and it doesn't sound good."

By the time I got to the square, half the town had gathered, some of them straight out of bed, with coats thrown over their pajamas. Three fire trucks were on the scene, and two ambulances, and three deputy sheriffs milled around aimlessly, as if trying to decide what to do next and who was in charge. The sheriff was nowhere in sight.

I parked down near the cafe—which wasn't on fire, although since I was being foreclosed on in two days, I didn't know why I should care. Toni pulled up, with Boone right behind her. How Scratch and Alyssa got there so fast, I'll never know. Imani was sound asleep in the backseat with a blanket tucked around her.

"What's going on?" Boone said.

"No idea. Let's get up there and see."

We threaded through the crowd until we got close to the front, where the deputies had finally set up barriers to keep the onlookers out of the way. The firemen were struggling with the Jaws of Life, trying to pry open the door of a pickup truck.

A battered red F-150 with its windshield shattered and its front end wrapped around the statue of a Confederate soldier.

Jape Hanahan was pronounced dead on arrival at the Chulahatchie County Hospital, but everybody knew he was a goner when he hit the windshield. Truth was, he'd been dead for years—suicide by alcohol. His body was just too stubborn to quit.

"What was he doing out of jail?" I asked Alyssa.

"That's the kicker," Alyssa said. "He bribed the sheriff with a case of booze, went home, and drank himself into oblivion. When he hit the square, his blood-alcohol content was more than twice the legal limit. No skid marks." She shrugged. "The ironic thing is, the sheriff resigned first thing this morning. Said he feels responsible for Jape's death because he let him out."

She'd gotten this information from the sheriff's office, where the deputy on duty gave her whatever information she wanted. With the sheriff gone, seemed he was glad to talk to somebody—anybody—who knew what they were doing.

Scratch came out of the kitchen carrying the last of the bacon and scrambled eggs, and then went back for grits and biscuits. Folks had to eat, even when the world was coming to an end.

"So that's it, then," I said. "The money's gone for good, and so is the Heartbreak Cafe."

We ate in silence for a few minutes. The sun came up, light in defiance of the darkness. I thought about Boone's liminal time, but there was nothing left to wait for.

· 34 ·

New Year's Eve arrived, with Chulahatchie reeling from its biggest scandal in decades.

I was still dead broke and facing eviction. Given all the upheaval in the sheriff's office, I hadn't been served the final eviction yet, but a day or two wasn't going to make any difference. The other shoe was destined to drop, today or tomorrow or the day after that. If I'da been stronger, I woulda just locked the door and turned my back on the whole shebang.

Still, I couldn't seem to stay away from the Heartbreak Cafe. I'd go over there every morning and make coffee and wander around like a lost soul on the way to Hades. I could almost hear echoes of the conversation and laughter, could almost see the faces of the people I had come to regard as family. Boone and Toni. Scratch, Alyssa, and little Imani.

Peach Rondell. Fart Unger. Even Purdy and Hoot, crazy as they both were.

"Bless their hearts," I whispered to no one in particular. It made me laugh. And then the tears came.

I swiped at my eyes and argued with myself. It wasn't like they'd died, I thought. They'll still be my friends. Still part of my life. But the Heartbreak Cafe would be gone. Nothing would be the same. It was like watching somebody you love give up the battle with cancer. Like watching a dream drift out to sea and sink beneath the waves.

At long last, grief pierced my gut like a blade. I could finally look at this old place with my heart instead of my eyes, and I loved it. Loved the way it felt, loved what it represented. It was the first thing in fifty years of living that I'd ever done on my own, my first real accomplishment. It was a monument to my ability to become what I'd never even dreamed I could be: a woman capable of taking care of herself.

Peach Rondell had seen it before I did, had written about it in her journal:

> Dell gives me an example of how to be strong, and thanks to her I have the will to go on. Maybe someday I'll work up the nerve to actually talk to her, to tell her that she's my hero and my inspiration.

I'd never been anybody's hero before. Never been an inspiration. Never been more than Chase Haley's wife.

But for a few more minutes, maybe another day, I'd be more than that. I'd be the owner of the Heartbreak Cafe.

This place had saved me, I knew that now. Even when I didn't want to be saved. Even when I wanted God and karma and the whole wide universe to just leave me alone.

The phone rang. I didn't move. I shoulda had it disconnected already. One more thing I needed to put on my final checklist.

Whoever was calling was a persistent so-and-so. It rang and rang, and finally, against my better judgment, I got up and answered.

"Dell?" It was Alyssa. "Listen, ah, could you come out here to the river camp?" Her voice sounded oddly strained. "As soon as possible."

"What's the rush?"

"Just come."

I hesitated.

The truth was, I didn't want to go out there. Didn't ever want to see the place again for as long as I lived. It had offered a place of sanctuary for Scratch and Alyssa, and for that I was grateful, but as far as I was concerned the place could burn to its foundation or be swept by a flood all the way down the Tennessee-Tombigbee to Mobile and the Gulf.

That camp had been Chase's baby, from beginning to end, and the very thought of it caused me nothing but heartache. I'da been happy never to see the place again, but I reckoned now I was just going to have to grit it up and go. I just didn't know if I had the fortitude to face the location of my husband's last and worst betrayal.

I remembered the river camp as a big box on stilts, built over a cement pad that served as storage for fishing gear and a shelter for Chase's boat and trailer—not to mention a hiding place for the truck. On the back side of the house stretched a broad screened-in deck overlooking a quiet bend of the Tennessee-Tombigbee, with steps leading down to ground level and a narrow path to the dock.

It was, as Scratch had once observed, "rustic." Cedar-plank siding, a silver tin roof, one large room with an unfinished wood floor, a stacked stone fireplace, and a kitchen separated by a waist-high bar. The place had two small bedrooms with a bath between—sufficient for a weekend getaway, but certainly nothing fancy or upscale. Envisioning the elegant Alyssa there stretched my imagination to its limits.

"Dell?"

I stared at the phone and heard Alyssa's voice repeating my name, muted and far away, like a child's secret stretched between two tin cans with a string. I tried to swallow past the knot in my throat.

"Sure," I managed at last. "Sure. I'll be there in half an hour."

The lower level, beneath the camp house, was shielded from view of the road by a stone wall that went all the way up under the foundation. The wall did nothing to support the structure, it was just there to hide the underneath storage areas from sight. On the back side, facing the river, it was all open, forming what amounted to a vast covered patio at ground level.

Chase's boat and trailer were parked to the far left, shrouded in a tan cover. The patio had been swept and washed, and now served as a play area for Imani, complete with a picnic table, several Adirondack chairs, a couple of overhead fans, and a porch swing hanging from the rafters. Scratch had been working, that much was clear. The place looked clean and inviting. A few things removed from upstairs sat in a neat line next to Chase's boat as if waiting for a pickup from Goodwill or the Salvation Army.

Scratch and Alyssa met me at the car when I drove in. I could see Imani down by the bank, digging for crawdads in the sucking mud. She looked up and waved and went back to her work.

"Hey, Dell." Alyssa hugged me and held on like somebody else had died. I hugged her back and held on, too, because all of a sudden I needed a sympathetic human touch. When you're fifty and single, you don't get touched very often, and the skin hunger can get pretty bad even if you're not conscious of what you're missing.

After a while we let go, and Scratch said, "Dell, you need to take a look at what we found."

He led me over to the lineup of cast-offs—the ratty old sofa Chase had taken from the house when I replaced it years ago, a couple of equally threadbare easy chairs, several end tables and lamps, old mattresses from the bedrooms. "I did some clearing out to make a little more room upstairs," Scratch said. "Hope you don't mind."

"You can set a torch to it, or a couple of sticks of dynamite, far as I'm concerned."

I stopped next to Chase's battered old mahogany desk and peered at an angular black contraption that looked like a giant spider.

"What on earth is this?" I said. "I never saw it before."

"It's a home gym," Scratch said. "A multipurpose work-out machine. If you don't want it, I wouldn't mind keeping it. It's really a nice one."

I shrugged. "Sure. Keep anything you want. But you didn't call me down here to ask me that."

He shook his head. "No."

"We found this," Alyssa said. "Wedged behind one of the desk drawers, when we moved it."

She held out a small, thin book with a dark green fabric cover—it looked like a ledger book, the kind you might use to keep track of business expenses. But when I opened it, there were no columns for income and expenses, no spaces for debits and credits. It was just a blank book with faintly lined pages. And it was full of writing. Chase's writing.

"We think it's a journal or a diary of sorts," Scratch said. "We barely looked inside, just enough to know it's personal, and you're the only one who ought to be reading it."

I held the book at arm's length, like it was a snake about to strike. "Thanks."

I didn't know what else to say. They weren't aware, of course, that I already had all the information I ever wanted about Chase's secret life. Whatever was in this little green book wouldn't be much of a surprise. The only surprise was that he had kept it in the first place. My husband, the jock? A journal?

I took the little book over to the picnic table and sat down. Alyssa said something about bringing me something to drink, and she disappeared up the steps into the house. Scratch stood there looking down at me.

"Take your time," he said. "We'll be here if you need us."

He laid his big hand on my shoulder and left it there, warm and comforting, for a minute or two. Then he squeezed it, and the pressure left, and he was gone.

I was alone. Alone with the memory of a husband who'd betrayed me, and a book that might tell me nothing, or might tell me more than I wanted to know.

· 35 ·

January 1

All right, I got this damned thing, and I'm determined to use it if it kills me. I hate writing, and I ain't much good at expressing myself, but I reckon it's high time I learned. Past time.

The diary went back to the beginning of last year, four months before Chase died. The entries, in a familiar erratic scrawl, were messy and difficult to decipher. But the meaning was clear. All too clear.

It wasn't just Peach Rondell. It was Ginger from Tuscaloosa, and Kathleen from Tupelo, and some girl he only called Babe, from God knows where—none of them lasting more than a week or two. He wrote about buying the exercise machine and working out so he could get his athlete's body back, and trying different kinds of cologne (cologne? Chase?), and how Babe had brought him a gift of black silk underwear, and how he felt sexy in it.

Shoot, I thought. *I don't need to be reading this.*

But still I kept on. It was like watching a train wreck in slow motion: brakes squealing, cars jackknifing, bodies flying, metal crunching. I didn't want to see it but couldn't turn away.

And then a woman only identified as J.

> *J's making me do this—writing all this down. She says I need to be more emotionally engaged. What the hell does that mean? I don't know how to do feelings. I'm a man, for God's sake, not some faggoty feel-good fairy like that Boone Atkins.*

Fury rose up in me at this. If I'd had a match, I would have incinerated the book right then and there. But I didn't have any fire except the one burning in my gut. I forged ahead.

> *I'm starting to get the point of what J says. I reckon I can feel those feelings and live to tell about it. It still don't seem quite natural, but I'm gonna keep on trying. I really am.*
>
> *I cried today. I was embarrassed and ashamed, but J said that crying is a sign of strength, not weakness. That only a real man knows the value of tears.*

In nearly thirty years of marriage I had never seen Chase Haley cry. The idea that he was doing it so freely in front of another woman caused the dragon inside me to stand up on its hind legs, roar, and belch flames.

I hadn't reckoned on being jealous. Funny, I didn't feel much of anything about the adultery anymore, but the thought of a few tears made me furious.

I flipped through some more pages and scanned through the description of Chase's affair with Peach. She might not have known who he was, but he sure as heck remembered her. The Bean Queen, he called her. *Easy enough to seduce, but not much to look at after all these years. Some women just go to pot when they hit forty.*

I gritted my teeth and resisted the urge to tear the pages into confetti. Just as I'd never told anyone about Peach and Chase, I would also keep my silence about these ugly words my husband wrote. One kind lie deserves another.

And then I reached the end. The entry on the day of his death, a kind of last will and testament. The final words of Chase Haley.

April 17

J asked me if I was finally ready. Ready to make a decision. Ready to make a change. I am ready. I've known it for a long time. I just didn't have the words to say it, even in my mind, even to myself. But it ain't the kind of change J's expecting, and I don't suppose there's any point in telling her the truth.

I wasn't sure I wanted to go on. I put my finger in the book to mark my place, closed my eyes, and took a deep breath.

I ain't been happy, not for a long time. Maybe never. Don't know if Dell's happy or not, she never says. Guess that means she's just going with the flow, not rocking the boat. But I can't do that anymore.

I know none of this sounds like me. Hell, it doesn't feel like me, either. It feels like somebody else is inside my skin, trying to get out. And I don't know if I want him to get out or not. All I know is that I gotta do something.

I been trying to change. Trying to find the man I used to be, the one who had dreams and wanted more and didn't just sit on his ass in front of the TV letting the world pass him by. But I can't seem to find him. I tried to get him back, the football jock, the handsome guy who could get any girl he wanted. I got me a few, too. But it didn't feel as good as I remembered.

I took a drink of the iced tea Alyssa had brought down, but could barely swallow it. There was a rock in my throat the size of a fist. I couldn't breathe, couldn't think. But I couldn't stop reading, either.

Nothing feels good. Nothing makes sense anymore. So I'm giving up. I never been the kinda man Dell deserved. She shoulda had better. She's a fine woman, and she oughta have somebody who acts like he's got a lick of sense. Not like me.

For months, he had been planning to leave, trying to figure out a way to break it to me. How long had this gone on without me noticing? How could I have been so blind?

Something nagged at me, tapping at the back of my skull like a woodpecker on the eaves. But I couldn't identify it.

So this is the end. Tonight I'm gonna tell the Bean Queen that we're finished. No more chasing tail, no more J. No more nothing.

My eyes filled up, and the pages of cramped writing floated underwater. I blinked, trying to see, trying to read the final words on the final page of Chase Haley's life.

I'll never tell Dell the truth about what I've done—all the other women, all the things I'm ashamed of about myself. She wouldn't understand. Nobody could possibly understand. If she knew, I reckon she'd never forgive me, and I couldn't live with that. Instead I'll have to live with not forgiving myself. Maybe the Catholics had it right all along. Maybe there is such a thing as purgatory, and it's right now, right here, in the life you have to go on living when you know you deserve to be struck down in your tracks.

There was a space, a couple of blank lines, and then he went on:

I'm going back. Back to Dell, back to my life. I don't know how I'm gonna do it, but I've gotta try. J says I've been attempting to recapture my lost youth, and I suppose she's right. But you can't get that back, no matter what kind of fool you turn into trying to find it.

How long has it been, I wonder, since I told Dell I love her? I shoulda said it more often; maybe saying the words woulda made it feel more real. Maybe we coulda been more

connected, instead of living under the same roof like two rest-
less ghosts haunting the scene of the crime.

I gotta make this work. I got to. There's nothing else out
there for me—I know, 'cause I tried like hell to find it and
came up empty. So I reckon I'll just have to live with the
emptiness, if that's what it takes, and fake being happy the
best I can.

Even if I'm faking it, maybe I can make Dell a little
happier. She deserves that much—deserves a husband who
knows how lucky he is to have a woman like her, a man who
pays attention and gives her what she needs and doesn't take
her for granted.

I sure ain't been that man, but maybe it's not too late.
Maybe I can still change. Maybe I can turn into somebody
I'm proud of on the inside, instead of feeling like a shit all
the time.

My mind balked and stuttered. I read the words over and
over again, just to make sure I hadn't imagined them or mis-
understood. Peach Rondell hadn't spared my feelings with a
compassionate lie. She had told the truth.

Last time I saw Doc, he warned me I was a ticking time
bomb, a heart attack waiting to happen. Gave me nitrates
for the chest pains, told me to take 'em regular. He also
warned me to stay away from the Viagra, but I been working
out, and got my weight down some, and feel good, real good.
Them little blue pills haven't hurt me yet. Besides, a man my
age can use a little help now and then.

My hands were shaking so hard I couldn't hold the book. It slipped from my grasp and fell onto the cement floor, and something fluttered out from between the blank pages at the back.

A receipt. Cash, $80.00.

To Dr. Julia Hess, Tupelo Center for Group and Family Therapy.

Nitrates and Viagra. A lethal combination.

Chase had brought the heart attack on himself.

A surge of sadness rose up in me, sadness colored by something like love. Poor Chase. Peter Pan. A little boy in a man's body, a boy who'd lost his self-image to the ravages of age and complacency, and couldn't find a way to get it back.

I could see it all on the screen in the back of my mind: Chase getting ready to come home to me, dressing in his nice clothes, taking the pills. And then when his heart started to seize up, calling 911 for help. A call that came too late to save him. Too late to know that I really might have been able to forgive him, if he had only just been honest with me. That we really might have had a second chance. That the distance between us wasn't all his fault.

I sat there for a long time, holding the book, fondling the pages, staring off into space. Waiting for the tears to come. Waiting for the grief to strike.

But it didn't come. What I felt was not pain, but pity. Pity, and no small measure of relief.

It was over. I had already done my grieving, all this past year. I had loved him once, or thought I had. Maybe what I took for love was nothing more than convenience, or security, or the soothing comfort of familiarity.

The real lessons of love had come not from my marriage, but from my widowhood. Late in life, in my fiftieth year, the world imploded and I was forced to learn how to open myself up and find out what real love was all about.

Real love wasn't possible until I myself became real. Until fate or destiny, or whatever force it was, intervened and cut me open heart and soul. Only in the midst of all those raw emotions, when I was at my worst, did I discover that people could still love me when they saw exactly who I was. Shadow side and all.

People like Toni Champion and Boone Atkins. People like Scratch, who forgave me for not trusting him even though we never said a single word about it. People like Peach Rondell, who saw my inner strength and took me for her hero.

And I realized something else, too. Chase's death, painful as it was, had been the catalyst for change, the door that opened onto a whole new life. I never would have wished it on him, or on myself for that matter. But I also knew I wouldn't—couldn't—go back to who I was before.

Funny how hindsight turns curses to blessings; how the one experience you're sure will kill you becomes the moment of your greatest transformation. If Chase had lived, I never would have faced those challenges, never would have grown, never would have found out what was inside me. Never would have developed into the woman I've become over the last year.

I like that woman. I like her a lot. She is my hero, too.

*   *   *

The temperature had dropped as the afternoon wore on, and I shivered. Out near the dock, Scratch and Imani were sitting on logs near a circle of stones by the riverbank, feeding sticks into a campfire. Imani was laughing.

I shut the journal and got up from the bench. "Everything okay?" Scratch asked as I approached.

I forced a smile and nodded, then reached over and dropped the little green book into the fire pit.

Fire has always fascinated me. It's mesmerizing, hypnotic, alive. You can watch it all night and never see the same flame twice. It gives off heat and light and sweet nostalgic memories on the scent of the burning wood.

Destructive? Yes. But even the destruction brings light. Even the destruction warms.

The cover of the book blackened and warped, and after a moment the edges of the paper caught. I could see Chase's blue scrawl on a page or two, and watched the orange flame rise up as my husband's last worst moments curled into ash and smoke.

One more door closed.

One more secret I'd take with me to the grave.

· 36 ·

Three hours until eviction.

We'd decided to make the most of it. The cafe was decorated to the nines—streamers hanging from the overhead lights, tables pushed aside to make room for a dance floor. Boone had brought a rotating disco ball, which threw glints of light around the room, in rainbow colors like sun off a diamond. The bar was loaded with platters of sandwiches and crab cakes, tiny quiches and fried apple pies.

We couldn't save the Heartbreak Cafe, but it had saved us. And so we celebrated.

I sat at a table with Fart Unger while Scratch tried to teach Imani to jitterbug. All knees and elbows, she kept poking him and kicking him in the shins, but he didn't seem to mind. On the other side of the room, Alyssa watched the two of them with undisguised adoration.

Peach came over and sat down. "You all right, Dell?"

The woman's powers of observation never ceased to amaze me. She knew something was up, but fortunately, she thought it had to do with the eviction. She kept quiet, and every now and then reached out and squeezed my hand.

The party was well under way when the axe finally fell. Boone and Toni had the music turned up full volume and were doing the boot-scootin' boogie with Imani, Alyssa, and Hoot Everett. Purdy Overstreet had a bright red feather boa wrapped around Scratch's neck and was trying to give him a lap dance.

"Dell!" he yelled above the music. "Somebody's here."

I looked. With all the lights on inside, the best I could make out was somebody standing at the glass door, peering in. I went to the entrance and turned the lock.

It was Kevin Ivess, the sweet young deputy who had been appointed interim sheriff after Warren Potts's promotion to the Chulahatchie Sanitation Department. Five or six years ago he had been a big burly halfback for the Chulahatchie Confederates football team, and he still looked like a kid, like he might be in high school. Blond, with a round baby face, rosy cheeks, and a sheepish grin.

Tonight the grin was missing. "I'm real sorry, Miz Haley." His voice cracked like an adolescent's. "But I got no choice." He held out a folded paper, which I knew must be the final eviction notice. "You gotta be out by tomorrow morning at 8:00 A.M." He looked away, into the restaurant, where the music was still blaring but the dancing had stopped. Everybody was staring at him.

I watched his discomfort and felt a twinge of sadness and sympathy. The boy was just doing his job, bless his heart. He didn't mean any harm, and I could tell from the look on his face that he'd rather walk through a nest of cottonmouths than have to evict me from the Heartbreak Cafe. None of this was his fault.

"Eight tomorrow morning?" I repeated.

"Yes ma'am."

"Well, that gives us time to ring in the New Year." I looked up at him. "Are you still on duty, Sheriff?"

"No ma'am. I got off ten minutes ago." He gave me an embarrassed grin. "But it's just Kevin, ma'am, if you don't mind."

"Well, Just Kevin, come join the party. We got plenty of food and some real nice company." I stood back and held the door open for him. "And leave the gun and handcuffs outside, if you don't mind."

"Five minutes to midnight!" Imani shouted.

The child had had way too much sugar and not enough sleep. She bounced like a Ping-Pong ball from one table to the next. "Four minutes! Three minutes!"

Most of the adults were partied out, and slouched around the tables waiting desperately for the year to turn so we could all go home and go to bed. Hoot and Purdy had toddled off to Hoot's house hours ago. Sheriff Kevin had made his exit at eleven, thanking me for the hospitality and the great food, and saying he had another engagement. Bless his heart, his mama taught him well. About time we had a sheriff with some manners.

Fart had left on Kevin's heels, saying he needed to take care of something, but he hadn't come back. Despite myself, I felt a little lurch of disappointment that he wouldn't be here for the countdown.

"One minute!" Imani squealed.

We all waited, then counted with her: "Ten, nine, eight, seven—"

"Happy New Year!" somebody shouted.

I turned. Fart stood in the doorway carrying what looked like a small laundry basket, the old-fashioned wicker kind with handles.

"It's not time yet!" Imani said. "Four, three, two, one!"

We all yelled together, and blew noisemakers, and raised our glasses. Toni, who had come prepared, shoved a disc of "Auld Lang Syne" into the CD player. Everybody circled up, swayed, and sang.

When the song was over, we all just stood there looking at each other. "My mama used to talk a lot about character," I said. "She said you could judge a person's character by what kind of friends they have. And if that's the case, then I'm a pretty darn good person."

Everybody laughed. "Anyway, thanks for coming," I said. "Thanks for being such good friends. Happy New Year, everybody, and good night."

"Not so fast," Boone said. "This party's not over just because it's midnight."

"I'm an old woman, Boone," I said. "It's past my bedtime."

"Well, you'll just have to tough it out a little longer," he said. "Sit down."

I sat.

Boone motioned to Fart, who brought the wicker basket over to the table and set it down in front of me. It was mail. Christmas cards, by the look of them, in envelopes of red and green and gold.

"These are for you, Dell," Boone said. "Sorry they're a little late."

"All of them? Surely not."

"Only one way to find out. Open them."

The first was from someone named Scott Killian. It said, "Merry Christmas, Dell, and thanks for the great food. See you in January."

Inside the card was a twenty-dollar bill.

"He works at Tenn-Tom," Fart whispered in my ear. "One of the guys who comes in with us sometimes."

There were more—lots more—from over-the-road truckers and the blue-haired pie and coffee ladies; from Tansie Orr and DeeDee Sturgis and the girls at the beauty shop. From Mama's old Sunday school classes and Daddy's old Little League guys, and just about everybody in town, if you want to know the truth. All with a bit of money—five dollars, ten, twenty. It mounted up.

And then, at the bottom of the basket, a handful of envelopes, each with a check inside: Boone and Toni, Fart, Scratch and Alyssa, Peach Rondell. All of them giving more than they could afford, I suspected.

An outpouring of love, to the tune of twenty-eight

thousand five hundred and ninety-four dollars. Enough for a down payment to buy the Heartbreak Cafe outright.

Plus another three dollars and fifty cents in dimes and nickels, from Imani, taped inside a handmade card to form the sentence:

I ♥ U.

Epilogue

Mama always used to say that love is never lost, even if it's not returned in the way you hope or expect. "Put it on out there," she said. "Lay your heart on the line, and don't be afraid of getting it broken. Broken hearts heal. Guarded hearts just turn to stone."

On April Fool's Day, Hoot Everett and Purdy Overstreet got married at the Heartbreak Cafe.

Scratch stood up for Hoot as best man. Imani served as flower girl. Purdy asked me to be her matron of honor, since Mama wasn't available. The Reverend Lily Frasier, the new chaplain at St. Agnes Nursing Home, officiated.

The place was packed—every table and booth filled except for the one reserved for the bride and groom. A two-tiered wedding cake dominated the center of the marble countertop, and everybody brought food. The place smelled heavenly: fried chicken and corn fritters and fragrant yeast rolls and triple chocolate brownies.

"Do you, Herman Melville Everett, take this woman, Priscilla Mayben Overstreet, to be your lawfully wedded wife?" Reverend Lily asked.

"I sure as hell do," Hoot bellowed.

"And do you—"

"Skip the formalities, honey," Purdy interrupted. "Dang right, I do. The old goat's already tipped me over, so we might as well make it legal." She arched her eyebrows in Scratch's direction. "I might be off the market, but you can still admire the goods," she said in a resounding whisper.

Everybody laughed.

"Then I now pronounce you husband and wife."

A great cheer went up. Hoot dipped Purdy back halfway to the floor and gave her a loud and sloppy kiss.

"All right, now," Purdy said when she had righted herself, "let's get this party started."

The food was passed around, and someone put on a CD of forties' music. Hoot and Purdy danced in the tight spaces between the tables, and once nearly caught Purdy's sleeve on fire when they waltzed too close to a candle. When they went back to their booth, I saw Hoot slip something out of his pocket and hand it across the table to Purdy. A small green bottle of his famous muscadine wine.

I stood behind the counter, watching.

Over by the window, Peach Rondell sat with Boone and Toni. In an eggplant-colored dress, with her hair and makeup done, Peach looked every bit the beauty queen she once had been. A bit rounder, perhaps, and more than a little older, but radiant nevertheless. She held Imani on her lap and was arranging her Bean Queen tiara on the little girl's head. Peach looked as purely happy as anyone I'd ever seen.

Scratch and Alyssa were on the floor dancing to "Stardust," or at least trying to dance. Scratch was so big he kept bumping into people's tables and having to apologize. At last the two of them gave up and went back to their booth, where they sat together on the same side and held hands under the table.

DeeDee Sturgis was there, too, and Tansie Orr and her husband, Tank, and a contingent of the girls from the Curl Up and Dye. They were all sitting together, exchanging stories and recipes with a bunch of the blue-haired ladies from St. Agnes, all of them shooting jealous glances at the bride.

Much to my surprise, Marvin Beckstrom had showed up, although I don't know why he came, since he wasn't the type to let himself have a good time, even at a wedding. Maybe he was just nursing his wounds, feeding on his failure the way you'll pick at a scab until it bleeds again.

On January 2, promptly at 9:00 A.M., I had presented myself at the Chulahatchie Savings and Loan with my basket of cash and checks in hand, and made an offer to buy the building that housed the Heartbreak Cafe. Marvin was late getting to work that day and by the time he showed up, jingling his keys in his pockets, the deal was sealed.

That defeat, along with his buddy the sheriff's new position as garbage collector, served to humble Marvin a little bit. Still, I could tell by the look on his face that he'd have given half a year's salary to put me out of business for good. Now for the rest of his sorry life he was going to have to walk past the Heartbreak Cafe every blessed day and count in his head the money he lost on that deal.

Sometimes we do get a little justice in this world. It probably doesn't say much about my character, but the thought of it makes me smile.

I felt a presence at my elbow and turned to see Fart Unger standing beside me, looking down at me with those blue, blue eyes. He was wearing a tuxedo—a rental, I suspected, since it didn't fit quite right up at the shoulders—but he couldn't have looked more handsome.

He gave me a crooked little grin. "Whatcha thinking about?"

I shrugged. "I don't know. This place. These people."

"Good folks," he said.

"You know, Fart, when I started this restaurant, I did it out of sheer desperation. I was pretty sure I was going to lose everything. And I almost did."

"Would you have done it any different if you had it to do again?"

I thought about this for a minute. "What else is life about, if not about taking the risk?"

"Looks like the risk paid off."

"Thanks to all of you. Everybody who supported me, believed in me. Boone, Toni, Scratch, Peach Rondell. You."

I sensed my face beginning to flush, and when I put my hands to my cheeks, I felt the warmth and knew that I was blushing.

"We're your friends, Dell. That's what friends do."

"But it's more than that," I said. "When we named this place Heartbreak Cafe, the name fit. But now look what's happened. Look at the smile on Peach Rondell's face. Look at Boone and Toni. Look at Scratch and Alyssa and Imani. Look at Hoot and Purdy, starting a whole new life together at eighty-something."

I thought about that long line of ghostly figures in the cave, stretching themselves out so that I could find my way into the light. I thought about Chase, and the fact that if he'd known acceptance like this, he might have been able to accept himself, and wouldn't have ended up dying alone. I thought about how good forgiveness felt, and about all the pain and healing the past year had brought. When I looked back on the difficult road I'd traveled, I could finally see the gifts, the grace.

"This place is magic," I whispered, mostly to myself. "It's a miracle."

Fart slid his arm around my waist and pulled me close to his side. He leaned down and looked into my eyes.

"It's not the restaurant, Dell," he said. "It's your heart. It's your great big luminous soul."

And then he kissed me.

Luminous. It put me in mind of the moon, hanging low in the evening sky, full and round and bright. Someday I'll have to ask Boone what it means. He's real smart; I'm sure he'll know.

But at the moment I got other things on my mind.

Like kissing back.

Heartbreak Cookbook

I got these recipes from all over: from Lillian, my mama; from my grandma, Olivia; from Toni's aunt Madge ('cause Toni doesn't cook worth a dang); and from Boone (who does). Even one from Purdy Overstreet, except that I had to steal it from her recipe box while I was visiting her and Hoot. I hope you enjoy 'em—and be sure to have your cholesterol checked.

—DELL

P.S. I tried to get Hoot's recipe for muscadine wine, but he said it was all in his head and he couldn't write it down. It's all in his head, that's for sure.

Good Lovin'
Cornbread Dressing

I use leftover cornbread and biscuits from the cafe for this, but I'll give you the cheatin' method; it's a heckuva lot easier. Makes enough to feed six or eight—unless Scratch comes to Thanksgiving dinner.

2 boxes Jiffy cornbread mix (or any mix will do; I just like Jiffy best. This is the small box, the size of a one-layer cake mix.)

2 cans clear chicken broth

2 onions, chopped fine

4 chicken bouillon cubes

1 bag seasoned croutons (white/wheat mix is best. Or you can use old biscuits or toasted bread.)

2 eggs

½ stick butter or margarine

Salt

Sage

A little sugar

NOTE: *I don't use celery because it messes with my digestion (more information than you wanted, I'm sure). But if you absolutely have to use celery, chop it up very fine, and sauté it with the onions. Some folks are horrified at the idea of cornbread dressing without celery, like it's some kind of betrayal of Southern womanhood. But in my opinion, dressing should NOT crunch when you eat it.*

Bake the cornbread according to label directions and set aside (an iron skillet is best). Pour the chicken broth into a large pot (soup size—this stuff expands), bring to a boil, and sauté the onions until they're soft. While you're at it, throw in the bouillon cubes and make sure they get dissolved all the way.

Take the pot off the stove, crumble in the cornbread, add the croutons, and stir it up until everything is mushy. Add more water a little at a time; it should be the consistency of thick oatmeal. Then add the eggs and butter. Season with salt and sage (lots of sage) until it tastes right. Add a little sugar (a tablespoon or so—it brings out the flavor).

When you're done, it should be thick but very moist—like I said, oatmeal. Spray a large casserole dish with non-stick spray, cover, and bake it on 375°F for about an hour. Then take the cover off and leave it until it's crispy and brown on top and set up and hot all the way through. (Another 20 minutes, probably.) The deeper your casserole dish, the longer it will take to bake.

You can make this ahead of time and put it in the fridge until the next day, but it'll take a little longer to bake if the dressing is cold. You can also freeze it for later if you want.

And no, don't stuff it inside the turkey. It'll just go all to mush, and that's not safe, anyway.

Toni's Creamed Corn Casserole

This is Toni's recipe. Like I said, she can't cook worth a flip, but this turns out great every time, even for folks who burn water. It rises up like a soufflé, and makes you look like a regular gourmet chef.

   1 box Jiffy cornbread mix (You get the idea we like this
      stuff?)
   2 eggs
   1 can creamed corn
   1 can whole kernel corn, drained
   1 stick of butter or margarine, softened
   ½ cup light (or fat-free) sour cream

Mix it all up, pour into greased baking dish. Bake uncovered at 375–400°F, 45 minutes to an hour, until brown on top. Takes about 3 minutes to put together. Serves 6.

Aunt Madge's Easy Yeast Rolls

Toni's aunt Madge gave me this recipe—I reckon she thought I'd know how to make the most of it, since Toni's a natural disaster in the kitchen.

   ½ cup sugar
   1¾ cups milk
   ½ cup shortening (you can also use oil)

1 package yeast dissolved in ½ cup lukewarm water (not too
   hot, or you'll kill the yeast)
4 cups self-rising flour
½ teaspoon soda (add to flour)

Heat sugar, milk, and shortening in a pan on the stove, stirring until the sugar is dissolved. Pour into a large mixing bowl, set aside, and let cool. When milk/sugar mix is cool, add the yeast/water mixture. With your mixer set on low, gradually add in the flour/soda mix. Keep adding flour until dough is thick and gummy.

Place in a large greased bowl (I use a plastic cake keeper turned upside down), cover with a clean dish towel, and let rise until double its bulk. Then cover with a tight lid and put in the fridge.

This will keep for a long time in the fridge. When you're ready to use it, slap a hunk on the counter, knead a little, and add a bit of flour so the dough isn't too sticky. Roll out or shape balls by hand and put into greased muffin pan. Then cover and set aside to rise again.

These rolls take a long time to rise. When they've doubled again, bake at 400°F for 20 minutes or so. Serves however many you make—but make a lot; people will keep coming back for "just one more."

Aunt Madge's Christmas Cinnamon Ring

This is a long-standing tradition for Christmas morning. I'm gonna give you two versions: the real way and the easy way. If you've got the roll dough made up already, use it. If you don't go to the trouble of making Madge's yeast rolls, you can use canned crescent rolls. You can use either Splenda or real sugar. If you use Splenda, this one is pretty healthy, as cinnamon rolls go. I reckon every little bit helps.

Softball-size hunk of Aunt Madge's roll dough (or 1 package crescent rolls—the big ones if you can find them)
Butter or margarine, softened to spread
½ cup or so of brown sugar (or Splenda blend)
A little white sugar (or Splenda)
Ground cinnamon

Roll out the dough. If you're using the real stuff, knead it and add flour until it holds together, then roll out a circle about the size of a pie crust. For the crescent roll dough, roll it out but DON'T break it apart into triangles. Lay it out flat and crimp the seams together.

Spread butter or margarine across the dough. Top this with brown sugar, a nice thick layer. Add a sprinkling of white, and top all that with cinnamon.

Roll it up the long way, so that you end up with a long, fat snake of dough. Crimp the edges together and put it in a greased glass pie pan, making a kind of circle or horseshoe with the dough. Use a deep-dish pie pan if you got one; this thing swells up.

If you're using the real yeast dough, cover with a dish towel and let it rise to double its size. If you're using the crescent rolls, you can bake it right away.

Rub a little more butter on the top, and a sprinkling of real sugar and cinnamon. Bake at 400°F until it's all brown and crusty, about 20–25 minutes. Serves 4–6.

Fart's Favorite Pumpkin Pie

My best recipe, handed down from Grandma Livi to Mama to me. This recipe makes two pies.

Pie Crust *(for two pies)*:

½ cup Crisco shortening (not oil)
1 ½ cups flour (plain, not self-rising)
½ teaspoon salt
4–5 tablespoons cold water

Cut in the shortening with the flour and the salt, then add the water a little at a time until it feels right. Divide in half and roll out thin.

A real cook will understand this, but the ability to make a flaky pie crust is a gift, and not something you can teach somebody. Go to the store and buy the Pillsbury ones in the red box at the dairy case.

Pie Filling *(for two pies—and why make one when two's just as easy?)*:

- 2 cups brown sugar (you can use Splenda blend if you're a health nut)
- 2 tablespoons cornstarch, and a little more
- 1 teaspoon salt
- 3 cups of pumpkin (2 cans)—*not* the pumpkin pie mix; plain pumpkin
- 2 eggs
- 4 tablespoons dark molasses
- 3 cups evaporated milk (2 cans)
- 8 teaspoons pumpkin pie spice

OR:

- 4 teaspoons cinnamon
- 1 teaspoon cloves (go easy on the cloves)
- 2 teaspoons nutmeg
- 2 teaspoons ginger

You'll need a BIG mixing bowl for this. Mix up the brown sugar and other dry ingredients, then gradually add in the pumpkin. Save the evaporated milk for last, when the pumpkin is thoroughly mixed. Fold in the milk at the end, and put your mixer on slow or you'll have pumpkin slung all over the kitchen. You'll think you've done something wrong, because the mixture will be thin, pourable. And a soft brown color, not bright orange.

Preheat your oven to 450°F. Use nonstick spray on your pie pans (deep-dish glass ones if you have them). Put in the unbaked pie crusts, crimp the edges to make it pretty, and then divide the filling between the two pies. Bake at 450°F for 15 minutes, then reduce to 325°F and bake for an additional 40–50 minutes. Takes a long time to bake. Pie is done when a table knife inserted in the center comes out clean.

Mama's Best Buttermilk Cake

This one's so good it oughta win an Oscar. It did, in fact. When I was twelve, Boone's uncle Oscar stole Mama's cake right off the table at the Holy Innocents Church Bazaar, and Sister Immaculata chased him on foot all the way to the courthouse square to get it back.

3 cups plain (not self-rising) flour
½ teaspoon salt
1 teaspoon baking powder
½ teaspoon soda
4 eggs
2 sticks butter or margarine
2 ½ cups sugar (save out ½ cup for the egg whites)
½ teaspoon salt
1 cup buttermilk
2 teaspoons vanilla
1 teaspoon lemon extract

Sift together flour, salt, baking powder, and soda. Separate eggs and hold out the whites; mix egg yolks and remainder of ingredients with the flour mixture. At the end, mix the egg whites with the remaining ½ cup sugar and beat until thick (but not stiff like meringue). Fold in egg whites and mix thoroughly but not too vigorously.

Bake in a greased tube pan at 350°F for 1 hour 20 minutes, or until the top is brown and crusty, and a toothpick comes out clean.

Purdy's Red Feather Boa Velvet Cake

Mama got this recipe from Purdy about a hundred years ago. She probably doesn't even remember it was hers to begin with, but I give her credit anyway. This is the recipe I snatched from the box when she wasn't looking, since I couldn't lay my hands on Mama's copy. It comes out the same color as that red feather boa she wears.

½ cup shortening
1 ½ cups sugar
2 eggs
2 ounces red food coloring
2 tablespoons cocoa
1 teaspoon salt
2 ½ cups plain (not self-rising) flour
1 cup buttermilk
1 tablespoon vinegar
1 teaspoon vanilla
1 teaspoon soda
1 teaspoon butter flavor

Cream together shortening, sugar, and eggs. Make a paste of the food coloring and cocoa, and add that. Mix salt and flour together; mix buttermilk and vinegar together. Add those in gradually, alternating flour mixture with buttermilk mixture, and blend everything together gently, but don't beat it.

Pour into two 9" layer cake pans greased with nonstick spray. Bake at 350° for 30 minutes, or until a toothpick comes out clean. Cool on racks and frost.

Frosting:

3 tablespoons flour
1 cup milk
1 cup sugar
1 cup butter or margarine
1 teaspoon vanilla

Cook flour and milk over low heat until thick. Let cool well. (Do this before you start the cake batter, and set it aside.) When the cake is done and you're ready to frost, cream together sugar, butter, and vanilla. Add to milk mixture and beat until stiff.

For people like Toni who don't cook: Make sure the cake layers are completely cool before frosting. Take one layer and turn it upside down on your cake plate (flat side up). Brush off the loose crumbs. Put a layer of frosting on the flat side, then gently position the second layer, flat side down, on top. Brush the loose crumbs off the sides and top. Frost the sides next, and the top last—that makes it prettier.

Boone's Best Oatmeal Cookies

Chase used to say that real men don't bake, but this recipe proves him wrong. All the nuns at Holy Innocents swear by these cookies—if nuns swear, that is. Probably not. At least, not out loud. But what do I know? I'm a Baptist.

1 cup plain flour (not self-rising)

¾ teaspoon soda

½ teaspoon salt

1 teaspoon cinnamon (double this if you like your cookies spicy)

¾ teaspoon nutmeg

¾ cup shortening

1⅓ cup brown sugar

2 eggs

1 teaspoon vanilla

2 cups old fashioned oatmeal

Mix dry ingredients together (except oatmeal). Cream shortening, brown sugar, eggs, and vanilla. Fold in flour and other dry ingredients, and add oatmeal last. Mix well; dough will be sticky.

Drop by spoonfuls onto greased baking sheet, and bake at 350°F for 12–15 minutes. Do not overbake; cookies should be soft and chewy, not hard and crispy. If you want, you can roll this dough up in wax paper, refrigerate, and then cut into circles to bake. The dough will keep in the fridge for several days.

For real decadence, add a bag of semisweet chocolate

chips. Boone tells me that chocolate chips will get you extra prayers.

Scratch's Comfort Sandwich

With a nod to the King of Rock 'n' Roll.

This is pretty unhealthy, especially coming from a man who had dreams of becoming a surgeon. But comfort food is all about comfort, now, isn't it?

2 slices of bread, lightly toasted (wheat is best)
Creamy peanut butter
Jelly (strawberry jam is best; grape will do in a pinch)
2 slices of Spam

Spread peanut butter on the two slices of toast. Add jam to the peanut butter (both sides). Fry up the Spam in a skillet. Lay in the meat, close 'er up, and perform a surgical incision diagonally from corner to corner. Good with sweet tea. Better with milk.

Grandma Livi's Fried Apple Pies

There's two ways to do this: the hard way and the easy way. But neither one is very hard, unless you're Toni.

The hard way:

2–3 apples
Sugar
Water
Cinnamon
Pie crust
Cornstarch
Vegetable oil

Core, peel, and slice your apples. I like Granny Smiths and Romes and Macintosh, but almost any firm apple will do. Cut the slices into chunks. Start with two or three apples; you can always make more if you get carried away.

Cook apples slowly with a little sugar (or Splenda, if you prefer), a little water, and lots of cinnamon. You can use apple pie spice if you want, or add in a bit of nutmeg. Don't ask how much sugar or spice; you just gotta experiment until it tastes right. Not too much water—you want the apples soft and tender, but you don't want a lot of runny juice. You can thicken it up with a little cornstarch if you like.

[*Note to beginners*: you have to mix the cornstarch with a bit of COLD water; otherwise it will make a mess.]

Make the pie crust recipe I gave you with the pumpkin pie [see page 300]. Roll it out and cut it into circles about

307

the size of a softball. Plop a spoonful of the apple mixture onto one half of the circle, fold the dough over, and crimp with a fork. Then fry it in a pan—use an inch or so of corn oil or vegetable oil, and make sure your oil is hot enough (but not smoking), so the pies will get crispy without getting soggy. Fry, flip, fry, flip—it's not hard, but it takes some time.

Drain the pies on a baking rack with paper towels underneath to catch the grease. This keeps the pies from getting soggy on the paper towel.

The easier (and healthier) way:

Go to the store and get a few of those roll-out pie crusts. Follow the directions above, and use Splenda instead of sugar. You can throw in a little brown sugar mix, too, if you like. Or if you *really* want to cheat, buy a couple of cans of apple pie mix and add a little more cinnamon and nutmeg.

Roll out the pie crust, cut, and crimp as instructed above. Then place in a glass pan (use nonstick spray) and bake at 400°F for ten minutes or so, until the pies are brown and crispy.

Unless you're pathologically honest (as Boone would say), you can do the cheat method and get away with it, and everybody will think you slaved in the kitchen all day. Why should they know any different?

Heartbreak Fudge Pie

This pie is so good it will break your heart and then heal it up again. It's my own recipe, and I offer it to you with love and thanks for sticking with me during my own year of struggle and healing. Come to Chulahatchie and have lunch at the Heartbreak Cafe, and I'll give you a slice of this pie and a cup of coffee, on the house.

Crust:

- 1 cup finely chopped pecans (you can use walnuts, too, but that's not so Southern)
- ¼ cup butter or margarine
- ¼ cup sugar
- 1 tablespoon flour

Finely chop the nuts. Cream together butter and sugar, then add the nuts and the bit of flour to hold it all together. Grease pie plate or spray with nonstick cooking spray. Makes one 9-inch pie crust.

Filling:

- ½ cup margarine
- 1 cup sugar
- 3 eggs
- 2 squares of unsweetened chocolate, melted
- 1 teaspoon vanilla
- ⅓ cup plain flour (not self-rising)

½ teaspoon baking powder
pinch of salt

Mix ingredients by hand. Place in the crust (above) and bake at 325°F for 35–45 minutes. Serve warm with a scoop of vanilla ice cream.

A Final Word from Dell

Right before she died, my mama said, "Dell, honey, lemme tell you something. When you come to the end of your days and are looking down the barrel of eternity, ain't nothin' gonna matter in this life or the next, except how well you loved the people you love."

Mama was right. As usual.

In the long run, nothing else counts. Not stuff you've acquired or accomplishments you've racked up, or any of it, no matter how important it seems right now. There's only one thing you can take with you to the other side. One thing. Love. Risky, outrageous, terrifying, soul-revealing love.

Love isn't just the most important thing; it's everything.

But then, you already know that. And so do I.

We just might need to remind each other now and then.